THE
DIABOLICAL

THE
DIABOLICAL

A BRUNO JOHNSON NOVEL

DAVID PUTNAM

OCEANVIEW PUBLISHING
SARASOTA, FLORIDA

ISBN 978-1-60809-529-2

Published in the United States of America by Oceanview Publishing

Sarasota, Florida

www.oceanviewpub.com

10 9 8 7 6 5 4 3 2 1

PRINTED IN THE UNITED STATES OF AMERICA

"We sleep soundly in our beds because rough men stand ready in the night to visit violence on those who would do us harm."

WINSTON CHURCHILL

THE
DIABOLICAL

CHAPTER ONE

THE LIDO CABANA bar sat far enough from the hotel and the beach that I could see anyone approach from either direction, a must for a fugitive on constant alert for those who wanted to ruin a life with an extradition back to the States for kidnap and murder. The cerulean sky, the white sand beach, and the temperature at three o'clock—an impeccable eighty degrees—created a perfect wedding day. The Punta Bandera Hotel and Beach Club, packed with tourists, would make it difficult to differentiate friend from foe. Didn't matter—I was ebullient over my friend's wedding. The tanned and sandy, all-but-nude visitors kept coming up to the bar, ordering pina coladas, rum punches, ice-cold daiquiris, and drinking them by the gallons. Their thirsty appetite kept my hands busy and my smile constant. The hotel didn't pay much in salary, but the tourists gave generously in the tip jar. Money we needed to feed and clothe our fourteen children.

Not all of them legally mine but loved just the same.

My wife Marie and I had rescued most of the kids from at-risk homes in South Central Los Angeles and brought them here to Costa Rica for a better life, and it warmed my heart to watch them thrive.

I raised my hand and waved at our mob of children making their way down the path from the hotel, herded by Marie with Rosie, our housekeeper, pushing two infants in a double stroller. The children wore tee shirts that mimicked formal black and white tuxedos, cute little penguins all happy beyond belief. Drago had brought the shirts from the States and insisted everyone wear them at the ceremony. I had one on under my aloha Hawaiian hotel shirt, ready for the festivities to begin as soon as Chacho relieved me from my bar duties.

Aleck and Alisa, parents of the bride, Layla, already sat at the bar doing some serious drinking—vodka martinis dry enough to drink in the Gobi. Neither approved of their daughter's marriage to my friend—my best friend, Karl Drago. "A socially inept, knuckle-dragging Neanderthal," they claimed—the sentiment more Alisa than Aleck. They forgot to mention Drago's heart of gold. No one would take better care of their daughter. No one.

Aleck and Alisa had once been our best friends in our little town of Tamarindo, Costa Rica. But now they blamed me for Drago's entry into their daughter's life. Two months earlier, Aleck, a local doctor, had delivered my son Tobias, one of the children in the double stroller. The day after the birth—a complicated, high-risk procedure—in gratitude to the couple, I agreed to escort Alisa in returning their daughter, Layla, back to Costa Rica from her college, USC—University of Spoiled Children. What I had not known at the time was that Layla had been held against her will with a ransom demand of one hundred thousand dollars and that I had been asked along for my particular talents in chasing violence, a reputation I was working hard to put behind me.

In the end, Layla came back with Karl Drago, her long, lustrous black hair cut just below her ears, a colorful dragon tattoo on her back, and with an infant child of questionable parentage that she'd picked up in LA. All of this apparently caused by me and hence the unjust acrimony.

Marie headed directly toward me at the bar with a huge smile. She went up on tip-toes. I leaned over and kissed her. When I tried to pull away, she grabbed my head and really laid one on me. She was happy. She loved weddings. She thought the one between Drago and Layla the most perfect union in the world. On top of the glorious wedding, I had also promised her that I'd never go back to the States and I meant it. She could now visualize a storybook life in a wonderful country with fourteen children. I couldn't blame her; I was just as overjoyed.

A few of the customers at the bar whooped and slapped the counter at the kiss. Marie let go, staring into my eyes. I stared back to let her know I loved her more.

Otis Brasher, a fat man in a seersucker suit, clothes too hot for the afternoon, took a wet cigar from his mouth and said, "Heh, heh, newlyweds, huh? Must be that three-week thing."

Marie, still looking into my eyes, answered him, "Nope, it's that five-year thing."

Brasher was a new live-in occupant at the hotel. He'd been there for two months and sat all day on the same barstool chugging down too-sweet grasshoppers. I'd seen his kind again and again. They flee the States as white-collar criminals or tax evaders and take up residency in the hotel until they get the lay of the land. Then they buy an estate next to other expat criminals.

We lived in one of those estates, abandoned by a criminal who craved the depravity Costa Rica lacked. He rented to us and returned to the States, to the turmoil caused by bumper-to-bumper traffic, gun violence, and masses of people too busy chasing lives they'll never catch. Traded it for the quiet serenity of Costa Rica.

The cheering brought me out of my trance with Marie. I caught a sour look from Alisa as she stared up the path toward the hotel. Drago in all his glory shambled along carrying his wife-to-be in the same manner as if walking across the threshold.

Drago wore 3X clothes, a huge man, his body underneath his tux tee shirt littered with scars from gunshots, stabbings, and bludgeonings. He was covered in tattoos that started on his feet and traveled the length of his body: Celtic crosses, Vikings with swords and angry expressions, gang members with bandanas just above their eyes pointing double-barreled shotguns—all tattoos from another part of his life that he'd left far behind. He'd grown his hair out to cover the tatts on his no-longer bald pate.

During the ceremony and for their honeymoon in Rio, Marie and I were taking care of Layla's infant child—the child rescued from a baby farm in California—Daphne or "Daph." The sad reality was that Aleck and Alisa wanted nothing to do with the child.

In the three weeks Drago and Layla would be gone, Marie had plans to both repair our friendship with Aleck and Alisa and convince them to love Daph. I told her "good luck." In my past life as a cop working the streets of south LA I'd seen too many Family 415's where one side digs in, refusing to budge; and that was Aleck and Alisa's position now. No way, no how. But once Marie sets her mind to something, I just step out of the way and keep my head down.

Layla at five foot four and a hundred pounds looked like an exotic doll in Drago's arms.

The crowd of local friends and even a few Drago had invited from the States, along with all the kids, moved in a slow-moving mob down the beach where a large tent-like shade had been set up in a coned-off area. Under the shade sat six round tables for ten and a mobile bar staffed with a congenial bartender. Off to one side the hotel had laid down a hardwood surface for dancing and a stage for the calypso band. It was going to be a night to remember on the sand under a moonless sky lit with tiki torches.

Drago had insisted on paying for the entire affair. I didn't ask where he got his money. But I knew. Before he'd met Layla, he'd sworn a vendetta against all outlaw motorcycle gangs. When he attacked, he maimed and mutilated, destroyed their drugs, and took their money. He'd promised me now that he was a father and a husband, he'd be leaving that life far behind. He had yet to state what he intended to do for a living. Maybe live off his spoils.

I wanted to tell him that I too had changed my life by moving down to Costa Rica, but a person can't chase violence and not expect it to bite back. Fate, like a recurring dormant virus, would periodically heat up and pull me back to the States. This had happened a number of times—old business as yet unfinished. After the last time two months ago though, I believed I was finally in the clear, free to settle down and enjoy the life I so desperately wanted with Marie and the children.

I couldn't wait to get relieved from the cabana bartending gig to join in the fun. I turned to see Chacho coming down the walk carrying a large round tray on his shoulder loaded with chopped fruit garnish for the tropical drinks. Then I realized I'd missed something.

Waldo.

While I worked my regular shift at the cabana bar the night before, Marie had picked up Drago, Daph, and Layla at the airport in San Jose. I'd forgot to ask Marie if Drago had brought along my nemesis, Waldo, Drago's hundred-and-thirty-pound Rottweiler. That dog loved to taunt me, and I didn't know why. Smartest dog I'd ever met, but rude. Drago spoke to him in German, and at times, I'd seen Drago give Waldo a complicated, multifaceted command. Waldo somehow knew how to accomplish the request.

Of course, Drago would have left him at home in the States. How would he get a dog that large on a plane unless he was put in a cage in the plane's hold. Waldo would never go along with a cage. I knew the devil-dog too well. He'd chew out of the cage then chew a hole in the belly of the plane, accomplish that trick without even trying hard.

Something bumped my leg. Startled, I jumped back grabbing bottles in the bar tray to regain my balance, almost falling on my ass. The bottles rattled and clanged. I looked down. Waldo was looking up at me, eyes black as Hades. He was wearing one of the tuxedo-printed tee shirts for the wedding. He needed one two sizes larger. He looked like an obese penguin in search of a fat sardine. He'd come under the bar's pass-through somehow, sniffing me out. He growled.

"Why me?" I asked him. "Why do you do this to me?"

He growled again.

Chacho set the round tray on the bar and leaned over to see who I was talking to. "Hey, what a beautiful *perro*." He picked up the pass-through, came into the bar, got down on one knee to pet the dog.

"Careful, that's a devil dog."

Chacho laughed. "Nah, amigo, this guy's a lover not an eater."

A shadow covered us. Drago appeared. "Let's go, bro, you're the best man. Let's rock this beach."

"You had to bring Waldo? Seriously?"

Drago shrugged, "He's the ring bearer."

"Terrific."

CHAPTER TWO

AFTER TWO HOURS of drinks and getting to know each other, the guests moved as a group closer to the water's edge and stood for the ceremony as the tidal water gently lapped the sand. With the sun low in the sky, the tourists interrupted their drinking and late sunbathing to wade in the water and watch. Weddings had that effect on people. Or maybe they'd never seen the likes of Drago, with dozens of other little penguins enjoying a tropical beach.

Cheers went up when the priest proclaimed "husband and wife." Marie clung to my arm and squeezed it, tears in her eyes. We stood close enough to Alisa and Aleck to hear Alisa mutter something about the wedding not being sanctioned because it wasn't in a Catholic church. I guessed that choice came from Layla, a strike back at her parents for not accepting Drago or Daph. They would come around eventually, especially if Marie had anything to do with it. Aleck already showed signs of cracking, the way he looked at Daph in the baby carrier Drago and Layla were holding.

The children romped in the sand playing games until hotel staff served dinner: fresh caught local fish with sautéed vegetables and brown rice. For some unknown reason, Waldo plopped down in the sand at the back of *my* chair. We sat one table over from the bride and groom and witnessed Drago tug on the waiter's sleeve, trying to hand back the plate of fish and instead ask for three steaks. Layla waved the waiter away and put the plate back in front of her new husband. Poor Drago. He'd just been put on a healthy diet.

I got up on the pretense to go to the bar to order Marie another white wine, found the waiter, and ordered the three steaks seared only and raw in the center. I asked that they be brought to me surreptitiously in a bag. Later I'd pull Drago aside and give him an early wedding present, because friends looked out for one another. And I wanted to ensure the wedding remain a happy place. Without meat, Drago tended to get a little peckish.

Twenty minutes passed and the waiter slipped me the bag. I set it on my lap. Waldo raised his head at the luscious scent that filled the air. Marie grabbed onto my ear and pulled my head down. She whispered, "Little mister, what did you just do?"

Oh no, we'd skipped right to "little mister," number three from the top of her anger scale.

I stuttered, "It's . . . It's for Waldo. We can't leave out Waldo, can we?"

Her expression suddenly shifted to sheepish. "Oh, of course not, I'm sorry. You're right, poor Waldo needs to eat too." She leaned down and petted Waldo's head. He didn't snap at her.

I whispered in a tone of mock indignation, "Your damn skippy he does. You ought to be ashamed accusing me like that."

She leaned up and kissed my cheek. "I said I was sorry, don't push it, bud."

Good. "Bud" was two levels down on the anger scale. Crisis averted.

Behind me, Waldo growled. He must've overheard the thing about the steaks being for him. I stuck my hand behind the chair and waved at him to be quiet. He grabbed onto my hand with his jaws, growled again, and shook my hand back and forth. "Okay, okay, let go."

I muttered, "Hold my hand hostage—what kind of dog does that?" I unwrapped one of the steaks and handed it to him. He caught it in the air and ate it without letting it drop to the sand. I tried to pet him, to make nice. He growled again. "Geez, I just gave you a prime steak."

Marie elbowed me. "Quit playing with the dog and eat your dinner."

When they cut the cake, for the photo op, Layla stood on a chair next to her husband and still wasn't as tall. But tall enough for the requisite cake-to-the-face gag everyone expected and pretended surprise when it happened. Behind us, Alisa puffed air from her lips.

The sun set, and we took a break to trundle the kids home for baths and bed. We returned to find the guests dancing to calypso music and taking full advantage of the open bar. The only lights on the moonless beach were tiki torches that flickered and gave off an ambience that would forever reside in our memories.

Memories Dad would miss. He wasn't feeling well and stayed home with Bea tending to him.

Drago danced with his new bride holding her with his arm around her waist, her feet dangling above the sand.

I'd only known him five or six years and could not be closer to a person—we were like brothers. He rarely displayed any emotion and this night, though not blatantly obvious, he was as happy as I had ever seen him. After the dance, I took him by the arm and said to Layla, "Excuse us for a minute. I need a private word with your husband."

She pointed a finger at me. "Bruno, don't you get him into any kind of trouble, you hear me?"

I put my hand to my chest and feigned surprise. "Me?"

She said, "I'll be over at the bar. Don't be long, okay, sweetie?"

"Okay," I said.

"Not you. You're not *sweetie*."

"Oh. Right."

I pulled Drago off into the dark. "What gives," he said, "I need to get another piece of cake before they take it away. I'm starving."

I took the bag now splotched with grease stains from under my shirt and handed it to him. "Don't say I never do anything for you."

He took the bag, the scent giving away the contents. "Dude, you're kiddin' me." He didn't have time to say anything else; he devoured the meat knowing he didn't have much time.

Costa Rica's top three exports were coffee, sugar, and beef. The Ticos really knew how to cook their beef. My mouth watered as I watched him eat. Marie had me on one of those diets as well.

In between gnash, Drago said, "Hey . . . ah . . .?"

"What? Just say it."

He nodded. "Would it be okay . . . if, you know, I call you while we're in Rio?"

Drago had a difficult time catching social cues and sometimes needed advice. He had not been sure Layla had been *into* him until I told him.

"Of course you can. But try and navigate it yourself first."

"Yeah, yeah, thanks, bro, you know I will. And I'll bring you back some beads or some shit from Rio." He wadded up the bag, wiping his hands on it, and tossed it into the night. He knelt, grabbed a handful of sand, and further cleaned his hands. "Oh, man, that was good. I owe you big."

"Here." I handed him some gum. "She'll smell it on you."

"You're right, thanks."

I patted him on the back. "You good? I mean, you happy?"

He broke into a huge smile. "Best day of my life."

CHAPTER THREE

GUESTS AT THE wedding slowly peeled away, seeking somewhere to sleep off the abundant food, the alcohol, the good cheer. I slow-danced with Marie in the flickering yellow globe cast by the tiki torches along with two other die-hard couples. I think they were actually wedding crashers—I didn't remember seeing them earlier at the ceremony. Marie had taken advantage of the celebration and drank more than her usual—three glasses of white wine instead of her standard one. She still carried a little baby weight since Tobias' birth two months earlier, but still looked ravishing in the black dress she'd revealed under the tux tee shirt now abandoned. She kept pulling my head down and kissing me.

I loved her so.

The band declared the last song of the evening and started playing. I looked around and found Drago and his young bride had slipped away under the cover of darkness. I whispered in Marie's ear, "Whatta ya say to a walk on the beach?"

She looked around as if confused, messing with my mind. "With who? Are you talking to me?" I pinched her bottom. She giggled, bent over, pulled off her shoes, and took off running into the shrouded darkness outside the tiki torches.

I'd only had one drink and easily caught up to her wobbly flight. I scooped her up, ran a little more. I gently laid her on the sand and kissed her. She grew amorous and kissed back, transporting us both to the other side of forever. She finally broke the kiss breathing hard, her fingers locked in my hair. "Hey, tiger, aren't we supposed to be lying in the surf with a kiss like that?"

She referred to the movie, *From Here to Eternity.*

"All right," I said, and stood, shucking off my penguin shirt and slipping out of my khaki pants.

She held up her hands. "No, Bruno. No, I was only joking."

"Oh, really?" I shucked my underwear.

She smiled. "Well, all right, tiger, va va voom." She took my offered hand, and I helped her stand. She slipped her black dress off her shoulders and let it deflate at her feet. She stood naked with no undergarments.

I uttered, "You are a cute little wench."

She giggled and took off running for the ocean, the gentle Pacific, with me in hot pursuit.

The water splashed cold at first and then shifted to smooth and caressing. I caught up to her in water chest deep. She wrapped her legs around my waist, her body hot against mine. She kissed me again, one of those never-going-to-forget kind of kisses. I eased her down on top of me.

She let out a little groan.

This was the first time we'd made love since Tobias was born and it was perfect, absolutely perfect.

I whispered in her ear. "I love you."

She started to whisper back when from the beach a male voice yelled: "Señor Gaylord? Señor Juan Gaylord? It's the police." His accent in heavy Spanish.

Flashlight beams came on and forked across the water's surface hunting for us. "Bruno, are they looking for us?" I pushed her head underwater and joined her. We stayed under as long as we could. We popped up gasping to find the beam had stopped over us. I stood chest deep in the water with Marie clinging to me, both stark naked and far too vulnerable. The poisonous bite of fate had again tracked us down and buried its fangs.

"Bruno, is it Rosebud?"

"Rosebud" was our bug-out code word. If I ever called Marie and said *Rosebud* in a sentence, she was to grab our go-bag and the children and catch a bus to Panama where we had money stashed just for such a contingency.

While working the cabana bar, I never used the name *Bruno*, not wanting to make it too easy for law enforcement to find me. I changed my name on my hotel vest every two to three months. The staff played along and thought it a humorous game. "Juan Gaylord" was the current name. The police had stopped at the hotel to ask about me, and they'd told them my current name.

A larger ocean swell picked us up off our feet and freed us from the sandy floor. I whispered to Marie. "They didn't call out for *Bruno*; Gaylord's my hotel name. We're trapped out here and don't have a choice. Wait here. I'll go in and find out what they want."

"No way, bud, I'm going into shore with you."

"Marie, listen, we have to think about the kids. We both can't get snatched up. Wait out here just for a few minutes. Let me see what's going on."

Tears in her voice: "Baby, what else can they want you for? We should swim out to sea. That's really our only chance. Maybe catch a fishing boat going by."

I couldn't believe the perfect night had flipped that quickly to a nightmare. "No, we'll drown, and it's not the best option. You stay right here. I'll go see what—"

"I'm going, and that's it. Get moving, little mister."

I held her behind me with both hands and made our way to shore. I yelled, "Hold on, we're coming. We'll be right there."

Off down the beach the hotel staff snuffed out the tiki torches one at a time, dimming the last of the ambient light.

I said to the men on the beach, "Please turn off your flashlights."

Some muttering in Spanish, then the lights went out. Marie half-floated holding on to my shoulders and whispered in my ear. "That's a good sign, right, that the lights went out?"

The depth of the water turned shallow all too soon, exposing us to the cool air and to the police on shore. My teeth began to chatter. I stopped ankle deep. "Wait here, babe, I'll get your dress." This time she complied. I hurried, not wanting to leave my lovely, vulnerable wife to the prying eyes and the cool air.

Three police officers in dark blue uniforms from Tamarindo Beach, a town of six thousand citizens, stood in a small throng waiting. One of them wore insignia on shoulder boards that might indicate he was the chief or at the very least the leader. He handed me my pants and the penguin shirt. I shucked them on with difficulty, the material getting caught on wet skin. I hurried down to the water with Marie's dress and stood blocking the view while she slipped it over her head. I put my arms around her to try and warm her up. "What do they want?" she whispered.

"I don't know." We padded barefoot back to where they stood. I said, "What's this about?"

The chief, who spoke in broken English, held out an open palm. "Please come with us."

Marie grabbed onto my arm and squeezed.

"Not until you tell me what this is about."

Marie whispered, "Is this Rosebud?"

The chief, no more than a shadow now that all the tiki torches were snuffed out down the beach behind him, said, "No, it won't be necessary for *you* to flee, Mrs. Johnson."

Marie wavered on her feet. "Oh my God, Bruno, they know our real name."

CHAPTER FOUR

WE STOOD IN the sand on the beach, scared out of our wits. I first shushed Marie then asked the police, "What is it I can help you with?"

A man shorter than the chief—also wearing a blue uniform—took a step forward and spoke in better English. "Mr. Gaylord, we need you to come with us."

The chief could double for the big screen actor Gilbert Roland, his black hair greased back with Brylcreem and a narrow line of a mustache on his upper lip. His black eyes resembled the marbles my brother and I played with when we were kids—knowledgeable and cunning.

Marie gripped tighter, digging her nails into my arm. I didn't flinch, the adrenaline from the threat throwing my body into full alert. I'd automatically shifted from a vertical to a horizontal stance—a horse stance—one foot ahead of the other, ready for the physical assault once I refused to go. Two officers were smaller and younger, the chief about my age, but I had weight on them and, most important, experience. Tamarindo was a quiet town devoid of murder and mayhem. There was no doubt I'd been in many more violent confrontations and knew "first with the worst" would win the day. The worst these cops dealt with were drunken tourists, which were usually already corralled by the hotel staff. The entire town was more concerned with public relations than minor public disturbances.

The same man who'd told me to come with him continued, "We will be happy to give your wife a ride home."

I peeled Marie off my arm. "Go with him."

She grabbed on again and yanked me down. "Please, please don't let this be happening."

"It'll be okay," I said, "trust me."

"How do you know that?" Her tone harsh, accusing.

The chief addressed Marie. "We are not here to cause you grief, madam. I promise you, my word of honor. We just need to talk with your husband."

"That's all?" she said. "Just talk?"

"That is correct, madam."

"Go with him," I said again. "I'll be along a little later."

Marie turned angry, pointed a finger at the chief. "We are friends with Aleck Vargas—he's going to be the next governor of the province and he won't like you messing with us." Marie never threw down the name card; it showed her desperation.

"I'm aware of Señor Vargas' status in the political arena. Now, please, we must hurry, Señor Johnson." He held his arm out. "Come."

I kissed Marie, a kiss without emotion, my mind speeding to get a foothold, find a way to work this out. None of it made sense. What the hell was going on?

All of us treaded through the sand to the wedding area now being broken down by hotel personnel. Chacho came up holding my huaraches and handed them over. "Everything all right, Gaylord?" He said Gaylord with a little too much emphasis.

"Everything is fine. Would you do me a favor and give Marie a ride home?"

"Of course, amigo."

The chief said, "But we would be honored to give her a ride. We are ruining your evening. It is the least we can do."

"Thanks. I'd feel better if Chacho took her."

"As you wish."

Marie gave me a hug and whispered close to my ear, "Is it Rosebud?"

"Hold off, I don't think so. Something else is in play here."

"You sure?"

"No. I'll call you."

She didn't answer, nodded, and left with Chacho. Some of the pressure lifted now that Marie was no longer menaced by the police. She too had warrants for her arrest for kidnap and murder. Costa Rica hadn't had an extradition treaty with the U.S. until the '90s. We liked Costa Rica better than Panama and chose lifestyle over safety, which had served us well until the high-profile wedding on the beach. Apparently, a foolish move. If the cop car headed toward the police station, I would do what had to be done to escape and evade. Knock some Tico heads together.

We moved along the concrete path beside the hotel that led out to the front.

Then out of nowhere I realized, this was about Drago. Drago had caused an incident somewhere and had asked for me.

We came out of the jungle trees and shrubs groomed by hotel staff and stepped to the front of the hotel onto the asphalt turnaround where the customers were dropped off and registered for their rooms. "How is Drago? How's my friend? Is he okay?"

The chief didn't answer. He opened the back door to a Volvo police car. I slid in and bumped into a mass of fur and muscle covered in a tee shirt.

Waldo.

He licked my face. "Oh, now you want to be friends when you're on your way to the hoosegow. Is this all about you? Did you do something wrong? Maul the wrong person?"

According to Drago, Waldo never just bit people—he mauled them. I'd seen Waldo in action and agreed wholeheartedly the dog knew his business—what Rottweilers were bred for. I leaned over and in a harsh whisper, *"Did you eat a policeman?"* Waldo took that opportunity to burp up steak breath right in my face.

The chief and one other cop, the one who spoke the best English, got in the front. We took off. I'd used this same ploy when I was a cop; put two suspects together in the back of a cop car and get them talking. Well, I wasn't going to fall for it.

The cop car didn't have a cage separating us. I leaned forward. "Did my friend Drago get into trouble? Is that what this is about?"

The chief shrugged. "I don't know a Señor Drago."

I sat back. "Did this dog have something to do with it?"

The car moved fast through the streets. "This is your dog, no? When we pulled up, he was out front of the hotel just watching. I opened the back door to the car and he jumped in."

"He's not my dog."

The chief turned in his seat. "Señor Johnson, he is wearing the same shirt as you."

I muttered, "Damn dog."

We drove a few more blocks. I finally asked, "Are you going to tell me what's going on?"

"It is better that I show you."

I didn't like the sound of that. I leaned over and whispered to Waldo, "This is all a ruse, and they're really taking you to doggie jail."

"Grrrr."

CHAPTER FIVE

THE POLICE CAR wove in and around the streets until I finally lost track of north and south, east and west, and Tamarindo was not that large. The second police car stayed right with us. The police radio in our car was oddly quiet, though I didn't know what the normal radio traffic would be in a town of six thousand people with only six police officers per shift. It was late, and everyone would be in bed. The police worked twelve-hour shifts, carried one sidearm, and kept a long gun in the cars.

I'd done my research on the department when we'd settled in Tamarindo. They'd never had a murder—or at least in recent history—that anyone could remember. Petty theft from tourists was the number one crime. The Ticos were allowed to possess three non-assault-type weapons once they applied for a permit. Not many owned guns. No drive-by shootings, no gang or drug assassinations, a quiet little corner of the world where white-collar criminals from the U.S. came to disappear and spend loads of ill-gotten gain.

Each time the cop car took a turn, I bumped shoulders with Waldo, who sat up higher on the seat looking through the windshield.

We came out on a wide boulevard, one I finally recognized. We'd gone through side streets to get there. But why?

Two other cop cars sat silent and dark in the parking lot of a strip center by a freestanding building in the same center. The building had been converted from a market into a thriving nightclub, El Gato Gordo—The Fat Cat, in Spanish. El Gato Gordo had a shady reputation as reputations go in Costa Rica. Tourists and expats could find most anything they wanted if they kept their request low profile, didn't talk about it, and paid ten times what the same vice cost in the States. I'd found out all of this while working the cabana bar overhearing conversations. Those same conversations said that the police stayed away, that the owner, an expat from the U.S., was paying off the police. El Gato was the only club of its kind for a hundred miles in either direction and Costa Rica wasn't that large of a country. In fact, it was smaller than San Bernardino, the largest county in California. From Tamarindo a two-hour car ride would take you to the Panamanian border.

I'd stayed far away from the club, not wanting to get wrapped up in any clandestine dealings. This town was my home and I wanted it to be for many years to come.

The chief and his patrol officer sat with us in the patrol car and waited. The chief dialed his cellphone and spoke in whispered Spanish that I couldn't hear; short and terse words. A tourist bus pulled into the parking lot with its headlights turned off—no lights at all for that matter—and stopped at the front door to El Gato.

I leaned over and whispered to Waldo. "What the hell's going on?" He licked my face. "Oh, now I see—once you get scared, you drop the bad dog routine."

"Grrr."

The chief turned in his seat with a concerned expression. "Do you always talk to your dog, Señor?"

"He's not my dog."

The chief nodded, his eyes moving quickly from the dog to me, trying to figure out what was going on in his back seat.

The door to El Gato opened. A dimmed yellow light sliced into the night. One patrol officer came out and stood in the gap between the bus door and the nightclub door. Suddenly another cop inside began ushering out patrons who looked harried and scared to death.

"Chief," I said. "*What is* going on?"

He waved his hand in the air. "Please, Señor, just wait a few more minutes and it will all become clear."

The bus filled halfway with patrons, started up, and took off into the night. The chief exited the Volvo police car and opened my car door. I got out and Waldo jumped out too.

"No." The chief held up his hand. "Not the perro. Have the dog get back in the car, please."

"He's not my dog and he does exactly what he wants."

"Please?"

I opened the cop car door and slapped my leg. "Come on, boy, get in." He sat on his haunches wearing the tux tee shirt that would look stupid on any dog, more so on a Waldo. He didn't budge. "See, I told you, he's not my dog." I closed the cop car door.

"Then he is your responsibility."

"Doesn't matter. Tell me what we're doing here."

The chief took out a long, narrow cigar and lit it. He puffed and pointed at me with the cigar between his fingers. "Costa Rica is not like your country." He waved his arm around. "This town, this county, is my responsibility. If something happens, I, me, I'm responsible." He poked his own chest, getting agitated. "Do you understand?"

"Yes, I do, and it is the same in my old country—there are people who are held accountable. And Costa Rica is my country now just like it is yours."

He stepped in close, smelling of cigar smoke and spices and hair grease. "No, you don't understand. I will be stripped of my rank and kicked out of the service and maybe even jailed." He pointed back toward the nightclub door. "My superiors might—no, they will—believe I had something to do with this." He took hold of my arm and pulled me away from the other three cops who had congregated and were whispering amongst themselves. "I am in a *muy malo* situation, Señor, caught between this world out here and what they in San Jose think this world really is. I cannot trust anyone. You understand now?"

Not really, but I said, "Yes."

"I need your help."

"I understand. I'll do what I can."

He came in close again, angry. "No, Señor, you do not understand. I know who and what you are, Señor Gaylord, and that never mattered before as long as you kept to yourself. You help the children, that is a noble undertaking. But you will help me figure this out or I will take you down with me. *Now* do you understand?"

"Take it easy, step back. Don't threaten me. I don't care if you are the chief of police. As a citizen of Tamarindo, I will do the best I can to help the police. But don't you dare threaten me. If you do, that proves you really don't know me."

He stared for a long moment. "I'm sorry. This . . . this whole thing has me . . . not being myself. Come, I will show you. Then you will understand."

He led the way to the door of the nightclub, still talking. "We are not experienced in this kind of thing and I have heard you are an expert. Normally we would call San Jose and they would detail a group from OIJ—Organismo de Investigacion Judicial."

I said, "I don't know where you're getting your information, but since I have lived here, I am only a humble bartender trying to make a living for my wife and children."

He stopped. "Don't make me out for a fool."

"I'm sorry, go on." Somehow, he'd heard I'd worked narcotics in my past life and that's what this was all about. Had to be with Costa Rica being so close to Panama. The chief and his men had made a big seizure and didn't know how to handle it; the money count, the dope, the guns, the interviews needed to show possession.

He opened the door and held it for me. I stepped up and peered into the gloom, peered into a version of hell I had not seen in many years.

CHAPTER SIX

Inside El Gato Gordo, the stench of burnt gunpower mixed with urine and feces and soured beer—an odor that corroborated what my eyes were telling my brain. I now understood why the chief worried about his job. Costa Rica had experienced its first "active shooter."

Tables lay on their sides with chairs and broken glassware mingled in mashed food and sweet liquors, all signs of a stampede; frantic people fleeing for their lives.

Six bodies—four male and two female—all dressed for the nightclub life littered the floor. All in different death poses, most with expressions of indescribable terror, mouths open, eyes wide. Edvard Munch's *The Scream* had nothing on these poor folks.

International news personnel would flood the once-innocent town of Tamarindo with loud, overbearing reporters filling the hotels and buzzing around like locusts. Our family would have to lock down until it was all over. We couldn't afford to have our faces splashed across the world for law enforcement to identify me—or Marie, Dad, or Bea.

I'd been estranged from my mother, Bea, my entire life until four months ago, when she showed up in our hotel suite in Glendale, California. I still had trouble calling her *Mom*.

The children too. Their parents wouldn't be looking for them, but an ambitious LA cop might. What an unholy mess.

Beside me, the chief puffed his thin cigar like a steam engine pulling a train up a grade. His black eyes glassy, his mind on the edge of shock; the nicotine stimulant probably the only thing keeping him upright.

I stepped over to the bar, poured a brandy into a glass, and handed it to the chief. "I'm sorry, I didn't realize. How can I help you?" He didn't hesitate and tossed down the elixir to bolster his frayed nerves.

His body shuddered with relief. He pulled a chair around and sat. Sweat broke out on his forehead. His tanned skin went pale.

I needed to distract him, or he was going to DFO, a ghetto term that meant, "Done Fell Out." I offered my hand. "Chief, I didn't get your name."

He nodded, put his cigarette in his thin lips, and offered me his hand. "Franco Hernandez."

I shook his hand as my cellphone buzzed. I didn't want to answer it, but Marie would be beside herself with worry. I checked the phone. A text from my adopted son Eddie Crane:

IF YOU KEEP YOUR FEET FIRMLY ON THE GROUND, YOU'LL HAVE TROUBLE PUTTING ON YOUR PANTS.

Eddie was a great kid, one of the first we'd rescued. His constant fear was that he'd somehow be thrown back into the violent world we'd saved him from. He dealt with his emotions with humor. When I didn't come home with Marie, he'd worry. He'd recently started sending me jokes, what he called "observational humor," until I was home and he saw that I was safe. He had an innate ability to make me chuckle at the most inopportune times. Though not this time, not with the death and mayhem that lay at my feet.

"Please, Señor Johnson, no cellphones, no contact until we can get this sorted out."

"I understand—it's my son." I showed him the text message to reassure him of its insignificance.

He nodded and looked at me like I was crazy.

I put my phone back in my pocket. "I don't know how you'll be able to keep this under wraps."

I noticed Waldo had snuck in and sat in the corner on his haunches still wearing that ridiculous tee shirt juxtaposed against a violence that still oozed from the air and would forever haunt the place.

Oh shit, I was also wearing one of those shirts.

"I know we can't," the chief said. "I just want a head start before I get frozen out of my own crime scene, frozen out of my life and my career. Please, Señor Johnson, tell me what you see." He waved his arm around the death room.

"I worked the streets of South Central Los Angeles and then I chased violent criminals. I never worked homicide."

He waved his hand again as he rapidly puffed his cigar, his other hand lighting another as the one in his mouth burned down to a nub. "But you have more experience than all of us. Please, tell me what you see. Tell me what we should do first." He yelled something in Spanish. The policeman who drove us to El Gato Gordo hurried in with a notepad and pen ready to take dictation.

I nodded and let my mind slip back to the old days working South Central LA when I'd come upon or was dispatched to a violent scene with dead bodies. An event that happened at least once a month— sometimes every other week if the Crips and Bloods were in an active feud.

I took a tour through the carnage to get that first observation, that first impression—sidestepping the pools of fresh blood. Then I opened the pass-through and checked behind the bar as well. I counted ten shell casings, bright brass, 9mm expended rounds on top of the "L" part of the bar and down on the duckboards. I came back to the chief.

"I'd say one shooter. He came in, got up on the bar, and picked his targets. He used a nine-millimeter handgun with a double-stacked magazine. This was not a random act. This guy is a professional."

The steno police officer kept writing.

"Are you sure?" the chief said. "All these people and just one shooter?" He held up one finger.

"Anybody of yours wounded?"

He shook his head. "No, those people you saw get on the bus are witnesses—the ones we could corral. Some fled before my first man got here. He was very close and heard the shots."

"No one else wounded. The shell casings all in one place. It was one shooter."

The chief shook his head. "*Dios mio.* Continue."

"No one else was hit—except who he targeted."

"Then why so many?" the chief asked.

"The shooter wanted two things: one—confusion and chaos, which he accomplished; two—he wanted his true target, the one person he came for, mixed in with the rest to delay or stymie your investigation altogether."

The steno said, "Excuse me, *como se dece, stymie.*"

"Confuse or stop."

"Gracias, Señor."

"What else?" the chief asked.

"The shell casings are in one place. So the shooter was calm with a steady hand. He didn't move around while shooting. Based on where the shell casings landed, I'd say he was standing on the bar commanding high ground—another tactic of someone experienced in violence."

The steno stopped writing. "That's correct, that's what the witnesses said. He came in, climbed up on the stool and onto the bar. That is amazing how you can see all of this from what is left behind."

"What else did the witness say?" I asked.

The steno cop looked to the chief who nodded to go ahead. The steno cop referenced his notebook for accuracy. "The witness said that the man wore a plain blue ball cap down low over his eyes and a scarf up over his mouth and nose. He had on a gray raincoat; the witness said it was a London Fog. When the killer was up on the bar, the witness got a good look at his shoes, He said they were wingtips, black wingtips."

"What would you do next?" the chief asked. "We have to hurry. I cannot delay much longer before calling the OIJ. Our only chance of keeping our jobs is to solve this before OIJ does. So, tell me what to do before they take over. What would you do next?"

"First, you need to know the real target. That might get you to a motive. Motive might get you to the suspect. Deconstruct the scene, see who was shot first. The shooter would want to put down his target first, then invest in the mayhem and chaos."

The chief nodded and stood, a little wobbly on his feet. He waved for me to follow him as he wove in and around the bodies until he came to a man wearing a white linen suit who lay face down with two exit wounds in his back, the material of his jacket saturated with blood. The chief stood by the dead man and gestured for me to turn him over. "This is why we will all lose our jobs and maybe even end up in carcel—in jail."

I squatted, took hold of the shoulder, and eased the man to the side. Then I fell back on my ass, startled. The man was Aleck Vargas, the doctor who'd delivered our son Tobias, my friend. This was Layla's father. Drago's new wife's father. This was our friend dead on the floor of El Gato Gordo.

CHAPTER SEVEN

I STOOD IN El Gato over the dead body of Aleck Vargas, the next governor of the province. Marie would be emotionally crushed. His daughter, Layla, on her honeymoon. Alisa, his wife, had to be told.

I had just seen Aleck and Alisa at the wedding, not two or three hours before. And the chief was right, this would be a category five shitstorm, one that would flatten the town of Tamarindo with a smothering stink and forever taint the town with a murderous reputation. A storm our family would have difficulty weathering.

"Was his wife, Alisa, here with him?"

The chief shook his head and lowered his tone even though no one else was alive to hear. "No, he was here with another woman, his *amante*."

"One of these two women?"

"No."

"Was she on the bus that left?"

He shook his head. "No, we will have to identify her by talking to all the witnesses."

Sweat now broke out on my forehead. The situation continued to get worse. "Okay. You and your man step back to the door." I took out my phone and told Waldo to sit and stay. Oddly, he complied. I walked outside and took photos of the parking lot, the cars, the entire surrounding area. I took one of the front door, entered, and took general photos first of the crime scene, then stood up on the bar and took overalls again, sidestepping where the suspect might've stood. I wanted an interior overall, but I also wanted to see what the suspect saw. How he saw it.

I wished I had booties, gloves, and hair cover. I was dropping DNA all over the place. My DNA was on record.

I froze. Was that what the chief really wanted? A fugitive American wanted on murder charges? I'd be the perfect patsy. I looked back at him. His expression still carried the look of a harried man about to drop in his tracks from stress. If he didn't find the shooter outright, I might be his plan B.

I didn't like being someone's plan B.

"Okay," I said. "Now close-ups. Follow along and write exactly what I tell you, no shortcuts, you understand?"

The patrol officer nodded. I stopped at the closest victim, a man. I described him: height, weight, hair color, and then took photos. I took out his wallet and identified him, took photos of his driver's license and everything inside. I took photos of his wounds, his hands and jewelry. I took the flashlight from the steno officer and shone it around. "Here," I said to the chief, "hold it right here." He did. I captured a picture of the blood splatter on the wall.

I moved to the next man lying on his stomach. I would have to remember the sequence of photos and not get them mixed up. The overall photos would help. I took photos and moved him as little as possible to get his wallet. I opened it.

From a crouch I sat back on my butt, stunned. My hand going into a pool of blood from the next closest person, a woman.

The chief said, "What? What's the matter? You know this man?"

"Yes, it's Salvador Perez."

"What? Are you sure?" The chief grabbed a handful of black hair and pulled it back to see his face and then let it drop with a thunk.

"Hey!" I said, "Take it easy, he was a friend of mine."

Color flushed the chief's pale face. He waved his arm around. "All of this is because of him." He kicked Salvador's corpse.

I stood and wiped my hand on my pants. "I'm not going to tell you again—leave him alone."

"Señor Johnson, this man was the target, not Señor Vargas. Salvador Perez had his filthy hand in everything from Tamarindo to San Jose and was a very close friend of the *Mordida*. I have been trying to arrest him for years. He is too smart. He is a *zorro*, a fox."

Mordida was a bribe or payoff.

Sal worked as a private eye but was more of a fixer. He had saved my family twice from the evil that tracked us to Costa Rica. Most recently, he'd made two bikers disappear who had menaced my family and had written a phone number in indelible ink on my son Toby's back. Scared the bejesus out of the poor kid. Toby had night terrors for weeks afterward. I lost no sleep over Salvador taking the two bikers for a long boat ride out into the Pacific chumming for sharks.

I knew Salvador as an honest stalwart man, bold and fearless. Maybe once in a while, he did cross the line, but it would have only been to right a moral wrong. One thing for sure, the chief was right, Salvador could've been the target and all the others just fodder, white noise to cover the assassin's intent. Now we had two possible targets; that only served to further muddy the water.

A lump of emotions rose in my throat as I patted Salvador down. I found his cellphone, palmed it, and set it by my foot to be moved to my pocket when I stood. I called out all the items I found, rings, comb, money clip with American dollars, and a small .380 pistol in an ankle holster, a stainless steel, Walther PPK, a James Bond gun.

When I pulled it out the chief exclaimed, "See. I told you. The man is no good. Nobody but bad people carry a gun. No, Señor, this man, he was the target. This proves it. This is good, we can tell the OIJ—give them Salvador."

I ignored the chief's prejudice, sniffed the gun, checked the loads, wiped everything off, and put it all back just the way I found it. Except the cellphone.

The gun had not been fired.

The chief returned to his confusion, trying to work out in his head the story he'd tell OIJ: if he knew of Salvador's purported nefarious acts, how come the chief didn't do something about it? The chief was right back in the jackpot.

I stood and stretched the kink in my back. "Chief, do you have someone who knows how to draw?"

"Like portraits? That's what you are talking about?"

"No, a diagram of this room, someone who can place all the bodies and furniture, the shell casings, every little item, draw it to scale. Scale is important here."

"Yes, good idea. Our traffic accident investigation team can do it."

"They will have to be careful not to disturb any evidence."

"I understand." He stepped away to talk on his cellphone. I bent over on a pretense to check Salvador's watch, palmed his cellphone, and stuck it in my pocket. I wasn't sly enough. The steno officer caught the movement and raised an eyebrow. I could only glare to silence him.

The chief came back. "Time is short. I will have to make the call to the OIJ."

We hurried through the other victims with the photos and personal inventory. Nothing of note presented itself, but the investigation had just started—we might not know something was important until later on. A homicide investigator once told me he made a suspect in a case because the first investigator on scene had written in his notebook the grass was wet with dew and didn't have any footprints. Everything was important until it wasn't.

I asked the chief, "How badly do you want to mess up the scene?"

"Explain?"

"I'd like to dust the bar for footprints and at least two or three of the shell casings."

He thought for a moment puffing, puffing, puffing, creating a cloud in the ceiling above us. "I am going to be suspended and locked up anyway, so go ahead."

"Seriously? Locked up?"

"Yes, there is no question. Now hurry, please."

I found some cleanser in the bathroom and lightly dusted the bar, then gently blew it off, bringing up some footprints. I used a ruler for scale and took photos from different angles with different light, the chief looking over my shoulder in awe. I ground up graphite used in a mechanical pencil the steno officer had in his clipboard and dusted three of the expended pistol cartridges. "Just what I thought, no prints."

"Meaning?" the chief asked.

"The suspect wore gloves when he loaded his gun. He's a pro for sure." I didn't want to add that the odds of finding him were nil. He'd already be on a plane or in a car crossing the Panama border for a long holiday. Mission accomplished.

After another hour I handed the chief my phone and told him my password: "Marie." I said, "Make two copies of all the photos, 8 x 11s, and put them all in a three-ring binder. Put the photos in clear sleeves; do not punch holes in the photos. One binder for me and one for you."

"Good, yes, I understand." He handed the phone to the steno officer.

"Don't tell OIJ that I'm involved."

"I am not a fool, *mi amigo*."

Least I was *his friend*. For now.

"When you get it done, drop my binder with the phone at my house. I also want a copy of the diagram."

"It will be done." He held out his hand. "Thank you, Señor. I am in your debt."

God, I hope so. I shook his hand. "*De nada*."

"Come on, Waldo, let's go home. I'm tired."

"We can give you a ride."

"That's okay, it's only a couple of miles. I can use the walk to think things over."

"I understand." He held the door open for us. The sun, still far below the horizon, had just started to color the sky with a purple bruise. Now the hard part, telling Marie our little corner of paradise had been corrupted with an incurable malignant cancer called blood and bone.

CHAPTER EIGHT

I SET A quick pace to get us home in less than an hour, Waldo keeping up without a problem, though with the penguin shirts we looked like Dumb and Dumber. The larger problem—I didn't know which one was Dumber. The sky color shifted from dark to pewter with the first signs of dawn. I found the tall double gate to the estate locked as well as the front doors. Marie had gone on high alert. Waldo entered like he owned the place and it was then, hours after Drago took off for Rio, that I realized he'd left me with his dog to care for. Of course, he wouldn't take Waldo on his honeymoon, what was I thinking? Waldo prancing around the nude beaches of Rio?

"Terrific," I muttered to him. He trotted over to lie down under the long dining room table. Halfway down the hall, I heard Tobias' cries. When I reached the master bedroom, I found Marie pacing, gently bouncing him, trying to calm him to no avail. She saw me and hurried over. "You're back, thank God."

"Here." I took our son. "You lie down and get some sleep. I'll take first shift, then you can relieve me."

"Is everything okay? What happened? What did that rude jerk want?"

"He just wanted some advice, that's all, no big deal." I wanted her to get some sleep before I dropped the bomb on her about Aleck. After that there wouldn't be any sleeping for a while. I'd pay dearly for the delay in telling her.

"So now you're a law enforcement consultant? Bruno, with our situation here, do you know how surreal that statement sounds?"

The walk home in the predawn and the warm, still air in the house brought on my own fatigue. Even so, her words made it to my brain. I could only nod and promise myself I'd think about it later with rested brain cells. "Get some sleep. Please?"

"You sure it's okay?"

"Positive." I followed her to the bed and with one hand pulled the spread over her and kissed her forehead. "You go ahead and sleep in. I got this."

"Thank you, baby, I'm so godawful tired. Just gimme two hours and I'll be right as rain, I promise. I'll relieve you in . . . four hours, just gimme four hours and . . ." A big yawn devoured her last words.

"Take eight. I'm wide awake."

She nodded, her eyes already closing. I didn't know how I'd stay awake for eight hours. Out in the living room I paced the floor, cooing to Tobias to no avail. Finally, I sat down on the couch, laid the two-month-old on my chest, covered us with an afghan, and hummed a lullaby. He could feel my heart beat and my chest rising and falling and quickly fell asleep.

Tobias' cries had been the only thing keeping me awake. There was something about a newborn child, the warmth, the scent of baby and baby powder that is comforting and lulling as if having a child makes everything right in the world. I closed my eyes with a promise not to fall asleep. I just needed to close them for a moment, that was all, just a couple of seconds, maybe a minute.

I woke to a cool spot on my chest recently vacated by Tobias. Rosie's aunt walked away with him. We'd brought her on to help with the newborn and all the other children. Our household chores overwhelmed three adults.

I still had to make my shift at the cabana bar so I wouldn't raise any suspicions. I lifted a hand to wave at her when a faint sobbing caught my attention.

Marie sat on the other side of me, tears running down her cheeks. In her lap she held a black three-ring binder thick with the report and abundant photos the chief had dropped off.

"Ah, man, I'm so sorry, baby. I didn't want to tell you until you got some sleep."

She tossed the binder on the couch and eased over to rest her head on my chest. "How horrible. What a nightmare. Has Alisa been told? I should go over there and be with her. Bruno, what's going on? Why'd this happen here of all places? This is our hidden paradise. We're raising our children here."

I didn't want to tell the rest—the part about if the chief goes down, he was taking me with him. "Is it on the news yet?"

She shook her head. "Not yet. I checked."

"The chief said he was going to keep it under wraps, but a thing like this, I don't know."

"The Ticos are a proud people and will be ashamed over what happened in their town. You add the chief telling them not to talk, and there won't be a peep out of them. It's the tourists that were there when this happened—that's where the leak will come."

Some of the kids tried to wander in; Marie held up her hand. "Nope, not right now. We're talking. Give a us few minutes, please." Eddie Crane stood in the doorway smiling, tossing a ball in the air.

"I'll throw the ball with you in a little while," I said, "before I leave for work." He nodded.

Rosie came out holding Daph, Layla's newly acquired child, and herded the kids into the kitchen. The savory scent from breakfast wafted in and made my stomach growl.

"Are you taking your shift today, like you said you were?"

"Yes, I don't want anything to seem abnormal. What time is it?" I checked my watch. I only had an hour.

She pointed to the binder. "Any ideas at all?"

"None, right now. I had to get some sleep first. I know it's not fair, but I was hoping . . . that you'd make some time to take a look at it and let me know what you think."

Normally that would be a weird question, a husband asking his wife to read a murder book. I sure didn't want her looking at the gruesome and grotesque photos. But a few months ago, when I'd been asked by a friend to find the men who took his granddaughter and to make them pay the price, it was Marie who solved the case by staring at the photos for hours at a time. She caught a minor detail even the FBI had missed.

She tugged on my penguin shirt and wiped tears from her eyes then suddenly sat back. "Ah, Bruno, you have a bloody handprint on your pants. Get in there and take a shower and don't let the kids see it." She slapped my leg without putting any oomph behind it.

Waldo trotted into the living room with at least ten stolen tortillas in his mouth and Rosie in hot pursuit. He jumped up on the couch, looking for backup from me. "Sorry, pal, you're on your own." He gulped down the floury treat and stared at Rosie as she scolded him in Spanish.

"Babe," I said, "would you please take that silly tee shirt off him." I was afraid he'd maul me if I tried.

She slapped my leg again. "Not a chance. You do it. He's your dog."

"*He's not my dog.*"

CHAPTER NINE

THREE MINOR SOUS chefs in the huge near-vacant kitchen worked diligently setting up for the night's meals, preparing the fish and meat and salads, the sauces. The chefs and waitstaff wouldn't be in for another hour. The sous chefs talked quietly among themselves. I heard several times, "a tigre negro," a black tiger or black cat, as I prepared my round tray with fresh fruit for the night's cocktails out at the cabana bar. Did they mean Fat Cat as in *El Gato Gordo*? Costa Rica had indigenous black panthers that were on the endangered species list. One is occasionally spotted in the jungle fringes around the town and a public safety alert goes out on cellphones.

Normally I joked with them, but the word about the police escorting me away from the hotel must've been going around like a virus. They were too proud to ask. If the news was out regarding El Gato Gordo, the sous wouldn't say a word about that either. Shame for their town would preclude them from mentioning it.

Maybe someone had spotted a big cat. Some got as large as two hundred pounds and could easily kill a man . . . or slap Waldo around like an errant child. When I first heard about the cats, I kept the children inside for a week until Marie told me I was being ridiculous.

The sous quit talking and I calmed down. I mindlessly sliced the limes, lemons, mangoes, pineapple, celery, passion fruit, kiwi, and melon balls, my hands doing all the work, my mind going over the previous evening's events, trying and failing to fit the pieces together. I didn't have enough of the pieces to complete a picture.

A lovely and lithe, long-fingered hand appeared in front of my face waving. "Gaylord? Earth to Gaylord."

I snapped out of my trance to find my boss, Darla Figueroa, the food and beverage manager, standing too close clad in her standard attire, a curve-hugging black dress with a white pearl necklace, stark against tanned skin, her brand; a brand she worked hard at maintaining. She ran a tight ship and as a leader was beyond reproach; always firm but fair. She wielded huge power in the running of the hotel and worked as *the* fixer when a problem arose in any department or with any unhappy guest. Her easygoing attitude and bright smile made her perfect for the job and made me wonder what they paid her. Whatever it was it wasn't enough, wrangling employees like me.

"Oh, hi boss."

"You zoned out there for a minute." She leaned in to read the nameplate on my hotel aloha shirt. "It is *Gaylord* this week, right?"

"Gaylord, yes, right." She went along with the name ruse after returning guests thought it humorous and added to the joie de vivre of the hotel.

Her expression shifted to concern. Her brown eyes could drill into one's soul. I'd told Marie about those eyes, and she'd pinched me. Hard. Darla's tanned skin was blemish free, smooth as a mocha coffee, and made the whites of her eyes and white teeth stand out even more. I didn't know when she had time to work on her tan— she was always at the hotel.

"I'm worried about last night," she said. "I need you to explain." She had one crooked upper right tooth that stood out and made her smile a tad crooked as well. It added to her mystique.

I'd only heard this tone in her voice three other times—all a precursor to firing an employee who wasn't "a team player." I stood on the razor's edge of unemployment. I had some favors in the favor bank with her, but if the word came out about El Gato Gordo and that I was there, that would be it, too huge a black mark linked to the hotel. I'd be back to tour guide for Americans who wanted to see a three-toed sloth and Geoffroy's spider monkeys out in the hot, sweaty jungle. Where a panther now skulked.

"Is this about last night? Was the wedding too loud? I apologize if it was."

She stared at me, not saying another word, an interrogation ploy I'd used on obstinate criminals when soliciting a statement against their penal interest. I smiled and tried to wait her out as a faint scent of Chanel mixed with the fresh mango.

She blinked first. She poked a perfectly manicured nail into my arm. "That's not what I'm talking about and you know it. Tell me."

I pasted on the best confused expression I could and feigned ignorance. I shrugged.

"The police?" she said.

I forced myself to relax and smiled hugely. "Oh, that. For a second there you had me worried."

"Gaylord?"

I looked both ways in a furtive gesture. "I . . . ah have been sworn to secrecy."

"In normal circumstances that might work with other people, not with me, and you know it. Give."

"You'll fix it with the chief if he gets mad that I talked?"

"You know I will."

And she could. Normally she had the chief tamed and barking for the seductive treats she tossed to him.

"They wanted me to identify a possible car thief."

"What's the big secret there? Was the thief staying at this hotel?"

This was her only real concern, the hotel came first above all else. "Well," I hesitated, looked around again for eavesdroppers. "The car was abandoned near our house and—"

"And what?"

"They found drugs and money in it."

"Drugs *and* money. The police never get the money and the dope together—it's one or the other."

She was one smart cookie. I shrugged. "I don't know, that's just what they said. I never saw any of it. They just wanted me to look at some pictures, some mug shots, no big deal."

She stared into my eyes a moment longer searching for the truth. Finally, she said, "Okay, good. Quit lollygagging and get back to work."

"Yes, boss, I'm on it."

I'd dodged a bullet. Maybe. If she found out I lied, I was done working at the hotel.

I hoisted the tray on my shoulder and carried it out. The bartender job was getting in the way. I had a few leads I needed to follow up, but at the same time had to maintain appearances. Now the boss would have me under a microscope. It couldn't get any worse. I suddenly looked around for Waldo and didn't see him.

Waldo could make it worse.

CHAPTER TEN

TOURISTS FROLICKED BY the pool and on the beach unaware of the local disaster that, once exposed, would forever paint their memories red.

White fluffy clouds scudded across the beautiful blue, throwing the world in and out of shade, creating shadows to hide from the heat.

I set the tray on the bar and opened the pass-through. Chacho came over and whispered, "Is everything okay, *mi amigo?*"

"Yes, fine, why?" Did Chacho know about El Gato Gordo?

He shrugged and moved his eyes askance as he spoke. "I was worried about you, *hombre,* the *policia* and all."

Shame wouldn't allow him to look me in the eye.

"Oh . . . ah that. No, they just wanted me to look at something . . . I mean, they wanted to know if I'd seen anyone driving a stolen car they'd found parked close to *mi casa.*" I kept with the same story I'd fed Darla.

"A stolen car, really?"

I'd forgotten stolen cars in the States were as frequent as stolen bikes in Costa Rica. A stolen car to the Ticos was big news.

Six dead in a nightclub was a tsunami.

"Everything is fine," I said.

He nodded, smiled. "Bueno. Ah, O Grande has been asking for you."

"Otis Brasher?" He was the obese American who sat at the bar all day in his sweat-stained seersucker suit sipping rich drinks colored green. He only took off his Panama hat to wipe down his bald pate with a clean and folded handkerchief he kept in his back pocket. He arrived at the bar when it first opened to get his "prime seat," a position that allowed him to perv on the semi-nakedness on the beach. He called them "luscious sandy jellyrolls." I made him as a stock market thief, inside trader on the lam from the SEC—the Securities and Exchange Commission—with a bag full of greenbacks.

Chacho nodded again.

I said, "He thinks I make a better grasshopper than you do." A grasshopper is a cocktail composed of 1 shot green crème de menthe, 1 shot white crème de cacao, and 2 scoops vanilla ice cream, blended to a smooth finish with a fresh mint sprig for garnish.

Chacho punched my arm. "Okay, mi amigo, let us have a taste-off. My grasshoppers will eat yours alive."

Sometimes his analogies cracked me up. I chuckled. "I think not. I have a secret ingredient." He'd spin his wheels trying to think of what that secret ingredient could be, and he'd watch my every move until I let my guard down while making one.

I closed the pass-through, caught up on drink orders, and joked with the tourists. I only had an hour until siesta. The Ticos took the midday break very seriously. Everything shut down so everyone in the country could take a nap. I didn't see the benefit when we first arrived but now loved the idea. Since I was an American expat, the beverage manager for the hotel, the notorious Darla Figueroa, scheduled me to handle the tourist drinks during the siesta. Unfair labor practices because I'd come to love the siesta.

I wiped the bar off with a fresh towel and washed glasses while my mind wandered off to rework the crime scene in El Gato Gordo. Going over it again—and again—body by body, shell casing by shell casing, reliving the scents, the colors, the awful death masks. The expression on Aleck's face, I would never forget; Aleck would haunt me in my dreams for weeks before he blended in with all the other members from my "blood and bone" memory album.

Otis Brasher finally caught my eye. "Can I talk you into another one of these?"

"Certainly." The man didn't have any lips, a physical attribute I unjustly assigned to criminals, usually child molesters. His mouth, a too-thin line, contrasted with the waddles of fat in his jowls. Broken blood vessels just under the skin made for a complicated road map on his cheeks and nose. Add the unkept bushy gray and brown eyebrows and he turned into a caricature in a Sunday comic strip, a man trying to cheat a cute little girl out of her lollypop.

I pulled a fresh blender and added the ingredients for a grasshopper, checked to see if Chacho was close enough to see, pulled a brown bottle of peppermint extract from my pocket, and added a dash. Otis leaned over before I pushed the PUREE button. "I need to talk with you."

"I'm standing right here, my friend, fire away."

"No, in private, it's very important."

I held my finger over the button on the blender, ready to push. "What about?"

He sat back and smiled, downing the last dregs to his previous grasshopper. "We're not in a private place, now are we?"

I nodded as I tried to work out what he wanted. Under normal circumstances I would have kindly rejected the man, letting him down easy, not wanting to fraternize. But after last night there would never again be a "normal" in our little paradise.

"I get a fifteen-minute cigarette break once the siesta is over." I had to find out what he wanted.

Two hours flew by. Chacho suddenly appeared at my side, his hands a blur, almost instantly catching us up on the sudden rush for bottled beer and fluffy pastel-colored cocktails with fruit garnish. "Go, amigo. I got this."

"Great, I'll be back in fifteen." I looked over to Otis. He'd slipped way during the rush. He never left the bar except to "tap a kidney—grasshoppers in and grasshoppers out." From ten in the morning until seven at night he sat and drank and stared at the talent on the beach. I picked up his empty martini glass tinted green and the half-crumpled cocktail napkin. On the napkin he'd written, "Rm 245."

I left the bar, walking fast.

CHAPTER ELEVEN

OUT OF OLD habit, when I knocked, I stayed to the side of the door to room 245. If a crook wanted you bad enough, all he had to do was point at "the window of death," wait for the knock, then shoot holes through the wood.

The door opened to a brightly lit room, the curtains on the balcony fluttering, windblown through the half-opened slider. That same wind enveloped me in Otis' scent of sour body odor, burnt cigar, crème de menthe, and oddly the contrasting essence of peppermint. He'd taken off the seersucker suit and his belly bulged against the buttons to his dress shirt, doing a valiant job holding fast against the onslaught. Instead of a belt, suspenders, the colors of the rainbow, stretched tight against his slumped shoulders.

Along one wall, he had stacked on the floor, waist-high, five rows of contemporary and classic mysteries and thriller novels. That explained what he did at night when he left the bar. He was a voracious reader of murder and intrigue. All the book bindings crinkled from use indicated he might have read them more than once, that or had no respect for books.

"Come in, take a seat. Can I get you something to drink from the mini bar?"

"Thank you, I'm good. Can we get right to it, I don't have a lot of time."

I stood by the closed door. Otis sat on the couch that had since turned a little swayback from his constant weight, the same place he obviously sat at night while reading his murder mysteries. On the end table close at hand was a recently oiled Browning Hi-Power 9mm pistol. The blue steel glistened.

I'd assessed the threat level. Otis in his obesity didn't move quick enough to worry about. I could open the door and be in the safety of the hall before he got to the gun and pointed. That model of Browning was single-action and the hammer had to be pulled back in order to fire, which added another second to evade. Plenty of time. A more important question though; what was a man like Otis Brasher, a dumpy white-collared criminal, doing with a handgun? *Just because he was paranoid didn't mean people weren't after him*, something my old partner Robby Wicks would often say when he and I were on the trail of a violent offender.

Brasher put his arm on the back of the couch. "Ah, you've spotted my little toy."

Little toy? A handgun was designed for one thing, to kill people.

"How did you get a gun in Costa Rica? This place isn't like the States where guns are on every street corner."

"That's in part why I asked you here. I want to hire you."

"Hire me? For what?" He'd dodged my question about where he'd obtained the weapon.

"For protection, of course."

This had never happened in all the time we'd been in Costa Rica; no one ever confronted me about my background and asked a favor.

What had changed? What was different?

El Gato Gordo was different, that's where my mind immediately took refuge; and I didn't like it. I didn't get the "of course." Why would he think an African American cabana bartender had the ability to protect him? This was coming very close to "Rosebud." Maybe we should've bugged out last night. Uprooting the children from where they were comfortable in their surroundings, throwing them back into the breach of the unknown, one laden with fear and night terrors. Of course, we were loath to make that drastic move without good cause, but was the need to stay connected to a home clouding good sense?

I said, "First, two questions. One, why me? And two, why do you need protection?"

His thin lips eked out a weak smile that blended too well with his entire persona; feeble, slug-like. I'd come to know him over the two months he'd stayed at the hotel sitting at my bar day after day killing off enough grasshoppers to save all the corn in Iowa from a biblical blight.

Visually, he came off as a fat old man, lonely with lots of time and money to waste. Someone who used to have a wife and kids, back in say, Omaha, and played bridge once a week with his neighbors, and on Friday night took the wife to get a steak and drink too much wine at the local watering hole.

Now he sat in an expensive suite in Costa Rica, afraid or paranoid someone was going to shuffle him off this mortal coil. Or something similarly derived from the books stacked against his wall.

He nodded and thought about it for a second and said, "I've had enough time to observe you, the way you watch everyone—watch everything that happens by the pool, on the beach, and at the same time the bar. All the while doing your job, talking to the drunk tourists, making them their drinks and taking their money. You're watching for something that's out there lurking. I just want you to do the same thing for me. And for your services, I'm willing to pay you say . . . a thousand dollars a day."

"A thousand a day?" That was an outrageous wage. If he stayed another two months, that would be sixty thousand dollars. That kind of money would go a long way to clothe and feed and educate the children.

"Paid in cash every night you walk me to my hotel room door and leave me in the very capable hands of Big Bertha." He nodded to the Browning 9mm. He *was* a nerd.

"For how long?"

"So, you're interested?"

"Maybe. You still haven't told me what's out there looking for you."

"Is that necessary information? Not for this kind of money, right?"

"No, if you only want me to alert you to a shift in the outside environment, that's one thing. If you want me to take action against bad actors, then no—I would need to know what exactly you are afraid of. Would I need a club or a bazooka?"

"You don't come off as faint of heart. In fact, I would take you as more of a person who knows how to handle himself in tight situations. And enjoy it. Are you ex-military?"

"What did you do back in the States?" I asked. How had he recognized my abilities if he were just an office pogue who walked off with a bag full of embezzled dollars, a fat and slow, white-collar criminal without real-world experience? Had I misjudged him?

"For a thousand a day, I would expect more than an alert to a threat. I would expect a neutralization of that threat." He'd ignored my question, yet again.

"What's changed? You've been here for two months, why now? What's happened?"

The thin smile again. He said, "You show me yours and I'll show you mine. Who are *you* and what are *you* wanted for?"

I put my hand on the doorknob. "Thank you for your time, Mr. Brasher."

"Wait. Wait."

I stopped.

"Okay, it was the wedding. All those people made me nervous, that's all. Too many people all at once invading our . . . ah, private tranquility."

"You're a bad liar."

He stared at me.

I said, "I would be happy to take your money, but I have a prior thing that I'm working right now, and I won't be at the bar as much until it's resolved." Did he know about what happened at El Gato Gordo? Was that why he wanted protection. "Otis, where were you last night? Did you go out?"

He shook his head; the waddles jiggled. "Nope, stayed in all night with my good friend Raymond Chandler and his enchanting *Lady in the Lake*."

I nodded, watching him and trying to decipher the truth from his mannerisms. The *lady in the lake* was a murder victim. Had he made that reference on purpose?

"I'm good with you watching out while you're here. Do you know someone who can cover for you when you're not? I'm not . . . ah . . . familiar with that world and wouldn't know how to solicit someone else. It was only luck that I spotted you. And, of course, this person's compensation would have to come out of your pay."

Something wasn't right with the entire deal, the way he spoke, the amount of money offered—the whole thing stank of latent skullduggery. "I wouldn't be fine with that arrangement. If something happened when I wasn't here, I'd be responsible."

"Ah, a man of conscience. Even better. The way I look at it, any protection is better than none."

"That's a lot of money for that kind of deal. Tell me the truth—who's after you? The law?"

He stared at me. "You want the job, as is, or not?"

Why now? Why me? If El Gato had not happened, I wouldn't have been as suspicious. I didn't believe in coincidences when it came to blood and bone sneaking up and taking a big bite out of my ass. To keep him where I could watch him was better than letting him run on his own while frequenting my bar. And why not get paid for it at the same time.

"Okay, it's a deal."

"Fine, tomorrow come in early before your shift. I'll need an escort to the bar at ten in the morning. Then you can hang around until your shift starts." He winked. "And maybe tell Chacho how to make your kind of grasshopper."

"I still get to leave to take care of this other thing. When I do, I'll try and have someone cover for me. If not—" I shrugged.

"I understand, just keep me informed, that's all I ask. I want to know when I'm able to sit back and enjoy my cocktails without having to worry about looking over my shoulder. That's worth a lot to me."

"See you at ten."

He put two fingers to his forehead and saluted me. I opened the door and slipped out, worried I'd missed something important that he'd said. Worried that this guy wasn't who he said he was. I almost tripped over Waldo sitting in the hall outside the suite door. At least someone had taken off that dumbass-tux shirt. "How'd you get here?" Waldo knew how to get to the hotel from the house and after that he simply followed his sniffer.

Otis came out of his room. "Hey, wait up. You're supposed to escort me back to the bar."

"Oh, right."

"You have a nice dog." He reached down to pet him.

"He's not my dog."

CHAPTER TWELVE

WE WALKED IN silence along with Waldo down the stairs and out the side door, avoiding the lobby to get down to the cabana bar. I didn't want anyone to see me fraternizing—a serious hotel infraction that could lead to days off and even termination.

Someone had taken Otis Brasser's spot at the bar. Like an ass, he stood in the couple's personal space and stared, making them squirm until they moved.

Chacho was slammed with drink orders. I jumped in, and we got them all knocked out. Waldo crashed a game of Frisbee on the beach with three twenty-something men in Speedos, their tanned bodies slicked down with oil and lightly sprinkled with sand. Soon a third of the beach had stopped to watch the hundred-and-thirty-pound beast leap lithely and snatch an orange plastic disk out of the air. He'd take the Frisbee to the closest other player and then retake his position. People clapped and cheered.

What a ham.

The cabana bar phone rang. Chacho answered it while I grabbed three Budweisers and served them to hotel guests visiting from England, pasty white with thick accents. Chacho held the phone out for me. "For you, amigo."

I took the phone. I'd assumed the call was from his long-time girlfriend Gloria who kept him on a tight leash.

"Hello?"

"Gaylord, was that your dog I saw you with in the hotel?"

"Who is this?" My mind kicked in and recognized the voice too late. Darla, the food and beverage manager, my boss. "I . . . ah came through the hotel returning from my break, but that dog isn't mine. He was just following along."

"I've had some complaints about that beast helping himself to the leftover food on discarded room service trays in hallways outside the rooms. When confronted, he struts around like he owns the place. Now I'm told he's out on the beach annoying the sunbathers."

"Not my dog."

"You're sure? Then I'm calling APU—the Animal Protection Unit."

"Yep, positive. Not mine."

"Good. If he was your dog, I would have to write you a blue sheet."

A blue sheet was something the industrious and always conscientious Darla Figueroa thought up when she took over the job eight months ago to track hotel employee infractions. Three infractions and you were gone, no questions asked; *adios muchachos*. The employees called them "bluies—*pequeno azul*."

She hung up without saying goodbye. I immediately felt bad. Drago had not asked me to take care of his dog, but as his best friend, I took it as my responsibility to look out for Waldo while Drago was on his honeymoon.

Damn dog.

Waldo chose that moment to come bounding over from his thrilling game of Frisbee. His large pink tongue lulled out of his mouth from thirst.

I yelled, "Go home." And pointed in the direction of our house.
He barked.

"I said go home."

He barked again.

"You better go home." I leaned over the bar and whispered, "They're coming for you, run."

"Grrr."

Chacho opened a Modelo beer. "Amigo, that's his beer bark."

I stood up straight. "His what?"

"His beer bark. He barks like that when he is thirsty. Come here, boy."

Waldo came around and under the pass-through and onto the duck boards inside the cabana bar. Chacho poured beer in a red plastic cup reserved for pool cocktails. Waldo lapped it up with his long pink tongue. Chacho said, "I've been putting them on your tab."

"*On my tab*? Are you kidding me? Then give him the cheap beer. Or don't give him any beer at all for that matter. Dogs don't drink beer."

"Oh, I tried. He only drinks Modelo."

"Damn dog *only drinks Modelo*."

The phone rang.

"Amigo, aren't you going to answer that?"

"Get that dog out of here. The Ice Princess thinks he's my dog and I'll get a bluie out of it for sure if he's not gone."

Otis Brasher now sat in his usual place sipping a grasshopper, chuckling at our exchange about a dumb dog.

I scowled at him and answered the phone. "Lido bar."

"Gaylord—"

I looked back toward the hotel. Where was she? How could she see Waldo inside the bar?

"Ah . . . yeah."

"Are you feeding the dog—that isn't yours—hotel beer?"

I closed my eyes and my shoulders drooped. "The dog's thirsty." I didn't know what else to say.

"APU is here. Grab onto that dog that isn't yours and who is drinking company beer. They are on their way down."

"Yes, ma'am."

"And, Gaylord?"

"Yes, ma'am?"

"There will be a blue sheet in your box tonight. Please sign it and put in the admin box. That will be all for now." She hung up.

I stared at the phone receiver for a long moment. The woman was a menace and now threatened my livelihood. Otis chuckled. "Nothing worse than a woman scorned."

"What are you talking about? I've never had relations with her."

Otis wagged his bushy eyebrows lasciviously and sipped his grasshopper.

Was there really a rumor going around the hotel? I'd never given anyone the slightest indication that— "Ah, to hell with all of ya."

I turned to grab onto Waldo, hold him as ordered, but he bolted back out to the Frisbee game. When he hit the sand, people cheered. He carried a huge smile on his Rottweiler mug, the returning gladiator half-drunk on expensive Modelo beer paid for on my tab. Drago gets a honeymoon, his dog gets an all-expenses paid vacation as if he'd won it on a game show, and I lose my job.

Perfect.

Two men dressed in gray uniforms with APU patches walked down from the hotel, skirting the pool. They carried long aluminum poles with steel cable loops sheathed in plastic at the end. This was Waldo's grim reaper coming to tax him for all his wanton flaunting of hotel rules. What would I tell Drago when he got back from his honeymoon? "Sorry, dude, your dog's in doggie jail."

When the APU men hit the sand, quiet blanketed the beach. Everyone turned to see the two men fan out, their loops at the ready to trap Waldo between them. Waldo looked on with the orange Frisbee in his jaws. His head shifted from one man to the next as they closed in on him.

A cry went up in many different languages. In essence, telling Waldo to run, flee for his life. Waldo ran over and handed off the Frisbee to the closest player then ran head-on, growling viciously, toward one of the APU men. The man backed up but then realized he was being watched by hundreds of people, didn't want to be a coward, and held his ground.

Waldo juked at the last second, changing direction. The beachgoers cheered. Waldo ran to the other APU man, ran around him in circles, not getting close enough to get snared in the loop. The man looked the fool trudging around in the deep sand being out-foxed by a dog.

The two men closed in on Waldo, using as a makeshift boundary a row of seven women lying on their stomachs, topless, asleep, unaware of the game afoot. Waldo ran across them all in a row. The women shrieked and sat up, forgetting about their nudity, their breasts in full public display. Sat up one at a time like a piano player sweeping the ivories. Another cheer arose. Otis held up his half-empty grasshopper and said, "Now that was quite titillating and worth the price of admission." Waldo took a victory lap and disappeared into the jungle shrubs.

Waldo, not the jungle! What about El Tigre Negro? What a strange role reversal, Waldo becoming cat food.

I turned around in the cabana bar worried about Waldo and immediately spotted the Ice Princess coming down from the hotel to personally supervise the failed beach operation, her expression grim.

Yikes.

CHAPTER THIRTEEN

WHEN I ARRIVED home, I found a note from Marie. She'd gone over to Alisa's house—apparently Aleck had gone missing and Alisa needed comforting. Marie would hate that she couldn't tell Alisa about her dead husband lying on the floor of El Gato Gordo.

It was past the younger children's bedtime. Down the long hall of bedroom doors, Alonzo, my grandson, was the first to peek out the door to his room then came out running with a big smile. I hadn't given him enough attention lately. I scooped him up and swung him around until he giggled. Some of the other younger children, all in their pajamas, came out to check on the ruckus.

I got down on the floor and wrestled with them, playing monster. Rosie came out of her room to see who'd disturbed her niñas in their nest. She wagged her finger at me. "No, meester, *no es bueno*." She backed into her room and closed the door. The older kids came out of their rooms to watch, carrying their cellphones and iPads. I soon ran out of breath—the kids sweaty and wide-awake.

"Hey," I said. "Why don't we make a fort?"

"Yay," came the chorus, "a fort. Let's make a fort."

Eddie Crane sat on the couch, his face in his phone. "Your ass is gonna be grass when Marie gets home."

"Language, please, Mr. Crane."

My phone buzzed in my pocket. Eddie had sent me one of his notorious text messages. I'd read it later.

Little children riding on my feet, clinging to my legs, I hurried to the linen closet. I took out an armload of sheets and carried them into the expansive dining room. The kids knew the game and pulled the chairs out into different configurations. I shook out the sheets to cover the chairs and table, making a semi-intricate covered maze underneath.

All of us crawled on hands and knees through the sheeted makeshift halls and rooms, me roaring like a lion, the kids screaming when I attacked. I bumped into Eddie Crane, too old to play lion fort, or so he'd said.

"What are you doing in here?" I asked.

"I think I lost a quarter under the table."

"Is that right?"

"Yeah, why?"

"Just askin'. You go that way. I'll go this way, and we'll herd them all into the middle and feast on their tender little bodies." I bumped my eyebrows up and down.

He smiled. "Okay."

We herded the sweaty laughing children under the table and roared as they screamed and laughed.

Everyone froze when the front door opened and then closed. I held my finger up to my mouth and then put my two hands to my face and closed my eyes. All the kids immediately understood, dropped to the floor, and closed their eyes, feigning sleep. A couple fake-snored. I lay down next to Alonzo with my arm around him. I saw Eddie Crane slither out on the other side of the table from the front door, seeking cover in the kitchen.

Chicken.

I hissed to the snorers to be quiet. We waited for the storm—a mother angry, her strict rules violated—waited for her bellow of indignation. Not really. My Marie wasn't like that. She dealt out discipline with a stern expression based on the hard-earned respect of the children.

Marie came inside, saying, "Well, I guess I'll just go to bed since all the kids are asleep."

Hushed giggles.

We waited a minute longer, then I motioned for the kids to get up and follow me to the safety of their rooms. I got them all in a line in a half-crouch as we crept out of the dining room into the hall. As we passed the kitchen entrance, Marie jumped out, her hands looking like claws, and roared. All the kids screamed and ran to their rooms.

Marie play-punched me in the stomach. "Now we'll never get them to sleep."

"No, I wore them down. I did. They'll sleep like . . . like babies. You wait and see." I picked her up and kissed her.

I said, "Sorry you caught the duty over at Alisa's."

She lost her smile. "It was a good thing I was there. A woman from the OIJ came to the house and told her what had happened and asked Alisa to keep it quiet, not to tell a soul over threat of jail time."

"How did Alisa take it?"

Marie pushed on my chest; she wanted me to put her down. I complied.

She scowled. "How do you think she took it? I had to give her a sedative."

Marie had been a physician's assistant back in the States. That's how we'd met, the night my old boss shot me in the ass, took me in custody for killing Derek Sams, my son in-law. She'd been the one to stitch me up and care for me before I was transferred to the jail ward and after that a two-year prison term.

I followed her into the kids' room where we kissed them all good-night. After we eased the door shut outside the last kid's room, Marie said, "I'm going to take a shower before I go and get Tobias from Rosie's room." I nodded in agreement, fatigue invading muscle and bone and fogging the mind.

Then my cell buzzed—the chief of police, Franco Hernandez, wanted a meet. I texted him I would meet him in the morning. He texted back. NOW. I ignored that one and read the one Eddie Crane sent me earlier:

HOW DO YOU MAKE HOLY WATER? YOU BOIL THE HELL OUT OF IT.

I chuckled and showed it to Marie on the way to our room. She whispered, "That kid's sense of humor has a lot to be desired."

"I don't think so."

She went up on tiptoes and kissed my chin. "Of course, you wouldn't. The kid is a little Bruno clone. He worships you."

I steered her into the bathroom, one tiled floor to ceiling in mosaic. The skylight above let in the moonlight with a few stars until she turned on the light. I turned the light off, preferring the stars and moon. The shower was large enough for a small cocktail party. I slowly undressed her while she talked about the murder book from El Gato Gordo, the things she saw in the photos, conclusions regarding anything that came to mind. Nothing of consequence yet, she'd only just started working her way through it, wrapping her mind around the senseless violence.

I undressed while she turned on the shower, getting the water temp just right. We stepped in and soaped each other up. After we stepped out, I dried her off. I couldn't help it—Mother Nature took an interest and I got the inkling that immediately shifted to an obvious tingling.

She smiled and play-slapped my cheek. "You're a pig."

I picked her up and carried her to the bed that had been turned down by Rosie. Rosie had also left the French doors open to the master bedroom's private patio surrounded by a ten-foot wall and shrouded in shrubs in gigantic pots. Moonlight raked across the paver tiles, the soft rays reaching into the room. The warm Costa Rican air, humid from the close proximity to the beach, caressed our bodies as I made slow, quiet love to my beautiful wife.

Afterward I lay on my back sweaty and sated, sleep coming on in a soft wave. Just before I slipped over the edge of slumber, my mind tried to alert me to a hazard, a danger. But this often happened—it came from too many years of chasing the vile and the perverted, the corrupt and violent. I let sleep take me—the lurking threat still echoing in my brain.

CHAPTER FOURTEEN

I WOKE IN darkness, startled by Marie's hand gripping my arm, her nails digging in. The moon had moved on, leaving only dim ambient light hardly more than shadows, gradations of gray to dark black. I lay on my back naked and vulnerable but didn't move until I ferreted out the reason for my wife's distress.

She wasn't easily panicked.

I tried not to move my head and searched with my eyes. My vision finally deciphered the grays and found a man standing in our room. Quiet, unmoving. Menacing. The dead on the floor of El Gato flashed in my mind.

I tensed, preparing to lunge, attack this interloper and defend my house and family. I'd become El Tigre Negro and would rip his arms off, tear out his neck. I took in a deep breath, ready to—

"Señor Johnson?"

The voice was familiar, yanking on a distant memory. I sat up and swung my legs over the edge of the bed as Marie pulled a sheet over to cover her lovely nakedness.

"Who are you?"

"José Rivera."

"Ah, man. I'm sorry, José."

In all the commotion that had happened the night of the El Gato Gordo nightclub massacre and the preceding day, I'd forgotten all about Jose Rivera, Salvador Perez' best friend and partner in their security business. He was Salvador's right-hand man. The muscle. A most dangerous man. And there he stood in our bedroom looking to me for answers.

"Please," I said. "Wait outside. I'll be right with you." Jose did as I asked and stepped out on the private patio, disappearing out in the shadows. I got up, went to the dresser, put clothes on, and grabbed the cellphone I'd palmed from the crime scene.

Marie said, "Bruno? Jose Rivera?"

"Salvador Perez' man."

"Oh, right. But in our bedroom, really?"

"He's a little different. He doesn't abide by social norms and operates by doing things in economical ways, bypassing manners and etiquette. That's just the way he is."

"Tell him for me, he shows up in my bedroom unannounced again in the middle of the night, and I'll economically kick his ass." She said it while shrugging into a robe. "I'm going to get Tobias from Rosie's room. I want him gone by the time I get back."

I had no doubt she meant what she said. Jose was very capable but wouldn't have a chance against an angry mother protecting her brood.

She hesitated. "Bruno, I don't want this kind of thing anywhere near the children."

"I agree. It won't happen again."

Words without bite, I had no control over the outside world. I'd found out the hard way fate was a hungry hunter.

I caught up to her, hugged her, felt her shaking from the adrenaline. Jose had scared the hell out of her, and she'd tried to cover it with bravado.

The wall around the estate was ten feet high with broken bottle set in the concrete cap. How had Jose gotten in and back to our room? I'd have to rethink the security, something I would've called Salvador to handle; only now he was dead on the floor of El Gato Gordo.

When I came out of the bedroom, Jose stood in the shadows between two potted shrubs, only his glowing eyes giving away his presence. "Señor Johnson, was he one of them?"

I hadn't known he spoke such good English. He'd mostly stayed mute when I'd been around him and Salvador, Salvador doing all the talking.

I was confused. "*One of them?*"

"One of the *muerto at negrocios sucious?*"

He'd referred to the dead at El Gato Gordo, calling it a "dirty business."

"How do you know about that?"

He said nothing and waited.

"Yes, I am sorry, *mi amigo*, Salvador is dead."

He stood silent, his eyes staring off into the darkness digesting the horrible news, then he said, "When death smiles at you, you can only smile back."

What? That was a weird reaction.

He asked, "Who did this?" His tone took on an edge.

"I'm looking into it. I don't know but I will find out. Trust me, my friend, I will find out."

"You'll tell me as soon as you know, yes?"

It wasn't a request as much as a command. "Of course."

Jose asked, "What can I do to help?"

Salvador had always been the intellectual of the team, Jose the muscle, older than he looked and tough as old shoe leather. He kept his salt and pepper hair cut short in a military style and always wore plain clothes, old but well-cared for. He looked like he could hike all day and all night in the jungle toting a hundred-pound backpack.

I took out Salvador's cellphone and showed him. "Do you know the password?"

He took it from my hand and typed it in with the slow deliberation of someone not familiar with technology; a simple code, four, five, two, one.

"Thank you, this will help a lot."

"You will tell me as soon as you know who did this terrible thing."

"Yes."

But once I told Jose the name of the suspect, that person would be dead within the hour. I had to be sure of my facts. And more importantly, whether justice should be served without due process.

He nodded.

I said, "There is something else that you can help me with."

"Anything."

"There is a man who sits at the Lido bar every day drinking—"

"El gordo who waddles. Is he involved?"

"I don't think so, but I need him watched to see what he does. Can you do that while I check on a few things tomorrow? I need him safe too. Nothing is to happen to him. There might be people out to get him."

I couldn't tell Jose that Otis might be a suspect. Jose would kidnap Otis, take him somewhere—probably on a boat out on the Pacific—and make him talk.

"I understand. It will be done."

"Thank you." I stuck my hand out to shake. He took hold and squeezed, his strength collapsing my hand. He pulled me close. He stood quite a bit shorter than me, his eyes alive with determination. "You find something out—you will tell me first. Not the *policia*, *verdad*?"

While working on the violent crimes team with my old boss Robby Wicks we'd taken down the worst criminals Los Angeles could produce, and none of them equaled in that moment what I saw in Jose's eyes and heard in his words—a gathering storm of violence. Marie was right, even though Jose was a friend, we didn't want him around the children.

"Yes, I understand." He wanted his pound of blood and bone.

CHAPTER FIFTEEN

THE ADRENALINE FROM the Jose scare took a long while to bleed off. I finally fell asleep as the black of night started to turn gray.

The next thing I knew bright morning sunlight coming through the open French doors blinded me, and I held my arm up to protect my eyes as Alonzo played trampoline on the bed next to me. "Mama told me to," he said giggling and continued jumping. I laughed and pulled him down and tickled him. Marie stood over by the bedroom door bottle-feeding our newborn, Tobias. "You're going to be late for work. I let you sleep as long as I could. The kids have all gone off to school. You better hurry."

"Right. Right, thanks." I picked up Alonzo and carefully tossed him on the bed. He giggled. "Again, Daddy. Again." I was his grand-daddy, but he wouldn't know the difference until he was old enough to understand. I picked him up and tossed him on the bed one more time, then hurried to the shower.

Twenty minutes later my body hadn't cooled enough from the shower. I'd already started sweating in my clean clothes—the hotel uniform, an aloha shirt with the name tag "Gaylord"—as I walked the two miles to work.

I opened Salvador's cellphone with the password I got out of Jose the night before—well, several hours before, anyway. When I had more time, I'd download all the text messages, and also start a spreadsheet of the phone numbers called and received. Right now, the only thing odd were an inordinate amount of phone calls to the hotel where I worked. Salvador had been talking with someone at the hotel and it wasn't me. No way to trace which room—all the calls went through the switchboard.

Just before I made it to the hotel, Eddie Crane texted me. He was in school in class using his cellphone. He was a smart kid and school didn't challenge him enough. I'd have to talk with him about paying attention to the teacher. Then I laughed out loud at his text:

TWO CANNIBALS ARE SITTING AROUND A FIRE EATING A CLOWN, ONE SAYS TO THE OTHER, "DOES THIS TASTE FUNNY?"

* * *

Inside the hotel I made a beeline into the admin office and clocked in two minutes late, a bluie worthy violation and I'd just received one the day before because of—

I looked over my shoulder out the window with a view of the hotel pool, the cabana bar, and the beach. Where the hell had Waldo gotten off to? I'd have to check with APU to see if they had him in custody. Or if any of their agents had fallen victim to him resisting arrest. I didn't want to think about El Tigre Negro getting him.

I needed a couple of personal hours off while the cabana bar wasn't too busy. I would have to ask the Ice Princess, Darla Figueroa, for permission. Only no one knew where to find her. I had her paged twice to the front desk. No response. Odd. She always had her nose in everyone's business, that's what made her so effective.

I really needed to get over to Salvador's business office before OIJ did. Then I remembered I was supposed to escort Otis Brasher from his room down to his seat at the bar. I called his room. He answered and sounded indignant about my tardiness. He was probably having withdrawals—a grasshopper palsy. I hurried to his room. I made it to his door just as he exited. He wore the same seersucker suit as the day before and a Panama hat. I didn't want to get too close—his body odor was bad enough the day before.

"For the money I pay you, I expect you to be prompt." Before he closed his door, out popped Waldo.

"What the hell are you doing with my dog?"

"I thought you said he wasn't your dog?"

"Never mind, where did you find him?"

"He came wandering out of the jungle last night just before last call. He's a hungry little bugger. He ate two tall stacks of pancakes and three orders of sausage."

I looked down at him. He stared up at me unabashed without the least bit of humility in his expression. I growled at him. He growled back as we traversed the hotel hall.

Otis said, "You two don't get along, do you?"

I ignored the observation. "If I can find the Food and Beverage Manager, I'm going to take a couple of hours off." We took the same route through the hotel as the day before, bypassing the lobby.

He nodded. "You want to find her, she's probably on the roof."

"How do you know that?"

"I've spotted her up there using binoculars to look down on us peons. I told you I'm a little paranoid, so I've been watching everything."

That was how she'd seen Waldo playing Frisbee and drinking Modelo beer inside the cabana bar.

"I found a guy who's going to be watching you at all times. He's very capable. You don't have to worry about a thing when he's on the job. I've used him before, he's very dependable."

"That's okay, but don't make a habit of it. I prefer your services. Is Waldo a guard dog?"

"What—oh, yes; yes, he is. One of the best." The lie came a little too easy. The dog did whatever he wanted when he wanted. Guard dog, right. More like Modelo-drinking beach playboy.

"He seems to drink a lot of beer. Tell him to stay with me today as a little extra protection."

I spoke some gobbledygook words that I thought might sound like German. Drago bought Waldo in Germany and the dog only responded to German.

We came out of the hotel in the hot humidity that grabbed at my lungs. The humidity was one thing I'd never get used to after living most of my life in dry SoCal.

"What was that you just said?"

"German. Waldo only responds to German."

Otis chuckled. "That wasn't German." Otis said something in German. Waldo stopped and sat. He looked up at him. Otis said, "Splendid, we'll get along famously."

"Good. See you in a couple of hours." I took off, leaving him with Waldo as they negotiated the large pool area headed for the cabana bar that looked empty, devoid of Chacho and customers. Too early. Everyone was sleeping off the hangover from the day before. But Chacho was conspicuous in his absence.

I took the elevator to the penthouse floor and then walked quickly down to the end of the hall to a door marked Roof. A small index card with writing in lovely cursive said, "No admittance under any circumstances. That means you." I grabbed the knob; it didn't turn. Locked. But the automatic door return hadn't closed all the way. I pushed and stepped through to face a dirty, unattended concrete staircase leading up. I took the stairs up. The door at the top of the landing had a second index card taped to it with the same cursive writing. "Last chance. Go back under penalty of termination." This was how she spied on employees who worked around the pool, the walkways, the cabana bar, and even the golf course where they served a limited lunch and alcoholic drinks. I needed my job and turned to descend the stairs when the door jerked open to a surprised Chacho, rivulets of sweat streaking his face, his expression agitated. He never sweated and remained calm no matter how far behind we were on bar orders. "Amigo," he said, desperately. "What are you doing here? You have to go back."

With both hands, he tried to turn my shoulders, but I outweighed him by forty pounds and didn't budge.

"A better question is what are you doing up here? Who's minding the bar?"

He brought his hands down, gripping his fists. "I have to go. You didn't see me. You understand? You didn't see me."

"What's going on?" But he didn't say anything more. His head bobbed as it descended, and I realized Chacho was going bald. I hadn't noticed before.

I held the door open so it wouldn't latch closed and thought through my situation. The smart move was to do what Chacho said and get the hell outta there. But I'd never been one to do the smart thing. Darla Figueroa was spying on employees and she needed to know that we knew.

CHAPTER SIXTEEN

THE SUN RADIATED off the roof, raising the temperature ten degrees, thickening the air, making it a sauna. In Costa Rica I often found myself wishing for clouds to cover the sun, a respite from the heat. That moment on the roof was no exception.

What caught my eye first was a newer-looking galvanized steel pole attached with metal plumber's tape to the side of the elevator housing. A jerry-rigged job that would never pass inspection in the States. The pipe rose ten feet above the roof. Attached to the top of the pipe were four cameras; CCTV, pointed in different directions. She no longer needed the binoculars or to make the trek to the roof. She'd shifted to technology to help her with a 360-degree view of the hotel environs. The cameras were the reason for the index card warnings; she didn't want the cameras discovered.

The Ice Princess had the entire hotel grounds wired to spy, encroaching on the freedom of others. Lying along the edge of the elevator housing was a long aluminum pole with two fittings used to wash the windows—a squeegee and mop applicator to wet the glass. I picked up the aluminum pole, and one at a time, reached up and moved the cameras out of position until they shot a continuous picture of beautiful blue Costa Rican sky. Proud of myself, I set the pole down just as music—soft rock—wafted on the light breeze along with the scent of

Hawaiian Tropic coconut oil sun lotion that sparked memories of my childhood days at Redondo Beach. I followed my nose over to a large air-conditioning unit, one of three along the roof that kicked on, startling me and washing out the soft rock, the reason I hadn't heard the music when I first came onto the roof.

I leaned and peeked around the tall air conditioner unit. My mouth dropped open all on its own. Spread languidly on a thick blanket sunned a naked Ice Princess, her tanned body glistening with Hawaiian Tropic lotion. Long and lithe, smooth and tanned brown, with wonderful breasts and her sex trimmed and neat. She lay on her back basking with dark sunglasses reflecting the sun. Her skin was greasy slick with the oily lotion. No Ice Princess but a Sun Goddess.

Dios mio.

A miniature version of my long dead ex-boss, Robby Wicks, sat on my shoulder and whispered in my ear, "Don't just stand there like a dumb rube, offer to rub lotion on those lovely coconuts. You know I'd be all over that luscious piece of—"

I ignored him.

Maybe she hadn't seen me, and I could surreptitiously back away, escape without embarrassment and without an explanation for why I'd violated the orders on the index card. One of which said, "under penalty of termination."

The legal part of my mind said that since the cards were not signed or did not end with, "The management," they did not have legitimate grounds for punitive action. A true fallacy, the Ice Princess made up her own due process in her tyrannical dictatorship.

She stared up into the blue sky, and without moving her head spoke, "Why don't you take a picture? It'll last longer. Gaylord, what are you doing on the roof of my hotel?"

Her hotel? She was *only* the food and beverage manager—there was a hotel manager above her and the owner above him. *Her hotel,* the nerve. How had she even seen me? How did she know it was me? She possessed some sort of psychic power.

I froze anyway, not knowing if I should stay or run. Her simple words had turned me into a pervert wearing a trench coat, naked underneath; pure shame and self-loathing.

Before I could get my feet turned to make a humiliating retreat, she took her sunglasses off and turned on her side to face me, her breasts perfect, the areolas dark brown, the whole package beyond alluring.

"Come closer and quit hiding behind that thing."

I looked down to double-check what she meant and found I hadn't embarrassed myself further and that she was talking about the air-conditioning unit.

I stood up straight. My feet, without direct orders from me, did as she asked; the traitors. I swallowed hard, more a gulp really, my eyes taking in her long, muscular legs; the longest legs I'd ever seen. Had she always had legs that long? How will I ever be able to look at her again and not see . . . not see *all of her*? The woman could model in *Playboy*.

Still unabashed she said, "What do you want?"

"I . . . ah, came looking for you because I need a couple of hours off . . . you know, before it gets too crazy down at the cabana bar."

Why hadn't she pulled a portion of the blanket around to cover herself? I swallowed hard again waiting while she thought about the question. I tried harder to keep my eyes on hers.

She put the sunglasses back on and laid down on her back. "That's fine, Gaylord, be sure to clock out and then back in. You'll find a blue sheet in your box for ignoring orders about coming up on the roof." She flitted her hand at me in dismissal. "Beware, that's two strikes."

Like a scolded child, I fled. As I made it to the door that led down, I remembered Chacho had been on the roof, sweaty, his aloha shirt disheveled, fear in his eyes. No time to ponder it, I had to get moving, but the male part of my brain wouldn't let go of her naked image, her unabashed calm. And my God, those legs. I shivered and hurried down the stairs. I'd have to tell Marie about the encounter . . . or maybe not.

Ten minutes later, still in a little bit of a daze, I left the hotel grounds walking fast in the direction of the Tamarindo business district, a small area three blocks wide and three blocks long. Salvador had worked out of a house converted to an office on the edge of the district. My guess was that he operated outside the designated area, violating zoning laws. He knew everybody in town and even a few political heavies in the main city of San Jose who owed him favors. A country like Costa Rica ran on favors.

When we first arrived and set up our household in the expat's estate, I had the jitters and couldn't sleep, afraid of the children's vulnerability. So, at night, after Marie dropped off to sleep, I walked the town. Eventually, I walked every street, lane, and alley in Tamarindo and learned its quirks, the way it slept, the people that moved at night, the town a living, breathing organism. A town far quieter and civilized than Los Angeles. Quiet except for the constant sound of birds even at night; the veerys and Swainson's thrushes. What struck me most odd, the town lacked any graffiti. No gangs ran street corners, drove by with guns, or sold dope. Just a nice quiet town. A Utopia to raise children.

The shrubs on the side of the road suddenly shook and rustled. I froze.

El Tigre Negro?

I had no weapon, nothing but fists. A human can't outrun a two-hundred-pound black panther, nor fight one successfully without a weapon. Robby Wicks whispered in my ear, "You're not friggin' Tarzan—run, you fool. Run!" I turned to face the threat. Maybe it worked like black bears, turn and face them, make noise. My throat had turned too dry to speak. Run. Now. Do it. My legs wouldn't obey.

Tier one predators singled out the weak and the old to bring down and eat. I was neither. Well, not really.

Out of the shrubs popped Waldo.

"What the hell, dog! You scared the piss outta me!" He didn't answer and stood there looking at me like I was some kind of dolt. Maybe he was right. I was talking to a dog after all.

He still had sand on his back from another rousing game of Frisbee on the beach. I started walking again. He followed along. I stopped. He stopped. I started again. He did too.

Annoying.

How did he know where to find me? "Hey, are you some kind of 007 with a license to kill?" What was I thinking? Dogs didn't need permission to chomp ass. He didn't answer and just kept walking. He burped. If I'd been downwind, it'd probably smell like Modelo beer.

Twenty minutes later we entered the block of homes where Salvador had his office. We walked by it twice and once down the alley in the rear scoping it out. No cars from OIJ or cars with people watching the place.

I asked Waldo, "What do you think?" He gave me that dumb dog expression.

"Yeah," I said, "that's what I thought."

CHAPTER SEVENTEEN

SALVADOR'S OFFICE WAS a dilapidated house with a sagging tile roof; shrubs and vines and trees obscured the view from the street, leaving mere glimpses of wall, window, and door. Anyone could easily be lurking in the flowered greenery. The macaws and toucans made themselves known with pleasant sounds. A black cloud had slowed its journey long enough to dump some rain. When the sun returned, water vaporized into a heavy mist that rose off the asphalt and concrete sidewalk. The heat and humidity made my aloha shirt stick to damp skin.

I remembered the German word spoken by Otis to make Waldo stay and to sit. I said it to Waldo. He looked up at me as if I were an idiot.

Maybe I pronounced the German word wrong?

No, he knew what I wanted, he just didn't want to listen to anything *I* told him.

In front of the door, I raised my hand to knock and realized the door stood slightly ajar, revealing a sliver of dark interior. I stepped to the side; Waldo did as well as if he understood the danger. I used my foot to ease the door open. The overgrowth of shrubs and trees that encapsulated the house blocked the light, making the interior dark. Quiet, bleak with the scent of mold.

I quickly entered, button-hooked to the left, and waited for my breathing to come back under control and my eyes to adjust to the darkness. Without a weapon, I knew I was vulnerable—naked as the Ice Princess up on the hotel roof.

Waldo trotted in without stopping and disappeared into the gloom. His paws made the sound of treading upon papers. So much for a covert entry.

I felt the wall and found a light switch that didn't work. My eyes adjusted, and I spotted a long string to a single naked bulb hanging from the ceiling, the glass globe for the light lying broken in shards on the floor. When I pulled the light's chain, the bulb swung back and forth, making the shadows wobble and flicker.

The room had been tossed. Literally. The entire interior a jumbled mess, all the furniture upended, the desk on its side, file cabinet drawers pulled out, files and papers scattered, cushions on the couch slashed, large holes knocked in the walls. I moved from Salvador's trashed office to the kitchen where Waldo was half in the refrigerator now on its side, eating something from a pan that resembled leftover enchiladas.

Someone had been looking for something. This gave credence to the chief's hypothesis that the shooting at El Gato Gordo was caused by something Salvador was into. A search for leads would've been hard enough with the house/office intact. Now it would be impossible. And even worse, time consuming. That's what the previous intruder had wanted. To cover his tracks.

First, I memorialized the scene, taking photos of everything no matter how insignificant. Then I picked a corner and got started.

The proper search of a house this size would take six to seven hours—time I didn't have. I searched until sweat soaked my shirt through, my two hours almost up without finding anything. I had to get back to the hotel, back to the cabana bar.

In any case, the person before me had probably already found whatever had been hidden.

I came across pictures in frames that had been on his desk, photos of his family and photos of his pride and joy—big game fishing—standing alongside his conquests, hundred-pound silvery tunas.

And finally, a photo I remembered well, one of the Johnson family—me, Marie, and all our children on a sunny day right after a heavy rain had cleansed the air, dampened the flowers combining their fecund scent, adding to the wonderful memory, the pure unencumbered joy.

The photo was taken outside in front of the estate. Salvador had been part of our family and now he was gone. I left the photo in situ with all the others so as not to single it out.

Maybe I should've taken it.

I ran out of time and moved to the center of the room. I closed my eyes and relaxed my mind. I opened my eyes and looked not just to look, but looked to see, the same theory as searching. I turned slowly taking in everything in the room, playing a game, "what didn't fit," "what was out of place?"

Nothing popped. I closed my eyes longer this time, the clock running, tick-tock, tick-tock. I had to get back to the hotel. I had two strikes already. I needed the job.

But I'd seen the boss naked.

Focus.

I opened my eyes and surveyed the same things a second time: crushed or damaged furniture, the wooden desk kicked in, the two file cabinets torn apart, the floor littered with old case files, photos, magazines from the office table, broken lamps, newspapers—

Wait—newspapers. I hurried over. The newspapers were still folded but not perfectly and slightly skewed. Salvador had gone through them and taken the time to put them back together. The previous interlopers had left them unmolested on a wide ledge next to the back window. Newspapers from three different days, a Monday, Tuesday, and Thursday—all from over a year ago in the month of August. Why keep newspapers that old?

The *New York Times* was a thick daily; three combined became unwieldy. With no time left to examine them, I found a used plastic grocery bag and stuffed them inside. I took photos of all the rooms again and texted them to Marie along with the ones I'd shot earlier.

I opened the front door and turned back. "Hey, Bonzo, we gotta roll." Waldo sat up, gave a half-yip, looked around as if he didn't know where he was. Then he stood, shook his entire body to wake up, and ran out the door. I followed.

As soon as I stepped outside, I felt a gun slam into the side of my head. The owner spoke in rapid Spanish and told me not to move, said something about having holes in my head if I did. I couldn't catch it all, my Spanish wasn't that good.

A second person came out of the shrubs on the other side of the door, took my bag of *New York Times*, and handcuffed me. Tamarindo Police. Shit.

Waldo barked. And barked. I took it as him asking for permission to attack and maul. It sounded a little like Lassie going for help to tell them Timmy had fallen down a well. "Go. Run," I said. "Save yourself."

Waldo spun and took off. He chose that moment to listen to me, the coward. He could've at least hesitated a little, at least waited until I told him a second time to take it on the lam.

The two cops tried to jerk me along but Ticos as a people were smaller in stature. They put me in a cop car and hauled me off, zipping in and out of public streets, heading in the wrong direction for the police station.

Ten minutes later they pulled up and stopped in front of a house in the nicest neighborhood in Tamarindo, not too far from our house, several blocks over the bridge and three blocks nearer the beach.

CHAPTER EIGHTEEN

THE TAMARINDO COPPERS knew the layout of the house and escorted me through several well-appointed rooms professionally decorated in British décor circa 14th or 15th century, replete with a Castilian coat of arms above a massive fireplace and a suit of armor that stood on blood-red carpet. Tapestries hung from the walls as did antique candle chandeliers from the ceiling with burned-down tapers. The house owner was an Anglophile with expensive tastes.

They guided me through a double door in the kitchen to the outside, to the rear yard that had a large, lagoon-entry pool with a blue pebble bottom.

Chief Franco Hernandez sat at a wrought iron table shaded by a red and white umbrella with a Cinzano logo. He sipped from a fine white china cup. He wore house slippers and a red silk dressing robe.

The two coppers sat me down—still handcuffed behind the back—and put the bag of *New York Times* newspapers on the table. Chief Hernandez seemed disinterested as he used one finger to prod the bag open while his man, standing at attention, gave a report in Spanish.

He set his cup down. "You make me very angry."

"I'm not exactly happy about being snatched off the street, kid-napped, and dragged here when I'm supposed to be at work at the hotel."

His pencil line mustache twitched. "My friend, you weren't kid-napped, you were detained after burglarizing a home." His English had improved. "And forget that job at the hotel—you are working for me. Or have you forgotten?"

"I didn't steal anything."

Chief Hernandez wagged his eyebrows at the bag on the table filled with newspapers.

"That's not stealing. Those are just old discarded newspapers."

"Let's quit playing this silly game." He nodded for his two men to leave, then leaned over. "When I send a message that I want to see you, you don't put me off, *entiendes*? You come. You drop everything and come."

I eased back in the chair and looked around. "This is your *casita*? Very nice. You've done well for yourself on a chief's salary."

His face flushed. "Do these newspapers have anything to do with what happened at the nightclub?"

I shrugged. "I just wanted to catch up with what was happening back in the States."

"With papers more than a year old?"

He'd been sly pretending he wasn't interested in the newspapers and had checked out the dates. He knew his business, and now after the ugliness of El Gato Gordo had calmed down, he could think like a professional.

Looking around, I said, "Does this beautiful house have anything to do with the fact we are only a few hundred miles from Panama— the drug and money-laundering capital of Central America?"

He brought his finger up into my face. His eyes bulged a little, spittle flying from his mouth. "You push me too hard, gringo. You poke the bear, you get the claw. You took a cellphone from the crime scene, and I want it back or I'll throw your black ass in jail. You see if I don't."

"And I thought we were friends."

"Do not test me."

I leaned forward, making him sit back. "Go ahead and put me in jail. I'll have a long talk with the OIJ." I looked around at his pool and large house.

Fear in his eyes shaded his expression as if a cloud had passed under the sun.

"Now take these cuffs off and let me get back to work."

He waited, staring me down. He took a sip of coffee. After a moment of deep consideration, he said, "Maybe we got off on the wrong footing."

I said nothing.

"Have you found out anything?"

"No, but I'll have something in a few days. Can you send something to the FBI for analysis?"

His expression turned to excitement. "You have found something?"

"Maybe. Answer the question." I didn't have a thing but had to throw him a bone to keep him dangling on the hook.

"We have a state-of-the-art lab in San Jose."

I said nothing.

He nodded. "Yes, of course. The FBI. What is it?"

"I'll have it for you soon. I'll text you. Now take these cuffs off. I won't ask again."

He spoke loudly in rapid Spanish I couldn't follow. The two uniformed coppers returned, took hold of my shoulders, and stood me up. One of them searched my person and pulled out both cellphones, mine and Salvador's.

"Wait," I said. "I'm still looking into those numbers."

"Not anymore. You are moving too slowly. I'll deal with the phone now."

"Then you'll give me a copy of what you find?"

He didn't answer as the one cop took off the handcuffs. I reached for the bag of newspapers. He put his hand on them, glared at me, and said, "I too want to catch up on what's happening in the States." His words dripped with sarcasm.

I rubbed my wrists as I followed the two cops out to the cop car. They got in and took off, leaving me in the street. My two hours were up, and it was siesta time. I was supposed to be at the bar to relieve Chacho for siesta. No Ubers or Lyfts were available, not during siesta. I ran just as it started to rain again.

The damn interminable rain.

I made it to the hotel in thirty minutes, running eight-and-a-half-minute miles, the fastest in a long time, soaked to the bone, light-headed, and out of breath. Something else I wasn't used to; like the song said, "It never rains in Southern California."

I took the path around the side of the hotel instead of going through the lobby sopping wet. Only tourist kids played in the pool, not caring about the deluge of rain. Tourists three deep crowded around the cabana bar trying to stay dry under the palapa overhang and at the same time ordered drinks to nurture their buzz with exotic blended alcohol, waiting for the sun to return. Chacho did his best to keep up, his hands moving machine-like, his eyes glazed over, his mind somewhere else. I hurried into the cabana bar lifting the pass-through. He looked up, angry.

"Sorry, mi amigo," I said. "I promise to make it up to you. Go ahead and go."

He eyed me as his hands kept working to get through the surge. I jumped in and between us we still never caught up. We'd be out of fruit garnish soon and we needed another case of rum and three cases of Modelo.

No one crowded Otis. They stayed away, his body odor an invisible barrier. Maybe he was hygienically incorrect on purpose. He tried to strike up a conversation, but I didn't have time. Some tourist from Mexico drinking Modelo talked about a sighting of El Tigre Negro. I tried to listen, but the rain came down harder, drowning out all else with a loud thrum.

The rain stopped all at once and the sun peeked out. The outside layer of tourists moved back to the beach, still leaving two layers deep of people talking in different languages, their faces flush with alcohol. The hotel made a killing on the drink markup, the rain a welcome ally that moved everyone closer to the bar.

Drunk on grasshoppers, Otis leaned over the bar and said to me, "Heh, heh, for a while now I've needed to sneak off to the restroom but was afraid of losing my stool. Get it?" When I ignored him, he said, "This rain, huh?"

A four-person cluster with Australian accents paused at Otis' comment. One of the two women said, "Bloody hell, what a wanker."

I still said nothing as I made him another grasshopper. I slipped in the peppermint. Chacho jumped around me, his finger in my face. "Aha. I caught you. It's peppermint! It's peppermint!"

I was having a bad day all around. I topped off Otis' drink with the blender. He slipped an envelope across to me and winked. I opened it and found two thousand American, all hundreds, my pay for watching out for him for two days. With the excessive amount came guilt for not earning it.

The phone rang in the cabana bar. I grabbed it. "Gaylord, you failed to clock back in." I said nothing, listening to the silence, gripping the phone, her lovely naked image flashing across the big screen in my mind.

The Ice Princess said, "After your shift, would you please come to the office? And you can clear out your locker on the way." She hung up.

I slammed the phone down.

Chacho stopped making a mai tai. "What's up, amigo?"

"I just got fired."

He looked shocked. I was ashamed and let my eyes scan down his shirt. I said, "Chacho, my friend, your shirt is buttoned crooked."

His expression shifted to fear, a kid with his hand caught in the cookie jar. In this case, it was more like the nookie jar.

CHAPTER NINETEEN

As NIGHT DESCENDED, hotel employees dressed in sarongs like Polynesians lit the tiki torches around the beach, cabana bar, and pool. This wasn't Hawaii, but the hotel owner, Mrs. Samuel Brodie, had lived on Oahu for most of her life and missed the Hawaiian sunsets and the cultural rituals. The visitors didn't mind so much especially after a hard day of drinking pastel-colored drinks with little umbrellas. I kept waiting for Waldo to show up. I didn't miss him. I just worried what kind of mischief he could be up to, worried El Tigre Negro had gotten him. Not a good way to go getting dragged off into the jungle and eaten.

Dad showed a few minutes after sundown, pushing Mom in her wheelchair. She could walk fine but was too used to conning people to walk on her own two feet. When asked about it, she'd say, "It's always good to have an edge, one thing your opponent isn't ready for." Dad went along with it, which was totally against his strict moral code, and that said a lot for how much he loved her.

Dad appeared out of the darkness like an apparition, a mere sliver of the man he used to be. His emaciation always startled me. Like most people with their parents, my memory of Dad was of a vibrant and vital bull of a man. Now his white hair reflected the guttering tiki flames that shadowed his gaunt face. He parked Bea, my mom, at one of the recently vacated outlying tables and came up to the bar with a huge smile. "Good to see you, Son. We just got back from the city. Can I get a G and T for Bea?" He chuckled at his own rhyme.

"Sure, Dad."

Marie thought that my animosity toward Bea was rooted in jealousy, that Dad now paid more attention to his long estranged, recently returned wife—my mother—than to me. I didn't think that true at all. She'd left my life back when I was still in the crib, went to prison over a murder committed during the commission of a felony—the felony murder rule. She was released after twelve years and I still did not see her. She didn't come back into my life until forty-eight years after she left. That was three months ago and only when she wanted to shake loose a parole agent on her tail. A part of me did love her and yearned for her to be like a regular mother and not a retired con artist. But every time she appeared in a wheelchair with Dad pushing her, I got angry all over again.

I made Dad his gin and tonic to take to her while he talked about his trip to San Jose. I listened to him and watched the light in his eyes as he spoke about Mom. That light was the only reason I allowed her to stay in our house.

I couldn't handle the guilt of telling him that I'd lost my job—I had too much respect for him.

Dad turned and walked back over to sit with Mom. I took off my waist apron and said to Otis, "My shift is up. Do you want me to walk you back to your room?" Twenty little umbrellas sat on the bar in front of him, the day's tally of grasshoppers.

His eyelids stood at half-mast, the muscles in his face relaxed, his speech slurred. "Sure, why not. Had a nice quiet day. Let us retire." He took off his Panama hat and swept down in a bow and almost continued on over.

I looked around for the first time trying to spot Jose Rivera. He stood over by a palm tree, his khaki pants and khaki shirt blending in with the sand and palm trunk. I nodded to him and ran my bladed hand across my neck. He nodded in return and disappeared into the darkness. He'd be back tomorrow.

Although it no longer mattered, I took Otis the long way to his room, bypassing the hotel lobby. The farther we moved away from the tikis, the darker it became. The shadows absorbed us like one glob of mercury into another.

I said, "I won't be at the bar tomorrow."

He stopped dead in the path. I almost bumped into him.

"Why?"

"I got fired."

"What the hell for? You're the best bartender I've ever seen."

A comment in my earlier life I never thought I'd hear and wasn't so sure I liked at that moment.

"I have accumulated too many infractions, which add up to termination."

"What kind of boob would let someone of your caliber go no matter what the cause? I'll have a talk with the hotel manager. You see if I don't."

"Thank you for your concern, but I don't think it'll do any good. The manager gives my boss, the food and beverage manager, complete reign to do as she pleases. I'm not sure I'll be able to hang around the beach or the bar either. Past and present employees are forbidden to use the hotel environs. The edict is strictly enforced."

"This is unacceptable. I'll fix it, you wait and see if I don't fix it. I spend a lot of money at this hotel."

His overly slurred speech gave little confidence in his ability to accomplish his braggadocio.

We took a concrete path to the side door to the hotel, a walkway that wound circuitously through tall indigenous trees and shrubs, their cloying scent pleasant. The night birds sang their lovely songs making the world peaceful and calm. All these things Los Angeles lacked, another reason why I'd never return to the place of my birth.

Two men, thugs dressed in black, jumped out of the dark, one on each side of the path, and grabbed onto Otis who yelped. I instantly slugged the closest one in the side of the head as he moved to duck. Pain shot up my arm past the elbow and into my shoulder. I'd hurt myself more than I'd impeded the attacker.

From behind, a third man hit me with an object in the back of the head. The world exploded in bright lights and caused the ground to waver underfoot. I tried to shake it off as he swung again. This time I moved but not far enough, he struck my shoulder. Electrical nerve shock paralyzed my arm. Now I saw his weapon, a sock filled with sand and tiny rocks, a poor man's blackjack.

Intermingled with the grunting in the encounter came the snick of a switchblade. Otis plunged it into one of the attackers, who grunted and didn't slow. Still the tide continued to turn against us. These men knew what they were about and had done this kind of thing before. Otis must've hit muscle and bone with the blade instead of an organ.

Knuckles, grunts, thumps caused by bone against muscle, expletives, and speckles of blood.

One grabbed Otis in a wristlock as I spun to face my attacker. Just as a dark beast leapt from the thick shrubs into the melee roaring like a lion. *El Tigre Negro*. The beast bit his victim's shoulder and held on. The man squealed like a small child falling from a tall building, "Eeeek."

I side-kicked the knee of the closest one on Otis. The blow connected well, the crunch vibrating up my leg. I'd done him some real damage.

The attack broke.

I shook off the blow to my head, grabbed onto Otis, and shoved him into the hotel side door as he continued to yell something. Inside, he stopped us in our tracks and held onto the interior doorframe. "What the hell's the matter with you? He saved us, let him in."

"What?"

"The dog. Your dog's out there still fighting the good fight."

I opened the door to find Waldo. He strutted in as if nothing at all had happened. In the dark and the heat of the melee, I'd actually mistaken him for El Tigre Negro.

I hurried us into Otis' room, locked the door, checked that the slider was secured. My left eye swelled shut and my lip blew up like an inner tube. My shoulder and head throbbed with pain. Still, we fared better than the thugs who besieged us. They left with a knife wound, an injured knee, and a good mauling from Waldo. With the rain there wouldn't be any blood trail to follow. They would escape into the dark without pursuit or clue as to why or who.

Otis opened the mini bar, took out a handful of miniature booze bottles, waddled over to the couch, and sat down in his usual place, the swale in the cushions. He took out a hankie and wiped the sweat that covered his eyes and head, his face flushed red and bloated. Waldo jumped up on the couch next to him.

Otis downed a vodka and then a gin. Gasping, he said, "Get the dog a beer, he deserves it."

I retrieved a bowl from the kitchenette and found one of two Modelo beers in the mini bar fridge and poured one for Waldo who lapped it up. I whispered to Waldo, "Hey, bud, alcohol is bad for dogs." He paused in his slurping as if considering my warning, then went right back to it.

Otis waved his arm. "Help yourself, please."

"I don't drink. We going to talk about what just happened out there?"

"No worries, you more than earned your money. You did exactly what I paid you for."

I raised my voice. "Who were they and what do they want?"

Sensing the elevated tension in the room, Waldo again looked up from his bowl of beer.

Otis had twisted off the top to an Irish Cream and stopped. "Why the hell do you think I would know?"

"Don't pretend you don't know what's going on. I want to know. Now."

He shrugged and downed the Irish Cream. He chuffed, wiped his mouth with the back of his hand. "No matter what country— no matter where you go to vacation—there are always thugs waiting to relieve the rich of their money. And, buddy boy, I qualify as rich in spades. Sorry, no offense intended." He really was on-his-ass-drunk.

"You're saying what happened out there was a random robbery?"

He still had not caught his breath and nodded vigorously.

My face throbbed, my knuckles ached, and I'd lost my job at the cabana bar. I'd had enough for one day. I unlocked the door, opened it, peeked out. The hall was clear. I said, "Come on, Waldo, let's go home."

He looked up from his beer bowl and didn't move.

Otis said, "I think he likes the breakfast here, sausage and pancakes." Otis patted his head. "He's good company and an added layer of protection."

"Fine." I turned to leave.

"With your dog here and Big Bertha I'll be okay. Don't worry about me."

"I'm not."

Otis struggled to his feet. "Wait. Will you be back tomorrow to escort me to the bar?"

I slammed the door as I left.

CHAPTER TWENTY

I STOPPED IN the hall at a maid's cart and swiped a folded room towel, then stopped at the ice machine in the soda alcove and prepared an ice pack for my face. I made my way to the lobby exit using one eye to see. The ice helped a great deal on the other.

In the lobby, Darla Figueroa came from behind the concierge desk where she'd been talking with Mary St. John, the concierge. "Gaylord, may I have a word, please?"

I waved my hand as I kept walking. "No need, I know, I've been sacked."

She stood up straighter, pulled her shoulders back. "Gaylord, my office, now." She hurried over to me. "Dear God, what happened to you?"

I pulled the towel away, so she could see the full extent of the injury. "I walked into a door. I'll be filing a claim against the hotel."

I wouldn't, but I was trying to put her back on her heels. Not much luck—she had an iron will a jackhammer couldn't crack.

She let one of her rare smiles ease across her lips. "My dear boy, this is not the United States, and Costa Rica is not as litigious. Now, my office, please?" She held out her arm.

Had she made it an order instead of a question, I would've blown her off and walked home. I didn't know what I was going to say to Marie.

I followed along behind Darla trying not to watch the way her hips swayed in the body-hugging Hawaiian holoku dress. She entered her office and moved behind her desk where she remained standing, her arms folded across her chest.

"What's going on?" I said. "I really have to get home."

"You have taken all the fun out of firing you."

"This is what you brought me in here for, to gloat?"

She stared, her eyes boring a hole through my head. She held her arm out again. "Please, take a seat."

I sat. I don't know why. Maybe it was that lingering scent of Hawaiian Tropic lotion. Or maybe it was how Dad had instilled in me and my brother, Noble, to always respect women.

"Would you like your job back?" She said it without expression.

I smelled a trap. "Depends. Does it come with a raise and an apology for what happened?" I pulled the towel down once again to show her the damage to my face the thugs had caused. She must've seen the incident on her spy cameras but then I remembered the fight happened too close to the building, out of view of the cameras. If she had even realigned them after my visit to the roof.

She waved her hand in dismissal. "Don't be ridiculous. I'm offering you your job back if you take care of one little hotel problem."

I moved to the edge of my seat. "What kind of problem?" Maybe she wanted me to realign the cameras I skewed, toss out an obstreperous drunk by the pool leering at the ladies. But knowing her, it was more like sweeping the front drive of the hotel or washing the tall windows. She'd love that.

She asked, "Does it really matter?"

I almost said, "What kind of job? Policing the roof from rogue sunbathers?" But I held my tongue. I needed my job back. I didn't want to tell Marie I was no longer employed. Those fat tips at the cabana bar kept our household afloat. Drunk tourists on vacation were appreciative and liked to show it with lots of greenbacks. Darla was right, it really didn't matter. What kind of problem could the hotel have that I couldn't handle? If I got the bar job back I could continue to work for Otis and his generous salary, only we'd have to have a "come to Jesus talk" about who was after him.

"No," I said, "I guess it doesn't." She had not left any option; she knew she had me boxed in but good.

She used a single long fingernail painted dark red to slide a card key to a room across the desk. I picked it up. "What kind of 'little' problem do you have in this room?"

"Nothing you can't handle." Her eyes softened as if trying to work me, something I'd never seen her use on me. "It's room 602 and I expect complete discretion in this matter. You are to tell no one." She'd shifted and honed the last words to a sharp cutting edge.

I stood, a little woozy on my feet from the thumps I'd taken to the head; probably a mild concussion. No doubt the issue at hand was some kind of sex-capade or narcotic den in room 602, something that needed covering up to protect the hotel's delicate reputation.

Darla was the hotel fixer and I'd just been enlisted as her lieutenant. She'd get the big salary and I'd do all the dirty work just to stay even, just to keep my job.

Better to do what she asked than be regulated to that jungle tour guide hunting for the three-toed-sloth and Geoffroy's spider monkeys. I headed for the office door to get on with it. I wanted to get home to Marie and the kids.

"Ah . . . Bruno?"

I stopped and didn't turn around right away. She'd used my real name instead of calling me Gaylord. That had never happened either. Our relationship had definitely taken a hard left.

But why had she changed now? I turned.

"Never mind, we can discuss it later after you handle this . . ."

I nodded as if being a puppet to her puppeteer was okay and left her office. I crossed the lobby, tossed the towel with ice in the ashtray next to the elevator, and pushed the "UP" button. The look of my injured face might be all that was needed to resolve the problem in room 602. Evidence that I'd give no quarter if they didn't cease and desist their illicit activity. A chance to use the cliché, "You oughta see the other guy."

In the past, while working the cabana bar, I'd overheard a *dark net*–type rumor that at one time the hotel had been listed on that website as a meet place for "sexapalooza," a place where swingers met up for couple exchanges and/or multiple couplings—meaning orgies. Darla worked in a single-minded way, at the sacrifice of the hotel employees, to recover the hotel's tarnished reputation. But every once in a while, that ugly little vice again raised its wicked head. After Darla's naked performance on the roof, I wasn't too sure she'd mind so much.

The elevator dumped me off on the sixth floor, the hallway ominously empty. Now in front of the door, I raised my hand to knock and decided surprise might give me the advantage—show them the hotel meant business and didn't care about decorum. I slid the key in the lock, stepped inside, and froze.

"Oh, shit."

I reached for the gun that had been on my hip for decades, muscle memory from a time long past.

I was unarmed.

CHAPTER TWENTY-ONE

THE PEARL-HANDLED SWITCHBLADE stuck out of the man's abdomen as he lay on the bed in hotel room 602. The knife an abnormal appendage.

His sandy-blond hair hung thick over a craggy face and made him out younger than his late forties. For a professional thug, he carried some excess weight. The dark clothes absorbed the color red from the blood and emboldened the darkness in the clothing. Little blood marked the hotel's bedspread.

The knife was inserted in such a way that the dead man bled out internally. He'd made it all the way from the downstairs exterior door where he and his two friends had attacked us. He'd flopped down on this bed and died. Otis had killed him, stuck the knife into flesh and bone without hesitation. Stuck him in exactly the right place—or was awfully lucky. The dead man knew enough not to remove the blade, leaving that job for a medical professional. Had he made it that far.

This was Darla's *little problem?* What did the Ice Princess classify as a big problem?

I realized I'd been standing with the hotel door open, stepped in and closed it. Waited. Listened. There had been three men who'd attacked us, and I didn't have anything in my hands.

How had Darla Figueroa found out about the death in 602? Something had alerted her to the problem—to this public relations nightmare.

I peeked into the closet to the right; lots of clothes on hangers, men and women's clothes; a suitcase sat open on a suitcase stand, black and red lacy negligees on top. No thugs lurked inside there.

If Waldo was with me, he could easily sniff out an ambush in the suite—someone hiding behind the other side of the bed or in the bathroom.

There was nothing for it. I moved in quickly, ready to react if assaulted, and found the room empty.

The man's eyes stared straight up at the ceiling, awestruck as if the ceiling possessed the answer to the universe. Like any well-versed homicide investigator, I stood and looked at him, "looking to see," and startled when the room phone rang.

I didn't answer it, a racket that further jangled my nerves.

The man had skinned knuckles on his right hand from punching me or Otis. Most likely me. In another world with more logic, I would easily match up his knuckles to the lumps and bruises cluttered around my eyes, lips, and nose.

He wore no jewelry, not even a watch. I checked his clothing—mid-range, not expensive, and with no clue as to where he came from. He didn't carry a wallet, just a money clip with two hundred and twenty dollars.

I found a military-type tattoo on his shoulder, a gloved fist holding three lightning bolts and two crossed rifles underneath.

The phone rang again. I picked it up and listened.

"Gaylord, will you be able to handle this little problem or will I have to call someone else?"

She spoke like dead bodies dropped in her hotel once a week and that she had alternate suckers like me to do her bidding.

I whispered into the phone as if the dead man might hear, as if he didn't know he was already dead and I'd give away that critical information. "You're asking me to become an accomplice to murder after the fact?"

"Murder? Don't be silly. Just take care of the ... ah, over-beveraged guest."

"This is more than I bargained for."

She said nothing, the silence excruciating. I didn't want to commit a crime in my own backyard. I already had enough warrants waiting for me back in the States.

At that moment I stood in a crime scene.

I said, "All right, but my bluies get wiped clean ... in fact, no more blue sheets for me from now on."

"We can talk about that." She held onto her power, her control, with an iron fist.

"Is this the dead man's room? How did you find out about it?"

"Do you really want to know?"

"Yes."

"The couple staying in that room found our over-beveraged guest sleeping on their bed."

A real Goldilocks story.

"An over-beveraged guest with a knife sticking in his gut? Aren't you worried that the couple will be a loose end and will tell someone?"

"No, I've spoken to them. I've already given them another room, comped, of course, an upgrade with a view."

"A comped room isn't going to be enough to keep them from talking."

"They registered under Mr. and Mrs. Bob Johnson."

"I see. Sounds like you lucked out this time."

A getaway tryst where neither person wanted anyone looking into the dead man on their bed. They wouldn't want their faces splashed across the news media for their spouses to see.

"Living right creates its own luck. Handle it, Gaylord, and let me know when it's done. Get that excess baggage off the hotel grounds and you can have your job back." She hung up. She was one cool customer not letting a dead body get to her.

I called a friend down in the bellhop office who knocked on the door and left the baggage carrier in the hall. I pulled the knife out of the deceased and rinsed it off in the bathroom sink. I rolled the man up in the bedspread, folding the ends over on the inside like a burrito. I got him up on the baggage carrier and rolled him out of the hotel room. With the late hour, not many people populated the halls and the ones that did paid me and the burrito no mind.

When the elevator opened, Darla Figueroa stood behind the front guest counter, her arms folded across her chest. I rolled the burrito across the lobby. She moved her head—barely perceptible—from side to side, angry, her lips a thin straight line of red lipstick. I smiled and waved, headed for the front door. I guess she preferred that I had exited out a side door.

Tough.

Outside, the tropical birds of the night chirped and sang as a light mist fell, making the moonlight reflect off the asphalt, turning the dull black to glistening obsidian. I rolled the baggage carrier along the hotel access road, past the private hotel bungalows for the rich who desired privacy and a view of the golf course.

As soon as I came upon public property I crossed the street, looked both ways, and dumped the poor man in the roadside shrubs where he wouldn't lie very long before being discovered. No one deserved to be tossed aside like so much garbage. I wrapped the bedspread up and brought it along.

I started to roll the carrier back from whence we came and realized the dead man added to the El Gato Gordo tally; he made number seven in a paradise that had not seen a murder in the last twenty years.

Violence acted like a virus—it was contagious and deadly. Violence was also a way of making a person distinguish between what's important and what wasn't. Our kids were more important than anything else in the world. We'd have to seriously consider moving to a safer environment. If one even existed. At the very least I needed money to build in a saferoom, a big one to conceal all our loved ones to shield them when evil came knocking.

Forty minutes later, I'd dropped off the bedspread in the hotel laundry, the carrier back in the bellhop closet, and walked home.

*   *   *

I entered our house quietly and got a root beer out of the fridge. The kitchen light came on, blinding me. Eddie Crane in his pajamas checking up on me. He never slept well until I was home safe.

"What happened to your face?"

"Nothing much. I was jumped by three professional thugs, real heavyweights who were trying to kill me. I had to fight for my life." I mimicked a fight, shadowboxing with left hooks and uppercuts.

"Fine, if you don't want to tell me. Mom's going to be mad you tripped on the way home. She thinks you should have a car instead of walking back and forth to work."

I headed toward him. "Give us a kiss."

"Ewww." He turned heel and left. It worked every time. He was of an age too old to show affection.

Marie shuffled into the kitchen in her slippers, sleep in her eyes, not awake enough to notice the injuries to my face. I quickly shut the light off before she spotted the evidence and escorted her back to the bedroom. She crawled back into bed and asked, "Why are you so late?"

I covered her up and lay next to her. I told her everything, about the search of Salvador's office, the cops grabbing me up and the conversation with the chief, how he took the cellphone and the newspapers that had to have some kind of significance. I didn't tell her about the fight outside the hotel room with the three thugs or about the dead man in the hotel. The morning would be soon enough. When I knew she'd fallen back to sleep, I told her about the naked Ice Princess sunbathing on the roof.

I took off the aloha work shirt, my muscles aching from the beating, my face throbbing. I stepped out of my pants as my cell buzzed. Eddie sent me a goodnight text message.

WHEN A LITTLE KID ASKS YOU TO SMELL HIS FINGERS IT ALMOST NEVER SMELLS LIKE VANILLA.

What a nice way to end a day that I wanted to forget, the contrast too heavy not to notice; a switchblade, three thugs, a dead body versus an innocent little kid talking about vanilla.

CHAPTER TWENTY-TWO

THE PHONE JANGLED me out of a dream that vaporized as soon as I opened my eyes. I reached over and looked at the caller on the cell; the Lido cabana bar at the hotel. Light sliced in through the open edge of the closed curtains. Marie must've closed them to give me more time to sleep. I answered. "Chacho, que pasa, amigo?"

"Turn on the news." This wasn't Chacho's voice. The Ice Princess. She'd called from the cabana bar phone. She knew I wouldn't answer if she called on her phone.

She hung up.

I reached for the controller and flipped on the television to the local news channel. Marie never wanted a TV in our bedroom. She said it would overburden our relationship, snuff out "open and clear communication." With all the kids at different ages we never got a shot at the news or our favorite shows on the living room TV, so she'd relented but kept strict control over "the when" and "for how long."

The news panned a shot of the hotel sign on the road at the entrance to the turnaround then shifted to the hotel golf course. I sat straight up in bed, my heart pounding. The news cameraman zoomed in on a dead man buried up to his waist in the hotel golf course sand trap at the ninth hole. His hands had been posed with a sand wedge lining up a chip shot; a grotesque tableau. The woman newscaster for *Channel Six*, Rebecca Sanchez, the Darling of Costa Rica, spoke in rapid Spanish I didn't need translated.

"Shit."

I slid to the foot of the bed to get closer to the TV. Marie came in the room and sat next to me. She gently put an ice pack to my face.

"You going to tell me about your face?"

"No."

She stared for a moment more deciding not to delve further into the issue, choosing her battles. "Bruno, what's happening to our little slice of paradise?" She'd obviously heard the news.

She didn't ask if I had something to do with *the dead golfer on the ninth hole on the hotel golf course, the one buried to the waist in the sand trap.*

Just thinking it out loud sounded ludicrous.

"I don't know, babe, it's really just a little blip. Once they get this mess at the nightclub cleaned up, it'll get back to normal, I promise."

She nodded, a little morose. "I called the *New York Times*. They're sending us copies of those newspapers."

I hugged her. "Thank you, that's great." I tried to pull back and kiss her.

She pinched me hard on the stomach. "Naked on the roof? Long, long legs? Seriously?"

"I . . . I . . ."

I didn't know what to say. I thought she'd been asleep when I told her the night before. No matter what I did she always outfoxed me. "I think I should get into work." Pointed to the TV. "Today's going to be a real mess. Tourists from other hotels are going to come over to lookee-loo; the bar's going to be a mob scene."

She nodded. "I was reading the murder book and I think we should try and find out more about the woman Salvador was meeting for drinks."

"We don't know her name yet, do we?"

"It's Gloria Perez. According to the murder book, she was lying close to Salvador. The next closest person anyway."

I froze. I knew a Gloria Perez, but Perez in Spanish was like Johnson or Smith in English, a very popular name. Gloria, not so much.

Marie noticed how my body had stiffened. "What?"

"Chacho's girlfriend's name is Gloria Perez. I forgot, she's a waitress at El Gato."

"Ah, Bruno, not Chacho? Do you think he knows?"

I didn't answer. The OIJ still had a lid on what happened. No families had been notified or we'd have heard about it in a big way.

"Bruno?"

"What? Huh?" My mind had wandered to the roof of the hotel, Chacho's mis-buttoned shirt, the naked temptress tanned and oiled, a sleek sex machine that hummed with a need to be serviced. Why else would she put the index cards up as a warning and not lock the door to the roof? She was the Venus flytrap, Chacho the fly.

She couldn't lock the doors without giving poor Chacho a key— Darla conflicted, not giving up control for privacy.

Marie repeated her question. "Do you think Chacho knows about Gloria?"

"He was at work yesterday, so I don't think so. The OIJ is keeping a tight lid on the shooting. They could never get away with it in the States."

"Are you going to tell him?"

"Gloria worked there. I don't see how I could keep from talking to Chacho about her."

"If you don't tell him what you know about . . . about what happened at El Gato Gordo, and he finds out you knew, he's going to be angry. He's a good friend and deserves our support."

I said nothing. Chacho, a happy-go-lucky guy who let nothing get him down, was going to be crushed. It hurt to think about it.

Marie keyed in on my silence. "What? You're not telling me something."

We'd lived together too long. She knew my quirks and tells; she read me the same as a champion poker player no matter how hard I tried to cover my reactions.

"Yesterday on the roof. I mean, when I was going through the door to the roof, Chacho was coming out."

She waited, then said, "That doesn't mean anything, just because there was a beautiful naked woman, tanned and oiled up . . . that doesn't mean . . . ah, hell." She couldn't even talk herself out of the duck theory. If it walks like duck, talks like a duck, looks like a duck, it's a damn duck.

"Later on, when I worked with Chacho in the cabana bar, I noticed his shirt wasn't buttoned straight."

"Ah, Bruno, I thought better of Chacho."

"He might not have had a choice. You don't know what this woman's like. She—" I caught myself too late. If Chacho didn't have a choice, how come *I had*?

Marie got up and took a quick step to leave. I caught her wrist and pulled her back to sit on my lap. "Where are you going?"

"I'm going to get a ball bat and go talk to . . . to this Ice Princess who sounds more like the devil."

"And do you think that will make things better or exacerbate them?"

Her eyes turned fierce. "Oh, it'll make things worse, make them untenable, but I'll feel a hell'va lot better."

"The woman has not made a pass at me." I pulled Marie into a hug. "And rest assured, I'm only gaga over one person."

Marie smiled. "Where is she? I'll kill her."

I chuckled. "Let me deal with the problems at my work, and you can deal with yours at the clinic. How's that?"

She nodded and kissed me, but her smile disappeared.

"What?"

She pulled away, went to the side of the bed, and opened the nightstand. She pulled out the murder book where she'd concealed it from the children. She'd been studying it in her spare time. She thumbed through the tabs until she found what she was looking for. She brought the book over, her finger pointing at something on the page, a name of one of the shooting victims.

"Ah, shit."

CHAPTER TWENTY-THREE

NOW TWO WOMEN involved in the nightclub shooting had the name Gloria. Both victims. Both unable to tell us what happened. The shooting at El Gato Gordo continued to spew loose ends at an overwhelming rate. Without any direct suspect, everyone associated with the victims became a person of interest—the more victims, the more leads. Information already uncovered had not yet narrowed down to one suspect. The name Marie pointed to was the woman who'd been closest to Aleck, both dead on the nightclub floor, but seven feet apart. When the shooting starts, people panic, start to move, shift and shuffle in the chaos.

Aleck, the doctor who had delivered our son Tobias, had died in the vicinity of a woman named Gloria Quesada. The enormity of that crime scene started to make my head ache as the wave of violence radiated out exponentially—the same as a big rock dropped in a still pond. Had the woman Aleck was seeing escaped in all the chaos? I needed to focus on her identity.

Stepping out on Alisa? No, not Aleck. Gloria Quesada had to be random, there at the club with someone else. Chief Hernandez said that Aleck was meeting his girlfriend. How did Hernandez know it was his girlfriend he was meeting? Hernandez had to have it wrong.

Rosie came in and handed Tobias to Marie. We both cooed over him. I reveled in his smile—the joy it gave me. His cuddly softness, his scent of baby powder—all of him made me want to skip work and stay home.

I wolfed down a quick breakfast and ran to work. Two news trucks from the main networks in San Jose sat in the hotel parking slots. The crews must've taken rooms in the hotel to be close to the action, the gruesome story of a golf game gone awry.

I headed right for the Ice Princess' lair, not to espouse my fealty but to explain where I had actually deposited *Sam Snead*, a name as good as any for our John Doe.

I entered the lobby. Darla Figueroa left her perch watching over the operation from behind the front check-in counter where customers lined up to check in.

She said nothing, her flinty expression difficult to read since she always looked angry. She headed to her office. I followed along, again trying not to watch the way her body moved under her dress, force the naked long and lithe, tanned and oiled image from my memory. That coconut scent . . .

She entered her office, waited for me, then closed the door. She moved around to the other side of her desk, crossed her arms, and said nothing.

I held up my hands. "Before you blow a gasket, I didn't leave that guy on the ninth hole in the sand trap lining up a chip shot."

She waited, letting the pregnant pause grow to a third trimester. "I know you didn't." She pushed some buttons on her computer, and the TV screen on the wall lit up displaying a video of me unrolling the burrito across the street from hotel property, the property covering almost a mile of the access road.

"You could've taken him farther away from the hotel than across the street." She waved her arm angrily. "There's a thousand square miles of damn jungle out there and you dump him across *the street?*"

"Half a mile down. I didn't think he should go too long before he was discovered. His people will want to know what happened to him."

"Oh, so I've chosen a white knight with a conscience to champion the reputation of this hotel?" She shook her head in disgust. "Do you have any idea what kind of shitstorm you caused?"

"Where's Herb?"

Herb Templeton, the purported manager of the hotel. In all the time I'd worked at the hotel, I'd never laid eyes on him; only heard his name invoked by the food and beverage manager. She said Herb mostly managed from afar. From the balcony of a plush home up on the hill. He watched with a telescope and commanded by telephone.

She half-mumbled and waved her arm. "When this shitstorm broke, he caught the first plane out of here. He said he needed to use up some vacation time before he lost it."

"Aren't you the least bit interested in how this dead guy ended up in one of the hotel rooms?"

I didn't know what else to offer in my defense. A feeble rebuttal at best.

She pushed a couple more buttons on her laptop. The TV shifted to another video that must've used infrared cameras and displayed the fight at the side door to the hotel when the three thugs jumped us. I cringed when I took the blows to the head and face. All I could do was shrug. She had me cold—or as my old boss Robby Wicks would say—"Had me dead bang."

She slowed down the video, the part where Otis shoved the knife into Sam Snead. I'd seen many gruesome things in my career, but seeing that blade slide into human flesh made me grimace and turn away.

She shut off the video. "I don't know your relationship with this man, this killer who's taken up residence in my hotel, but I want him gone before he causes any more mayhem."

"You want me to kick Otis out?"

"He's your friend."

"He's not my friend."

"Then what is he to you?"

"I won't do it. It's not my job. I'm a bartender and that's it."

"You're what I say you are."

I needed to change the direction of the conversation or risk punching out my boss.

I asked, "Who moved the body and why?" Another question I never thought I would ever ask.

She hesitated, staring me down. "Who else?" she said. "The police chief. He's not happy—and I quote, 'You let your hotel slop get dumped off in my town.'"

"You're kidding me. Chief Hernandez had the guy buried in the sand trap? He said that?"

Her hard expression softened as she looked down at the desk. "He and I are no longer on good terms. We were, but now he's angry about something, and I can't figure out what it is. I can normally work him like a lump of clay, but the last couple of days, he's been a real bastard. Do you know the chief?"

She'd finally opened up—sounded like a real human with emotions.

"He's acting out because—" I caught myself. I almost let slip the shooting at El Gato Gordo. She'd softened me up on purpose, and I almost fell into her web.

"Because *what?*" she asked, back to her old self. Just that quick—a chameleon with sharp teeth, a reminder that I had to watch myself and never again let my guard down around her.

"I guess because I dropped a John Doe in his area. The town hasn't had a murder in twenty years."

She came around her desk and stepped into my personal space, up close, inches away. The faint scent of coconut lotion made me swallow hard. With a red, perfectly manicured fingernail, she poked the skin below my neck, the exposed vee of my aloha shirt. The touch sent a shiver up my back.

"Don't kid yourself, cowboy, there's been plenty of murder and mayhem—it's just been covered up to protect the reputation of Tamarindo."

I took a step back, sweat beading on my forehead, her eyes drilling into my cranium trying to uncover my deepest secrets. I shook myself like a wet dog and took another step back as she followed.

"What's the matter, Bruno?"

"No. No. No. I have to go." I spun and opened the door to the office.

"Gaylord?"

I turned back and said, "Just so you know, my wife, Marie, has a ball bat."

Darla transformed back into the Ice Princess, her mouth a tight line. "You're at the bar by yourself today, cowboy. Chacho asked for some time off."

Chacho never took time off. He needed the money to support his extended family. "Is something wrong?"

"Nothing that concerns you. His girlfriend has gone missing." She looked up from her desk, a paper in her hand. "You don't know anything about his girlfriend, Gloria, do you?"

"No, why would I?"

"Go to work, Gaylord, and on your way down to the bar, take a case of gin, two of rum. And check the beer—it's low, critically low." She knew everything that went on in the hotel right down to the bar stock.

Bizarre.

I saluted with two fingers. "Yes, ma'am."

I exited and hurried to get Otis.

CHAPTER TWENTY-FOUR

FIRST, I STOPPED in the kitchen to prepare the drink garnish and found one of the sous chefs had already set me up. In fact, he'd done a much better job. I picked up the heavy platter, hoisted it to my shoulder. "Thank you, Jaime, I owe you one."

Jaime waved a thick-bladed butcher knife he'd just used to cut the head off a large game fish with a chomp and a crunch. "Anytime, mi amigo. Hey, can I ask you a personal question?"

I hesitated. "Maybe . . . sure, you helped me out today. Whatta ya want to know?"

"Why is everyone all of a sudden calling you El Gato Negro?"

"What?" The heavy tray of garnish on my shoulder grew heavier. "Who's calling me The Black Cat?" I hoped this new revelation in no way connected me by rumor with the nightclub shooting.

Jaimie kept waving his knife as if it were an extension of his hand. He had gang tattoos on both hands and neck with three teardrops below his left eye—all black ink—so he'd gotten them in prison. The one on his neck, "MS13," meant he was a member of the most dangerous street gang in South America, Central America, and the U.S.—a vicious gang with over a hundred thousand active members. Yet, a nicer guy you'd never want to meet. To me, he seemed like a guy trying for a fresh start in life, and I intended to give him that opportunity. He worked hard and when he could he helped out others—not characteristics of a dangerous gang member.

He shrugged. "Everyone has been saying you're the Black Cat."

"Tell you the truth, I don't know—this is the first I heard of it."

But it wasn't. I'd heard tourists and hotel employees talking about the *Black Cat*, I just thought it was a panther prowling about on the town outskirts. What a fool I'd been. "Thanks again, Jaime, I owe you."

He brought the knife up to his forehead in acknowledgement, his eyes locked on me as if trying to decide an important question.

Out at the cabana bar, I set everything up, made five Bloody Mary cocktails, extra spicy, for a group of hungover early risers, and headed out to escort Otis to the bar. I'd gone five steps when the cabana bar phone rang. I was leaving my post without relief, an Ice Princess felony that warranted two bluies instead of one. That had to be her on the phone.

Why was she watching my every move? Then I realized she had video of me in a fight with three thugs, one of which ended up playing the back nine forever caught in a sand trap.

Didn't matter. After the attack the night before, I couldn't leave Otis unprotected. As I passed under the camera, I waved to Darla and held up two fingers to indicate I'd be back in two minutes.

Over the last few days, the entire atmosphere of the hotel had shifted. No longer the bright sunny safe haven with blue ocean water, swaying palm trees, a caressing soft breeze, a respite from the crushing everyday grind—instead, the Lido bar had turned into a vortex of violence.

Over the PA, the Ice Princess' voice came out loud and clear. "Gaylord, please respond to the blue room." That's what she called her office. The room wasn't painted blue, it was just a place where bluies were issued without emotion, a place where work lives were ruined. She specified the blue room on purpose to keep the other employees on their toes, letting them know they could be next, that the Ice Princess was always watching.

Two minutes later, I knocked on Otis' door. After a second when he didn't answer, I pounded on the door.

He yanked it open. "What's the rumpus? We're still eating breakfast. You're here earl—"

I grabbed him by the collar of his seersucker suit coat, the same one he'd been wearing for three days. His rotund body jiggled with excess fat as I jerked him out into the hall.

"Hey. Hey, what the hell? What's going on?"

Waldo slipped out the door before the automatic return closed him in. At the same time, he gobbled down two large buttermilk pancakes with chocolate chips, eating them on the run without dropping one little ort.

"I'm late for work. Chacho took the day off."

"Chacho's day off should in no way impose upon my schedule. Not for the kind of dough I'm layin' out. Wait. Wait. I haven't had my morning ablutions."

I didn't slow and held on to him.

"Let go. Let me go."

He said something in German. Waldo ran ahead, turned, and braced. He growled. There wasn't any doubt I was about to replace his sausages—the part of his breakfast I'd interrupted.

I stopped. "You're supposed to be my dog."

"I thought you said he wasn't your dog?"

Otis shrugged out of my grasp and pretended to be indignant while straightening his coat. "You need to make up your mind—you're confusing the poor dog. Now, we're going back to the room and when I'm ready, I'll call you."

I looked down at Waldo, then at the obstinate Otis and decided I didn't have time to mess with them. I reached into my pocket and tossed Otis the switchblade I'd extracted from Sam Snead's abdomen. "Here, this is yours."

He caught it. "This isn't mine." He looked at it with real incredulity, real enough to win him an Oscar.

Of course he'd deny it. He knew where he'd stuck the knife and that his victim wouldn't have survived.

I said, "The hotel management has you on tape sticking your knife into a human."

He stood up straighter and fussed with his suit, a nervous tick. His face flushed red from fear. "The hell you say? Video?"

"That's right and she wants you gone before anything else of a violent nature occurs at the hotel."

His eyes stared off down the hallway as he apparently tried to work the problem. "I . . . didn't see any cameras. Are there cameras covering that area? Hey, those guys weren't humans, they were animals, killers. Self-defense, I'm claiming self-defense."

It took a moment for Otis to recover his composure before reverting back to happy-go-lucky Otis. "I'll deal with that. Don't you worry about it. If they have video, they also know what happened was self-defense."

He now sounded less convincing on that second part.

I shrugged. "I'm not worried about it." A fat lie that caught in my throat. I didn't need a murder warrant that would force me to move farther south to Panama.

"Listen, I'm paying you big money to take care of my interests, you understand? I want you to get that videotape. I don't care what it takes. I'll give you a bonus, ah . . . five grand if you get that tape."

I moved in close to intimidate him. "You're not telling me every-thing. Who were those guys who attacked us?"

He pulled back. "Exactly. *They* attacked *us,* buddy boy, not just me but us. Think about that. How do we know they weren't out to get you? Huh?"

He must've seen my expression shift from confident to confusion. Of course, he was right, it really could've been my old life coming back to bite me in the ass. It wasn't out of the realm of possibility. I'd angered a good many people, including vengeful outlaw motorcycle gangs who'd never rest until they evened the score. Sons of Satan had dispatched bikers to Costa Rica to menace one of our kids. Those two bikers went for an all-expenses-paid fishing trip with Salvador Perez and Jose Rivera and never returned.

But if the three thugs last night had wanted to kill us—me or Otis—there were easier ways. They'd send one dude with a gun, not three mouth-breathers with blackjacks. Then I realized the attack was meant to either make a statement—or more likely—take one of us into their custody for warrants or to extract information. Why else use blackjacks?

"They wanted you for something you've done," I said. "And don't try and throw it back on me. Why are you paying me so much money to protect you if you didn't think someone was trying to get you?"

"Okay, okay, you gotta point." He looked from side to side up and down the hall. "I married into some money. Fact is, she was a rich spinster with a monkey's ass for a face. I'm not kidding, a real Boogawolf. Her dad knew what time it was and wanted a prenup. We went back and forth until finally good ol' Doris came through and insisted on the wedding without the prenup. I'd pulled it off. I waited a respectable time, got control of a couple of the biggest accounts, some stocks and bonds, and took it on the lam. Her daddy is beyond pissed. Not because of the money, but because I broke his precious daughter's heart. He said he'd get me. That's what that little incident was all about. No big mystery. You did your job and I appreciate it. I'll give you a bonus for it and another one if you get that damn tape back."

"You're a real pig."

"Hey."

"I'll see you down at the bar." I'd given him my word that I'd protect him and I'd keep it. I'd protect him to the best of my ability. "Otis, take a shower, the customers are starting to complain."

"You're a rude bastard. I'm your boss so cut out the disparaging remarks. And I want that tape. You hear me? Get it."

I said, "Come on, Waldo, let's go down to the bar."

Waldo looked at me with sad eyes—at least they looked sad to me. He walked by me and followed Otis into the hotel room. He probably wanted to finish his breakfast, or he would've chosen me instead of Otis.

Yeah, that's what happened.

CHAPTER TWENTY-FIVE

As I HURRIED back to the cabana bar, I replayed everything I knew about Otis—all that had happened since the first day I'd met him. The man was not who he made himself out to be. I didn't believe his gold digger story, not for a minute. And he was something more than a white-collar criminal hiding out in a popular hotel in Costa Rica, living off of his ill-gotten gains. That's what he wanted everyone to believe. Maybe his poor hygiene was part of that act; it kept folks at arm's length. And why would a white-collar criminal need muscle to watch his back? The thugs from the night before were pros. Pros didn't come after white-collar criminals, not without good reason. More important was the way he'd wielded the blade and stuck it into poor Sam Snead.

I made it back to the bar and found some unhappy, near-sober tourists who were late at getting their drunk on. I caught up after fifteen minutes of flinging glasses and beer and metal mixing shakers.

Darla Figueroa was right—I was almost out of rum and gin and most of the beer selections. No way could I leave now—the daily rush had already started. People on vacation, who, when at home, would never dream of drinking so early in the day.

In a lull, I spotted Jose by the same palm tree. I waved him over. I leaned across the bar to speak to him in a low whisper while his eyes took in the injuries on my face. I told him what had happened the night before and asked him to look into it. We were still missing two of the men, one with a bite on his shoulder from Waldo's intervention and the other with a broken knee—if not broken, then at least real sore. He nodded that he understood. I reached over and grabbed his shoulder. "First, can you go to Otis' room and escort him down here. Then I'll watch him until you come back."

He nodded and disappeared into a throng of tourists coming up to the bar.

Two young girls in bikinis and nice tans asked for strawberry daiquiris with extra rum floated on the top. I smiled and talked with them while preparing their order. This was the tough part of the job. They spoke with British accents and loved the hotel, thought it was the best kept secret in South America. I didn't correct them on their geography.

When they walked back toward the beach, I turned and spotted Chacho coming down from the hotel negotiating the walkway around the pool, trundling a dolly stacked with cases of booze, the stock I should've picked up before my shift started. My day began at a run and I still had not caught up. The dead guy—now known as Sam Snead—on the ninth hole remained the topic of conversation, the folks buying at least a third more pastel-colored fluffy drinks and shots of hard liquor, out of fear of the virulent strain of violence possibly visiting *them* on their vacation.

Oddly, Chacho never mentioned Sam Snead, his expression focused entirely on the job at hand.

Earlier, Otis had appeared out of nowhere and now held up his glass indicating he'd like another grasshopper. He wagged his eyebrows. "The guy who picked me up at my room—was that *Hose-A*? The guy who's supposed to be watching my ass when you're gone? I couldn't pick him out yesterday. We gonna have *Hose-B* next time you're gone? Get it?" Otis was already drunk on his ass— must've been hitting the mini bar for breakfast. His hand always shook with a palsy until his third or fourth drink of the day. He'd started drinking at the cabana bar with a steady hand.

I opened the pass-through and helped Chacho with the resupply. "I thought you were taking the day to look for Gloria?"

Bent over, he stopped shuffling the cases of beer and stood up with a concerned expression. "I have already looked everywhere. Amigo, she must've left town. But I don't know why. She'd never leave without telling me. Never."

When things slowed down, I'd have to break my promise to Chief Hernandez and tell Chacho what happened at El Gato Gordo, an obligation I was not looking forward to.

Three hours later, the tip jar stuffed with greenbacks, we caught a lull in the action, some of the hard-core drinkers taking a break, getting some food to soak up all the booze. I asked Chacho, "Do you know a guy named Salvador Perez?"

He looked at me funny. "No, why do you ask?"

I hadn't thought out an explanation for my inquiry if he asked. "Ah, just . . . ah, he's a friend of mine, and I wondered if you knew him?" I chickened out. I couldn't tell him while working—he'd take off at a run headed for El Gato. I know I would, given the same circumstances. If he took off, I wouldn't be able to leave the bar unattended to chase him.

Yeah, at least that's what I told myself.

Chacho looked around furtively. "No, amigo, I don't know him." He kept checking out the beach and the concrete boardwalk in front of the cabana bar. "But I've had this feeling someone is watching me."

I asked, "Who's watching you? What does he look like?"

Chacho shrugged. "Don't know, it's just a feeling. You know what I mean?"

He was probably talking about Jose watching Otis, caught the vibe from Jose's eyes always on the cabana bar.

"Hey," I said, "I'm going to take a fifteen-minute break before siesta, that cool?" I needed to start eliminating suspects from the list that continued to grow. If I hurried I could mark one off during my break

"Si," Chacho said. "Come back with some more rum and vodka. I'll restock the beer again when I return from siesta."

"Gottcha. Be right back." I picked up an empty plastic liter root beer bottle, a drink not on our soda dispenser selection hose, but kids asked for it all the time. I left the bar in a hurry, and Waldo immediately appeared at my side. "Oh, no you don't. You don't get to come along whenever you want." I pointed. "Go back."

The dumb dog sat. "I didn't say *sit*. I said *go back*." He looked at me with his big brown eyes.

"Otis, call your dog."

Otis toasted his tenth grasshopper, his eyes blurry. "Ain't my dog. You said he was yours." He turned back around and pounded the bar with his other hand. "Cheecho, my man, hopper me up, would ya, son?"

"Stay!" I told Waldo. "Stay."

He still just looked at me like I'd lost my mind. I took off again. Waldo followed.

"Damn dog."

CHAPTER TWENTY-SIX

WITH A DOG in tow, I had to change course and bypass the lobby entrance. That meant shifting to the same side door from the night before—where we'd been jumped. Waldo slowed and sniffed around the concrete where the fight occurred. Maybe he caught the blood scent—even with the rain, a dog had that ability.

"Go on, boy, follow the scent."

Waldo looked up with his favorite stupid dog expression and sat.

"Never mind."

I entered the hotel and moved down the maze of hallways to Otis' room. I used the master card key from the night before, the one Darla gave me to take care of Sam Snead. I opened the door.

On the way in, Waldo all but knocked me down. He headed right for the couch and sat in his usual place. Otis had left the morning breakfast dishes scattered about the table. Waldo craned his neck from his sitting position, took the small maple syrup urn from the tray in his mouth, and upended it, slurping the sticky nectar that ran down his chest and paws and the couch.

Perfect.

Maybe housekeeping would be able to clean it before Otis got back tonight and figured out someone had been in his room.

I didn't have much time. I selected a paperback book from the discards stacked against the wall, *Man with a Gun*, by Robert Daley. Good book, I'd read it twice during my two years in prison.

I took the book and Otis' gun, the Browning Hi-Power 9mm, from the table by the couch, into the bathroom and closed the door. I filled the plastic root beer bottle three-quarters full of water. Next, I put the book in the bathtub, set the bottle filled with water on top, stuck the tip of the gun barrel in the neck, pointed into the water.

And hesitated.

I had never done anything like this before, but when I thought of it, the idea sure sounded logical. The plastic bottle would dampen the gunshot; the water and book would slow the bullet down. Well, in theory, anyway. I pulled the hammer back, turned my head away, grimaced, and pulled the trigger.

Water blew out all over the place, spattering my face and arm. The bottle had ruptured at the sides, the noise muffled like I expected. I picked up the book, wiped off the water, and quickly thumbed through the pages with holes in them and found the bullet all the way at the back.

The bullet nose had flattened. I picked up the expended shell casing and looked at the tub more closely. Oh shit. The poor man's ballistic test had dented the fiberglass and left a little crack in the bottom of the dent. The tub would leak now, but only a little at a time. Couldn't be helped. I pulled the rubber anti-slip mat over the hole.

The rifling on the bullet needed for identification was still intact. Mission accomplished.

No way could Otis have pulled off the shooting at El Gato Gordo. He was too fat and slow to climb up on that stool without assistance. And he was never sober long enough. But I still needed to eliminate him. Three thugs jumping us was just too big of a coincidence and it happened too close to the nightclub shooting.

I opened the bathroom door cautiously and found Waldo on the couch watching me, his long pink tongue still at work cleaning the syrup from his muzzle and paws.

I moved to the closet, opened the door, and froze.

Otis had a pair of black, wing-tipped shoes.

But everyone his age had wingtips, right? I turned them over, laid a quarter by the shoes for perspective and photographed the soles. I put them back and started to close the door when I noticed the gray London Fog raincoat hanging in the back.

Otis had a 9mm pistol, wingtips, *and* a gray London Fog. What the hell? The Duck Theory applied here, and Otis was quacking.

Loudly.

Back in the States as a street cop, I would've had probable cause to arrest Otis for six counts of homicide. I took out the coat and examined it for blood spatter and didn't find any. I checked the pockets—empty.

After photographing the coat, I put it back and closed the closet door.

I texted Chief Hernandez to meet me at the cabana bar. In the hotel room, I put everything back just the way it was—except the damaged book and the dent in the bathtub. I opened the door to leave.

"You coming?"

Waldo got up, stretched, yawned, and stood there. "Come on, move it. Let's go." He looked at me with no intention of making my day any easier. I couldn't leave him inside the room. I hurried over to the mini bar concession on top of the counter, picked out a full-sized Snickers bar, opened it, and stood outside the hall holding it down low. He casually walked out the door trying not to look interested in the candy, but I knew better.

"Don't let me rush you."

I closed the door, tossed the book and the obliterated plastic bottle in the trash of the room service cart in the hall, and headed back to the bar. I took a bite of the candy bar.

Waldo growled.

"Sorry, pal. Better luck next time, huh?"

He charged and nipped at my leg. I dodged. He made another try, his jaws clacked together, missing my private parts by inches.

I ran.

He could've caught me if he'd wanted; instead, he kept his canines just in range to taunt me all the way out to the cabana bar.

Damn dog.

CHAPTER TWENTY-SEVEN

CHACHO DIDN'T COME back after siesta and Chief Hernandez didn't stop by either. Something must've happened with Chacho or maybe he'd thought of more places to look for Gloria.

I couldn't get what I found in Otis' room out of my head—three pieces of evidence that matched the nightclub killings. Throughout the remainder of the shift I kept looking over at Otis. He'd see me, raise his grasshopper glass, and shoot me that goofy smile. He was too much of a victim to be a violent predator. But some serious evidence pointed to him, even though my instinct said no way. For much of my career I'd strictly followed the rules of evidence wherever they led me, but sometimes those same rules walked up and kicked me in the ass.

Even though Otis fit the Duck Theory, I still wanted to rule him out. Lots of people wear wingtips and have London Fog raincoats. Costa Rica's annual rainfall is one hundred inches, and some areas get as much as twenty-five feet of rain. For that much water you're better off with a scuba tank than a London Fog.

As for the 9mm, the caliber is the most popular round on the market. No. Otis was nothing but a fat obstreperous old drunk—no way could he have pulled off a mass murder. No way.

And as silly as it sounded—his name was *Otis*. I don't like to classify people, but this guy was a dweeb with a capital D. He just got lucky sticking that knife. That's what happened—just a visit from lady luck when three violent men forced his hand.

The night crew for the cabana bar came on at eight, Jaime, the sous chef, pulling a double shift, and a beach blond from Malibu named Lisa who lived to lie in the sun and swim in the ocean.

Jaime said, "We got this, El Gato. You don't need to clean up— we'll take it from here." His eyes looked glassy like he'd been smoking weed. I looked to Lisa to see if she agreed that it was okay to leave without doing my cleanup, but she was already in conversation with three tourists, good-looking men her own age who spoke with Greek accents.

Jaime looked like a thug with tattoos on his neck, face, and hands. Nice enough guy—but why did Darla allow him to serve as bartender?

I slapped the bar. "Otis? You ready to go back to the room?"

His head swayed from side to side on its own, his eyelids at half-mast. This was as drunk as I'd ever seen him. On the bar in front of him lay fifteen little umbrellas from the dead grasshoppers.

Marie forever corrected me, "They're not umbrellas, silly, they're parasols."

Otis shook his head. "Naw, look." He tried to wave his hand over the parasols and almost fell off his stool. "I'm goin' for a record. If I continue to pace myself, I can make twenty."

I pulled off my apron, came around to the outside of the bar. I waved at Jaime. "Thanks, man, I'll take you up on your offer so I can get this guy back to his room."

"You got it, El Gato." He made his hand into a gun with his index finger for the barrel, his thumb for the hammer, and pointed at me. His lips formed the word, "Pow."

I stopped and hesitated. The way his eyes looked, the way he spoke and acted, reminded me of the hardcore gang members I used to chase back in LA. The murderous ones. The ones without a conscience.

I snapped out of it, picked Otis up under his arms, damp and odoriferous with sour body odor. I had to fight off an automatic gag reflex. Almost not worth a thousand dollars a day. We took the short route past the empty pool and through the lobby. No way did I want to risk that side door again. The Ice Princess wouldn't dare mess with me, not now. I was her fixer who kept a black book that involved her.

When we got to his room, I had to help Otis with his card key to open the door. I tried to guide him to his bedroom, but he'd have none of it. He broke away, wobbled, almost fell on his face, made it over to the couch, and fell face first into the cushions, out cold. While he was out, Housekeeping had done a miraculous job cleaning the place, not that Otis would've noticed.

After handling Otis, I went in the bathroom and scrubbed my hands and arms, but I still reeked and badly needed a bath.

I said to Waldo, "You coming with me or staying for breakfast with your new best buddy?"

I tried to keep the jealousy out of my voice. I didn't want him to think I liked him.

He gave me his best dumb dog expression, turned, trotted over to the counter, got up on his hind legs, and snatched the last full-sized Snickers bar out of the mini bar concessions. He came right past me. I followed him out the door and into the hall. "Hey, pal, you want me to open that for you?"

"Grrr."

He munched on the candy bar, wrapper and all.

We made it across the lobby without any Ice Princess sightings. No doubt she was in her lair, watching our every move on her cameras. At the front door, I turned and waved, hoping she'd see and know that I knew she was watching and no longer cared about violating her policies.

It had not rained for a couple of hours. The night birds sang, and the full moon lit the way in a beautiful tropical night filled with the scents of moisture and sweet flowers. No need to hurry home. I'd enjoy the quiet evening despite the odor of Otis that clung to me.

We made the first turn just past the golf course heading inland away from hotel property when I stopped. Up ahead, a man stood to the rear of a car covered in deep shadow from the branches of an overgrown glory-bush tree. I might've missed him had he not taken a drag from his cigarette, the cherry red glow barely illuminating his face. Beside me, Waldo growled, the fur on his back rising.

The man said, "Amigo?"

CHAPTER TWENTY-EIGHT

OUT ON THE dark street, Waldo growled at my side. I didn't recognize the voice of the man leaning up against the car in the dark, and I moved with caution toward him. When he took another long drag off the cigarette, the cherry glow lit him up in an eerie redness. Jose Rivera—the man who worked with Salvador Perez in the security company—the man who'd been helping me watch over Otis. I relaxed and moved in close to talk.

"*Buenos noches, Señor Johnson.*"

My eyes adjusted to the darker tone in the shade cast by the trees. "Yes, it is a nice night. What are you doing here, my friend?"

Another drag off the cigarette. Out of old habit I took a step away from him as he marked himself as a target in the dark. Old tactical habits die hard. We stood for a silent moment.

Something rustled in the shrubs and trees close by. I reached for the gun that wasn't there. Jose remained unmoved and continued to smoke.

A small deer broke out of the tree line and crossed the street, something I was still getting used to. Wildlife never made an appearance in South Central Los Angeles, except for ghetto wolves, feral dogs that came out at night in packs to terrorize cats and sometimes people.

Waldo bolted across the street after the deer and disappeared into the dark. He was great at catching the orange Frisbee, not so much with lithe nimble brown deer.

I chuckled at a memory. When I was with Marie and a deer made an appearance she'd casually say, "Oh, dear." The mere thought of her warmed my heart.

In his lifetime Jose had spent a lot of time out in the sun, his face nut-brown and crisscrossed with age lines. Gray hairs streaked the raven hair he kept cut short. Salvador had told me that Jose had fought in the guerilla wars in Honduras and El Salvador and now resided illegally in Costa Rica, quite at home out in the jungle. He had no family and lived off the land, staying off the radar except to help his friend Salvador in his security business. And like me now— minus one good friend.

Jose took out a pouch and began to roll another cigarette. "These men who hurt you, they are here for money, *muy malo hombres.*"

"Yes, they are very bad. How do you know they are here for money?"

He licked the edge of the paper, put the cigarette in his mouth, and lit it. He squinted from the smoke in his eyes. "They are Russians who have no business in this country."

"Jose, my friend, how do you know they are Russians?"

"Russian gang members, *muy malo.*"

"Yes, you said that, but how do you know?"

He stared at me as if deciding on his answer. Finally, he turned and opened the trunk to the old AMC Hornet we stood next to. The trunk light had come loose and hung from a wire that swung back and forth, illuminating the dead man inside.

I stood back, startled. "Ah, shit."

Had I told Jose to seek and destroy these men? No, I think I only told him what had happened and to look into it. This was his way of *looking into something.* Salvador must've defined his instruction better when he sent Jose out on a mission.

"Jose . . . ah, why did you . . .?"

Headlights lit us up, a car coming our way. I quickly shut the trunk. Jose's hand slowly disappeared behind his back where he most likely hid a gun. I gently put my hand on his shoulder. "No."

He looked up at me for a long moment, turned, and disappeared into the dark jungle—did it without a whisper of a noise. A ghost.

The car stopped fifteen feet away, the headlights marking me as an easy target. The blue rotating light of a police vehicle came on.

Perfect.

Why now? Lady Luck was not my friend. I fought the urge to plunge into the jungle, run until I could run no farther. But I was easy to recognize, too many people would know me by description. We lived in a small town and I was only about a mile from home.

I waited, my heart racing, standing next to a car with a dead Russian in the trunk. What could I use as an excuse: "I'm just walking home from work and stopped to talk to the nice man who fled when you pulled up"? The alibi even sounded lame to me.

Suddenly, all the lights in the cop car went off, dumping everything into blackness until my eyes readjusted to the moon. Now was the time to go.

Run.

My feet wouldn't cooperate.

The car rolled slowly forward, the tires crunching and popping on the tiny rocks that littered the asphalt. Then it veered to the left with the right side of the car stopping alongside. The rear window rolled down. "Señor Johnson."

Chief Hernandez.

I let out the breath I'd been holding.

Chief Hernandez said, "What are you doing out so late?"

"Walking home from work."

"That's not your car then?"

"No. I . . . I came upon it and was asking the man if he needed help when you pulled up."

"You're a poor liar. Get in the car."

I came around the other side and got in the backseat next to him. He smoked a narrow cigar and held a brandy snifter in his other hand, at ease in this new dangerous world. He said something in rapid Spanish I didn't catch. The driver got out, walked ten feet from the car, and stood in the moonlight where we could see him. The cigar smoke smelled sweet like cherries and mixed nicely with the bouquet from the brandy. The chief was wearing a dark burgundy satin house robe with black lapels. "I came as soon as I could," he said. "OIJ has me under house arrest. The bastards are all over me like gnats. I had to sneak out the back."

"I'm sorry to hear that."

He waved the snifter. "Let's dispense with the fake heartfelt sentiment. I assume you have something important for me; that's why you called?"

His English improved even more. I didn't like the way he showed up, casually dressed talking about house arrest. Something was off. He no longer seemed as pressured—or maybe this was a display of ego, his way to show control.

"No," I lied, "I just wanted to know if you got anything from dumping the cellphone records. You know, from Salvador Perez' phone you took from me."

He took a drag from his sweet cigar and blew the smoke my way. "We got a lot of names and numbers."

"What about text messages and emails? Those are where all the clues will be found."

He took the cigar from his mouth and stared at the tip. "I'd need a subpoena to access those records, and as I said, I'm under house arrest and not privy to the investigation."

"Why do you seem so relaxed? I thought you were afraid of losing your job and going to jail."

He smiled and stared.

"What?" I said. "Tell me."

"I think tomorrow you will have visitors from the OIJ. They want to talk with you."

I sat back in the seat. "Why me? I had nothing to do with what happened at the nightclub."

I'd had enough and opened the car door, stuck my foot out. "I'm not playing your ignorant little game tonight. I'm tired and want to get home to my family."

"You are going to jail for a long time, my friend. Enjoy your family tonight while you can." He took out his phone, punched in his code and played a video, the one from the hotel, the one the Ice Princess played for me, the one where I unloaded the dead man, unrolled him from his shroud—the hotel bedspread.

The video gut-punched me, took all the air out of the car and made it difficult to breathe. The Ice Princess had offered me up as fodder to take the heat off her for Sam Snead on the ninth hole sand trap.

"You see, my friend, I am no longer the focus of the problem. The OIJ have a bone in their jaws and are not likely to let go anytime soon."

"*You* buried that dead man in the sand trap, not me."

He shrugged and sipped his brandy.

Anger flushed my face. I sat back in the car. "Do you have access to the bullets or shell casing from El Gato Gordo?" I had to get him back on my side and in a hurry.

He put the cigar back in his mouth and shrugged again as if he had nothing in the world to worry about. That was the way I'd felt a couple days ago swimming naked with Marie in the ocean when this asshole walked up hat in hand asking for help.

I took out my phone and sent him the photos of the shoe soles of the wingtips for comparison and a photo of the London Fog.

He choked and sputtered and dropped his cigar. He batted at the red cherry burning his satin burgundy robe. "What? Who . . . Where did you take these photos?"

"Maybe I found them in *your* closet."

"*What?*"

"You quit playing ball with me and I'll bury you."

"You . . . wait . . . You can't . . . Where did you get this information?"

I reached in my pocket, took out the expended bullet and shell casing, and handed it to him.

His mouth sagged open in awe. "Is this . . . Did you find a gun as well, my friend?"

"Oh, now I'm your friend again?"

"Yes. I am so sorry, I was . . . I was only jesting, yes, I was jesting you." His English deteriorated when he got excited.

"Send that information, the shoe photos, the shell casing, and bullet along with ones from the crime scene to the FBI for comparison."

"You got the man. Who is he? We can arrest him and be heroes. You did brilliant work, my friend, brilliant."

"Send it to the FBI. The guy this stuff points to doesn't fit the profile. Something stinks. Be sure it's the FBI you give this stuff to, not OIJ. It'll box us in, cut down the moves we can make. Just do what I ask and try to keep the OIJ off my back for at least a couple more days and I'll try to get us both out of this mess. But you try to double-cross me again, I'll drop some evidence in *su casa* and then I'll make an anonymous phone call."

"*Mi amigo*, please. It's not like that."

"Just do what I ask and it'll all work out." The words had more confidence in the outcome than I did.

"I can't tell the OIJ something contrary now. They'll think I'm hiding something."

I pulled my leg back in, closed the car door, and stared at him as I thought through the problem. OIJ couldn't know it was me—the night video wasn't clear enough. It only depicted a man in shades of grays and blacks from a long distance and never a shot of my face, not one good enough for identification, especially if you didn't know me personally. That meant only one thing. It was just as I'd thought—the Ice Princess had offered me up to get the stank off her hotel. I'd become her sacrificial lamb. She'd told OIJ that the man in the video was her cabana bartender. A perfect play. A cunning woman. Cunning and dangerous.

I said, "Darla Figueroa gave you the video and told you how to put the noose around my neck. You and Darla Figueroa have worked together on other . . . ah, less than savory incidents, right?"

He nodded.

"You must have something you can hang over her head? Something you can use to get her to recant her statement to the OIJ, tell them she was mistaken and it wasn't her bartender after all. That he was at work when the body was dumped. She could do that easy enough."

He shook his head. "No, she is like an El Tigre Negro, clever, shrewd, hard to get a shot at before she melts back into the jungle."

"You tell her to recant her statement or I'm going to plant another dead Russian, this one on the eighteenth hole. Another dead golfer buried to the waist in a sand trap will ruin the hotel—no one will want to patronize a war zone."

He stared at me as if I'd lost my head. "Do . . . you have another dead Russian? Really?"

"What do you think?"

CHAPTER TWENTY-NINE

CHIEF HERNANDEZ DROPPED me off at the front gate to our home. I waited for the red lights to his car to disappear before I turned to face the house, his words echoing in my brain: "Enjoy your family tonight while you still can." What a jerk. But he was right.

I unlocked the gate and before I could close it, Waldo trotted up out of the dark, head held high. "Well, pardon me, your highness."

He gave me a disgruntled snort, stopped at the front door, and waited for me to catch up. I opened the door and he entered the house as if the mailbox out front said, "The Waldo Drago Estate."

Only night-lights illuminated the inside. Past the gargantuan living area and down the long hall, Eddie Crane's head popped out of the bedroom door to see that I made it home safely. He stayed there waiting to see if I'd tell him to get back to bed. When I didn't, he smiled and came out, his cellphone lighting him up. Another kid popped out, and another, until Eddie, the pied piper, led the entire Johnson crew out in the living area: Alonzo and Bosco, my grandsons, as well as Toby and Ricky Bixler, Melvin Kelso, Tommy Bascome, Randy Lugo, Sonny Taylor, Elena Cortez, and Sandy Williams. All of them ten years old and under except Tommy and Eddie who were eleven.

Marie was volunteering on the late shift at the clinic. She was with the kids most of the day, but as hard as I tried, I knew I didn't spend enough time with them. They always craved more, and I loved them for it.

Eddie said, "I was telling Alonzo that you never gave me a Chariot Race rematch."

The other kids said, "Yeah. Yeah, a rematch."

Rosie the housekeeper appeared from the entrance to the kitchen holding her robe together. "No, Meester Johnson, no Chariot Race, la senora will be angry." She wagged her finger at me. Her English got better when she wanted it to.

Eddie leaned in toward me, whispered. "You gonna chicken and listen to her?"

"Maybe, depends on what's at stake."

Rosie said, "No. No. No. *Esta no bueno.*" Then she disappeared back into the kitchen. She was heading to her room where she watched over Tobias and Drago's little girl, Daphne.

"It's late," I said to Eddie. "I'm risking a lot if your mom comes home and catches us."

"What do you suggest?"

"I'm going to bet that if I win, you, little man, will have to trim the bougainvillea all along the west wall."

"Ouch," Eddie said. "That's a big bet. You always do that trimming and come in with all kinds of scratches."

He was talking about the spines on the bougainvillea. Those shrubs were a real pain to trim, but if you didn't, they could take over the whole place.

"There's a lot at stake and I think you're old enough to take on that kind of responsibility. What do you want in return?"

The kids yelled, "Ice cream. Ice cream." It always came down to ice cream. I understood that craving; my dad used to take me and Noble for hot fudge sundaes. We ate them on the hood of the car and watched planes land at Compton airport.

Eddie nodded. "Yeah . . . yeah, but not just regular ice cream, we want the Rocky Road, the five-gallon bucket in the chest freezer. The whole bucket. And tonight. Not just a promise for tomorrow— tonight right after the race. The whole bucket."

"You're really trying to get me in trouble, aren't you?"

"Bwak, bwak!" Eddie put his hands under his arms and flapped them like a chicken.

"You seem pretty sure you're going to win. Okay, you got a bet. I'm not worried about the ice cream, no way will you win."

"Okay, but . . . but because of those spines and all that work, it's still not a fair bet. I want a handicap. I get to pick your driver."

I chuckled. "Okay by me," thinking he meant one of the kids.

"Rosie," he said.

"What? You're kidding me, right?"

He crossed his arms, his expression smug. "Nope, it's gotta be Rosie."

The kids yelled. "Rosie, Rosie, Rosie."

He'd just chickened out. He knew Rosie would never go for it and he could ease out of the bet without losing face.

"All right, who's going to be your driver?"

"You going to get Rosie?"

"You don't worry about my end of this race, little man, pick your driver."

"Alonzo."

My grandson and smallest of the bunch. "Okay, but full protective gear."

"Goes without saying."

"Fine, I'll go get my driver." He'd chosen Rosie because of the weight difference. He was a smart kid and if I did happen to talk Rosie into it, he'd still have a huge advantage. "You kids go get all the protective gear you can find. Go." They took off in a mob laughing and talking, bumping into each other as they ran. I walked through the big kitchen to Rosie's door and knocked quietly. She opened it a little, still dressed in her thick cotton nightie covered over in a robe. "Jess?"

"Ah . . . Rosie, would you do me a big favor?"

"Maybe." She knew me too well to say "yes" outright.

"I need you to be the driver in the chariot race."

Her eyes grew huge. "No, *tu estas muy loco.* No. No. No."

She tried to close the door on me. "You can have all the ice cream you can eat."

She eased off the door and looked at her watch. I'd got her with the ice cream. She had a real jones for the creamy treat that Marie kept a tight rein on. But Rosie was worried, if she agreed, Marie might come home and catch us all in multiple house rules violations. She wagged her finger at me. "Not too fast, okay?"

"No. No. Just fast enough to win."

She hesitated one more time, looked over her shoulder in the dim room to check on the infants, then came out. This would be her first time as a chariot driver. In the past, before the prohibition, she'd only been a spectator suppressing her laughter, and I could tell she wanted to ride the sheet.

Ten minutes later the track had been cleared, the chairs and table in the dining room, the couch and chairs in the living room. Rosie sat on a king-sized bed sheet on the floor while wearing a roller-skating helmet that looked ridiculous on her, as well as elbow and knee pads. Alonzo sat on a twin bed sheet wearing similar gear. He looked so damn cute.

"No too fast, Señor Johnson. No too fast."

I looked at Eddie. "Keep it under thirty-five miles per hour."

He giggled, then turned serious. "If I lose, I'm going to get all cut up on those shrubs."

"Really, you're holding me up for more?"

He nodded and pointed at me. "It's gotta be the Rocky Road ice cream in the chest freezer."

Rosie clapped her hands. "Oh, jess, the Rocky Road ice cream."

I wanted to shake him up a little, give me a little more of an edge. "How do you know about the Rocky Road? That's supposed to be a secret for my fiftieth surprise party."

His mouth dropped open. "How did you know about the surprise party? Mom's gonna be mad."

"Rosie told me."

Rosie started to get up as she wagged her finger at me. "No, Meester Johnson, I did not tell you. No. No. No."

I pushed on her shoulder, and she sat back down. "Okay, Alonzo, Rosie, hold on." I moved to the front of the sheet, Rosie behind me, her feet pointing at my back. I picked up a corner of the sheet, one in each hand. Eddie did the same. "Remember," I said, "no crowding the corners."

"Quit stall—"

I took off dragging Rosie across the floor. The kids screamed and jumped up and down clapping. Rosie yelled, "Iiiyeee. No. No. No. Alto. Alto. Too fast. Too fast."

I looked back. "You shouldn't wax the floors so well."

I had the jump on Eddie, but he had less weight and immediately caught up and drew alongside as we jockeyed down the hall to the master bedroom. He had to slow to let me go in first or crowd me at the turn, a forfeitable violation. The race had to have at least one safety rule. Alonzo screamed with joy—Rosie just screamed. The kids followed along yelling.

We made it first into the bedroom and then into the master bath. This was the slowest part of the track as we had to stop and turn around. Rosie smiled at me when we did. She was enjoying the game but would never admit to it.

We bottlenecked at the bathroom door, Eddie trying to turn around and me trying to get out. In the bedroom the kids got up on our bed and jumped up and down and cheered. Eddie came out right on our tail but had to slow again for the turn into the hall. He yelled to the kids. "If you want Rocky Road, you better help me out here."

Tommy, his family buddy, reacted first. He jumped off the bed, passed Eddie's chariot, and tried to grab our dragging tail, the excess sheet behind Rosie.

"Foul," I yelled and increased speed. I took the corner into the kitchen a little fast to stay away from Tommy. Rosie bumped her head a little on the jam, but she was wearing a helmet.

Jimmy caught us in the middle of the kitchen, grabbed a corner of the sheet, and sat down on his butt. The sheet jerked and let out a little ripping sound but held together. Eddie caught me in the dining room as we circled the dining room table. He swung wide into the living room and across the finish line.

Everyone jumped up and down clapping their hands, cheering. I helped Rosie to her feet.

Eddie didn't wait for a judge's decision on the illegal weight shift after the race started. He ran to the second and larger of the two pantries, the one with the chest freezer, and came back with a five-gallon cardboard container of Rocky Road ice cream. The sight of which made me cringe. I was going to be in deep over this caper, no doubt about it.

I yelled, "Not on the table. On the floor. Put it on the bigger sheet—get on the bigger sheet."

Ricky handed out a spoon to everyone. Eddie pulled off the top and the locust hoard descended on that poor cardboard carton of

Rocky Road. Spoons clashed over the almonds and marshmallows. In seconds everyone had chocolate all over their faces, and running down their arms, including me. I loved me some Rocky Road.

Rosie and Alonzo still had on all their safety gear, wearing huge smiles. Waldo stood off to the side barking until I dug out a large scoop and put it on the sheet. He went at it slurping, his muzzle turning light creamy brown.

The front door opened.

In walked Marie, home early from her shift.

Everyone froze, their eyes going wide with shock. In a stern voice she said, "Nobody move. Not one inch." She reached into her purse, pulled out her cell, and shot several photos. She smiled hugely. "Now, someone hand me a spoon."

CHAPTER THIRTY

WHEN WE'D FIRST arrived in Costa Rica, we dreamed of a world without violence, and now we'd awakened to give that dream a kiss goodbye. First thing the next day, I called a contractor to convert one of the food pantries into a proper saferoom large enough to house all the family—so they could hide if I had to leave work to come and get them should the need arise. I needed a gun to complete my plan for their protection.

My breakfast soured in my stomach as I thought about the children, Marie, Dad, and even Mom in jeopardy—about my need of a gun.

I ran the two miles to work, taking a different route as I mulled over the shooting at the nightclub, Otis, the two dead Russian gangsters—confused about how violence like a black plague had sought out our peaceful little town. If Otis wasn't the shooter, then someone wanted him as a prime suspect. But who? It didn't make sense.

Leave motive for later.

Maybe it was just that simple, Occam's razor, and Otis did the dirty deed. I moved on to opportunity; if Otis was being set up, who had access to his room to obtain the Browning 9mm, his shoes, the London Fog, who was diabolical enough to—

That was it. Only one person fit that description in every way. I needed something with the Ice Princess' fingerprints to send to the FBI, confirm her identity, and find out if she had a criminal background. She fit the profile: her lack of conscience, her antisocial and manipulative behavior, and most important, an ego that entered a room two seconds before she did. Why had I not thought of it earlier? She fit perfectly into the puzzle covering most all the bases . . . except, of course, motive.

Damn.

One step at a time—motive would come later. At least now I had an investigative path to pursue, one that felt right. But at the same time, I would not leave Otis out as a possible suspect. Stranger things have happened. If he did pull off the shooting, staying in the hotel afterward was the stroke of an evil genius.

I showered in the employee locker room and put on a fresh aloha shirt. Before preparing the garnish in the kitchen, I stopped at Otis' room to escort him to the bar. When he opened his door, the sunlight from his open curtains and slider lit up his living area.

Waldo sat on the couch leaning over, eating his pancakes with chocolate chips from a plate on the table that must have just arrived. Next to the pancakes sat three side orders of the hotel's famous apple maple sausages.

How had Waldo gotten out of our house, past the locked gate, and beaten me to work? The dog had a little Siegfried & Roy in him. Wait, Siegfried & Roy were German American magicians who performed with white lions and white tigers in Vegas. Ah-hah, Waldo spoke German. Now it was all coming together, Waldo was part German, part white tiger.

Otis stood at the door, not allowing me to enter. He looked disheveled, his reek worse than the day before, if that were possible. His eyes were bloodshot, the tan, wrinkled skin on his face hung like a wet swimsuit on a clothes hanger. His whole body shook with a palsy. Poor bastard drank his limit the night before and now paid a heavy price.

He burped and put his hand to his mouth as if that ineffective stopgap could keep his gorge from rising and polluting our world. The sour stench from the burp made me step back. He swallowed hard, barely able to hold it together, speaking around his hand. "Come back at noon."

He slammed the door.

I yelled through door. "You take a shower and change your clothes, or you won't be allowed at my bar."

He'd be lucky to make it to the bar tomorrow, let alone at noon. His condition further proved Otis couldn't have pulled off the El Gato Gordo nightclub shooting.

Unless he was a true master of deception.

I needed Darla Figueroa's fingerprints.

*　*　*

In the kitchen, Chacho did my job preparing the garnish, his expression grim. His anguish broke my heart and I rued the moment he'd discover the truth about Gloria. He'd always had a huge smile with lots of white teeth and a sparkle in his eyes, all gone now. His love for life stomped into sadness and regret by a shooter without morals or conscience.

"Chacho, mi amigo, I need to tell you something."

Jaime, over by the stainless steel prep table, stopped dicing carrots, and said too loudly, as if his hearing had suddenly been impaired, "El Gato, last night someone at the bar was asking for you."

I nodded. "Thanks, Jaime." Lots of folks become enamored with their bartender. The alcohol the bartender serves lowers their social inhibitions. They want that same feeling again and believe the bartender played an intricate role.

I turned back to Chacho, but before I could say anything, Jaime interrupted again. "No, El Gato Negro, this person was a cop. I smelled pig as soon as she walked up."

"A cop asking for me?"

"No, she didn't say she was a cop, but I knew." He waved his knife, his eyes glassy, his eyelids at half-mast. "Trust me. I know."

"Okay . . . thank you. I'll take care of it." My mind ran a thousand miles an hour. Besides the cop asking for me, I'd just realized *Jaime* had *access* to Otis' room and the *ability* to do the shooting at the nightclub. The ability more so than anyone else. I didn't need his fingerprints to know his background. His tattoos told the story.

I now needed the Ice Princess' digital record shot by her surveillance cameras the night of Karl Drago's wedding, the night all of this mess kicked off, to see if Jaime prowled the premises or left the environs headed toward the nightclub.

To obtain the fingerprints and video was going to take some delicate juggling, some moves Sean Connery would appreciate.

I gently took hold of Chacho's arm and pulled him along. He didn't put up much resistance, his body filled with woe made him light on his feet. I opened the huge walk-in refrigerator, pulled him in, and closed the door that whooshed shut.

"What's going on, mi amigo, we have to work . . . the bar, it's . . . we have to get to the bar."

"I need to tell you something and . . ."

I didn't know how to say it. I'd made many death notifications in a past life and dreaded each and every one; the look on the poor folks' faces as they reacted to my words caused a shiver just remembering. Words that described a violent death always at the hand of another; a car crash or brutal murder.

Every murder was brutal.

Chacho looked up at me, his innocent eyes as large as a puppy's, a puppy I was about to kick.

"Ah, Chacho." My voice lowered all on its own as a lump rose in my throat. When had I turned into an overly emotional old man? "I know what happened to Gloria."

He grabbed my arm, excitement filling his face, the white teeth, the smile, the sparkle returning to his eyes. "Where is she? Where is my Gloria?"

I nodded—the only physical communication I could muster—and then forced out the words. "My good friend, Gloria is dead."

His mouth dropped open, his eyes going wide as he backed up until his back touched the shelf filled with stainless steel vats piled high with raw roasts, red meat marbled with fat. He shook his head slowly, then shifted into high gear.

He leapt forward, grabbed both of my arms. "Liar. You are a liar. She is in San Jose visiting friends. I know she is. She has to be." He turned and put his hand on the long handle to open the huge steel door.

I grabbed his shoulder. "No, she's not. She's dead. I am so sorry, Chacho."

He spun. "How do you know this? Tell me how?"

"I . . . I saw her."

He pulled back to punch me. He wasn't a violent man, wasn't a fighter. I saw the punch coming and could've stopped it. I deserved what he gave me. I should've told him a couple of days ago. The punch landed hard under my right eye. Bright lights of every color exploded in my vision.

I maintained my stance.

Chacho pushed open the door and fled.

CHAPTER THIRTY-ONE

CHACHO DIDN'T WANT the details regarding Gloria's death. We were too good of friends; he knew I wouldn't lie to him and *that* untold truth between us would ruin our friendship. He'd soon be back to find out the rest. But that would be it. After I told him, he would walk away, and we'd never talk again.

I picked up the garnish tray and walked out of the kitchen, down the hall toward the lobby. I wasn't supposed to traverse the lobby with any bar supplies and did anyway, the regret eating me up inside. I was looking for a fight.

Over the PA, the Ice Princess spoke angry words. "Gaylord, my office, now."

I'd cut the puppet master's strings and shifted my regret to a deeper anger over the way she'd tossed me to the lions, giving OIJ the video of me doing her bidding, dumping the dead Russian from one of her hotel rooms, off property.

I continued on, down past the pool, sidestepping little children slick with water who climbed out just to jump right back in. Their joy transferred to me, cut through all the trouble thick in the air, and made me smile.

Around the bar, an indignant mob wanted their alcohol fix, even though I wasn't late. I set the garnish down without putting it away and went to work, my hands doing the job without asking for help from the brain while my mind worried about Chacho and all that had happened in the last twenty-four hours.

When my head finally broke the surface of reality, I discovered Otis had arrived without escort. Three parasols already sat on the bar in front of him, grasshoppers I'd prepared and served without realizing.

Out on the beach, Waldo played Frisbee with three men from Brazil wearing DayGlo banana hammocks—speedos—his long pink tongue already hanging out from thirst. He'd be at the bar soon giving his "beer-bark," as Chacho had named it, wanting an expensive bottle of Modelo.

Poor Chacho. I wanted to weep for him.

A woman wearing a floral sarong that accented her figure and who had big brown eyes and sexy long fingers asked for a "gin and tonic, hold the gin." I stopped my frenetic movement and stared. Something about her screamed *pay attention, danger.* I didn't take my eyes off hers while I filled her order and set it in front of her.

"Gaylord? That's a strange name."

"My name's not Gaylord."

A smile crept across her face, not revealing her thoughts. That's when I realized who she reminded me of: a Los Angeles County Sheriff's deputy, Helen Hellinger. I'd worked with Hellinger on a child rescue; we now took care of her niece Stephanie. This woman at the bar was a Costa Rican cop, just like Jaime had said. The cops were watching me.

What a disaster. Darla Figueroa had set me up good and proper and I didn't know if I'd be able to extricate myself from the trap.

There was nothing for it. I decided to play it head-on. "That's on the house, Detective."

She tried not to react, but her head moved back just a hair and her eyes wavered a tad. She was good.

I shot her my biggest smile. "What? You're not going to deny it? Or are you just going to take a minute to think about it?"

She continued to stare and said nothing.

"My buddy who worked last night told me some cops were asking about me." I held onto the fake smile. "Did you want to talk? I've got nothing to hide."

I'd blown her undercover gig where she was supposed to befriend me and weasel out incriminating information. She brought her clutch purse up from her lap, opened it, took out a ten, laid it on the counter, and left.

"Come again, Detective." I said it loud enough for the entire beach to hear.

My cell buzzed in my pocket. "Probably Eddie gloating about last night's chariot race victory. I served three more customers before checking my phone.

Eddie: "Dad there's a strange man outside the gate watching the house. He has a bandage on his shoulder and neck."

My heart flopped in my chest and then dropped to the floor. The third Russian. He was at the house looking for me. His presence could mean only one thing—he wanted to get even, retribution for killing his two pals.

I flipped up the pass-through, yelling, "Waldo! Waldo!" I ran. He caught up to me at the pool, his brown and black fur speckled with white sand. "It's Eddie, he's in trouble. Go home. Go home."

The damn dog acted like he knew what I was talking about and took off running ahead of me, his tongue lolling out from thirst. He disappeared into a throng of tourists exiting the hotel doorway carrying towels and pool toys. Far behind me Otis yelled, "Hey? Hey, what about me? At least leave your dog."

I entered the lobby at a run, yelling, "I need a car. I need to borrow someone's car. Now!"

Everyone stopped to look at me. The employees, friends of mine, looked up from the desks and front counter—bellman, valets—all of them walked to work or took the bus. The patrons didn't know me, and would no way let me take their rental cars.

"My children are in danger, I need a car, now." If one of the tourists didn't offer up their keys in the next five seconds, I'd—

Darla Figueroa came running from the hall that led to her office. She hit the lobby kicking off her Christian Louboutin high heels. "Come on, we'll take my car."

I didn't have time to be stunned. I followed along, grateful and confused at her shift in character. I speed-dialed Rosie's cellphone. She picked up. Before she could say anything, I yelled, *"Alerta Roja. Alerta Roja."* Red alert.

"Dios Mio." She screamed. The phone went dead. We'd trained for something like this but never in all the world thought we'd have to use the home base emergency code, not in our little slice of paradise. She'd gather all the kids who were home and not in school, get them in the largest pantry. I'd put in a two-by-four to bar the door from the inside. That door wouldn't hold up against a determined foe.

CHAPTER THIRTY-TWO

I followed Darla over to the slot closest to the front door to the hotel, the one marked "Manager," Herb Templeton's slot. She was parking in the manager's space while he was out of town hiding from the PR fallout Sam Snead created on the ninth-hole sand trap.

I got into the white BMW sedan as she screeched the tires backing up. She shifted gears and smoked the tires heading out of the driveway.

I said, "Take the—"

"I know where you live, Bruno. Tell me what's going on."

"It's the third Russian—the third guy who jumped me and Otis the other night. He's at my house, watching it."

She nodded and paid attention to the road, the BMW continuing to accelerate in the narrow residential streets. Two miles would click by fast at seventy mph.

We came up and passed Waldo running out of steam, his gait nothing more than a goofy lope. "Slow down, that's my dog. Let him in the car."

She took her eyes from the road and glared at me for a half-second. "No dog's getting into this car. And I thought you said that wasn't your dog?"

"Gimme a break, would ya?"

"We're gonna talk after this."

"Yes, we are." I said it with venom.

We came to the last street—a right turn and then we'd be there. She came up on it too fast. She yanked up the parking brake, throwing the car into a sideways skid around the corner.

What the hell? She could really drive.

A man in a tank top with a white bandage on his shoulder, dressed in utility shorts, had just jimmied the lock on the front gate to the estate and was about to enter.

The skidding tires alerted him.

His head jerked around to see the white BMW sliding sideways toward him thirty yards away.

He was a pro and didn't panic. He'd studied his egress and ran toward us trying to get to the open jungle on the south side of the estate.

I had the door open before the car came to a stop and took after him. He put on a burst of speed, but running to work every day improved my wind. I got right on him and started closing the gap. He didn't have time to jump into his jungle exit and ran along the road in front of residential houses; houses on one side, jungle on the other.

Behind me came the slap of bare feet.

I chanced a look over my shoulder.

Darla Figueroa, the Ice Princess, ran on the hot pavement barefoot. And with a large handgun in her hand, one I recognized, one commonly used in Germany and Eastern Bloc countries, a Walther 9mm. *Son of a bitch, a 9mm.*

Up popped a quick image of her naked, tanned, and oil slick body on the roof of the hotel. The gun in her hand was incongruent with what I knew about her.

I resumed pursuit, watching my prey as I continued to gain on him. Behind me Darla yelled, "Move out of the way and give me the shot. Get down. Get down."

"Are you crazy?" She was a food and beverage manager for crying out loud, not some kind of trained shooter.

She wanted to shoot him for no other reason than menacing my children. Which was plenty good reason. I just wanted him alive to beat the crap out of him and find out exactly what was going on.

Then she could shoot him.

I moved over to block her shot even more. She began to fall back, the restrictive dress and bare feet not great running attire.

The crack of a gunshot caused me to flinch and almost lose my footing. I looked back. She'd stopped running and fired into the air two more times while hopping from foot to foot, the hot asphalt burning skin.

The gunfire spooked the guy in front of me. He cut to the right into the jungle on the south side of the street.

He instantly disappeared.

I followed headlong, not liking the lack of visibility. He could lie in wait and ambush me too easily in the shadowy dimness and dense undergrowth. I didn't know if he was armed. I know if I were him, I would be.

Twenty yards farther, the jungle fell away, revealing a little grassy knoll with a steep drop-off to a flooded stream, the sun blinding bright. The stream remained flooded most of the time due to the constant rainfall, its roar loud over all else.

From the left, the bamboo rattled. The man came out in a flying tackle. He hit me low. We tumbled onto the grassy knoll.

Hot pain slashed my back followed by a hot wetness. I had not seen the knife and broke away from him before he could slash me again. We separated. I bent over, my hands going to my knees. I was winded and cut.

He rose, an army killing knife in his right hand that caught the sunlight and glinted. Blood like little jewels dripped from the hilt, my blood.

His chest heaved, trying to get enough air. The bandage on his shoulder spotted red from his football move to take me down, the injury Waldo had given him. The knife scared me, this guy knew how to use it and I had nothing.

Worse, I wasn't a knife fighter.

"Why are you after Otis? Or are you after me?"

He had a mashed potato face, flat and lumpy with a ropy scar that ran from the bottom of his ear down to his chin. He didn't answer. I reached around to the pain and brought back a hand wet with blood. He'd tagged me good.

He took a step toward me. That answered the question of whether he'd flee while he had the chance. He intended to finish what he started.

"What do you want?"

He finally spoke, his voice like a bag of gravel. "The money that's owed us. Nothing more, just what's owed us. Where's the—"

Waldo leaped out of the jungle onto the thug's back, bowling him over. Waldo latched onto the same shoulder, chomping down.

The man howled and tumbled down the knoll, Waldo still latched on. They hit the stream, and both disappeared under the churning brown water. They didn't come back up.

The entire fight, if you could call it that, only took seconds. Flashes of images; the Russian's lumpy face and beady eyes, the glint of the razor-sharp military knife beaded with rubies, Waldo's leap from the bamboo cluster, the fall into the flooded stream.

And just like that, Waldo was gone.

"Waldo? Waldo?" I yelled his name, walking the bank to the stream until my voice turned hoarse.

I waited. And waited some more. A couple of colorful toucans looked down from their perch at the crazed man upset about his dog.

Waldo didn't come back.

I yelled his name, then, finally, one last time, in a whisper: "Waldo?"

CHAPTER THIRTY-THREE

I CLIMBED THROUGH the jungle to the road and trudged back home. I stopped where Darla had stopped and fired the 9mm into the air. I searched for the three expended 9mm shell casings from the Walther. I didn't know if five minutes had elapsed or an hour. I was about to give up when the sunlight through the tree canopy caught the bright brass casing just right and reflected a quick flash, enough to give the location to look. I found it and put it in my pocket.

The exertion, dehydration, and blood loss made me lightheaded. The walk home faded in memory like the last remnants of a colorful sunset; the smear of yellows, oranges, and reds a child's pastel finger painting. I was due in to work. Who was covering the cabana bar? It couldn't be but eleven in the morning. Who would escort and watch over Otis? I hadn't seen Jose, and the car with the dead Russian in the trunk had disappeared. I'd checked for the car on the way to work. Gone.

I rounded the corner and found Darla's white BMW re-parked in front of the house. Marie's VW van was parked cattywampus. Rosie with our children, ensconced in the pantry, the quasi-saferoom, had called Marie at work as per protocol. I tried to wrap my head around Darla's car parked in front of our house. Then it clicked in my foggy brain, *Darla was in our house talking with Marie. My Marie.* Callous and coarse meets sweetness and nice. I hurried through the gate, wobbly on my feet.

I came through the door, Marie on the phone talking to the police. She hung up when she saw me, relief plain in her expression. She had played the good mother and stayed put to protect her children instead of coming to look for me. She let the ball bat in her hand drop to the floor.

The Ice Princess drank from a wineglass while sitting on the ottoman talking to the four small children not in school, her feet up on a chair bandaged from being burned on the hot pavement. Marie had actually touched the Ice Princess' feet.

Marie rushed into my arms, tears brimming her eyes. Her hand immediately came back covered in red. She took a step away from me, instantly understanding the situation. "Kids, go to your room and play. Do it right now, please. Come on, chop, chop."

All I wanted to do was hug my wife, take in her scent, appreciate the air I breathe, the warmth of sun, my children.

When she saw the blood, Darla jumped to her sore and bandaged feet, her expression neutral as always.

Marie said to her, "Can you help him to our room? I'll get my bag."

"Yes, of course." She hurried over, put my arm around her shoulder, hers around my waist. I'd never touched the Ice Princess. She was warm and soft yet muscular.

But most important, she was actually human.

I didn't know what to say. "No one's covering the bar?"

"Don't worry about that, it's covered." She looked up at me. For a brief flash I caught a glimpse of another person, one with compassion and—It disappeared, turning back to the Darla of old when her hand snaked into my pocket searching until she found what she was looking for, the third shell casing that she couldn't find out on the street. Her eyes turned hard and unyielding; back to business.

My head swam with thoughts too loose to grasp. I knew I should smile at the beautiful woman helping me into my bedroom, so I smiled. I grabbed onto a thought and said, "Hawaiian Tropical sun lotion with coconut?"

She glanced over her shoulder to see if Marie had caught up and whispered, "Stop it, you're being a pig."

I smiled again. "Oink."

She let out a little laugh, the first time I'd ever heard her laugh. A day of firsts. Another thought grabbed hold. I lost my smile. "This changes nothing. I thank you for the ride when I needed it most, for coming to the rescue of my children, but I'm still coming for you."

I wasn't sure I even knew what I meant.

She smiled again and patted my chest. "Tiger, I wouldn't want it any other way." She held me up while pulling the comforter off the bed to keep it from getting bloody and laid me down on my stomach. "You're one lucky Tiger, you have a wonderful wife."

"I won't argue with you there."

Marie hurried into the room. "Won't argue about what?"

I said, "That you have the nicest legs in Costa Rica?"

"You're delirious."

Darla, her arm red with my blood, asked, "You mind if I wash up?"

"No, of course not. Right in there."

Marie cut off my shirt and started an IV, all business. "This isn't that bad. You've just lost a lot of blood. I'll disinfect the site and staple it closed. A couple of days in bed and you'll be good as new."

"I . . . ah, really don't like the idea of a stapler. Can't you use . . . like . . . what, superglue or something?" My words warbled in air that had turned thick.

"Quit being a big baby and lie still."

She prepared a syringe with a topical anesthetic and injected the site.

"I'm sorry," I said.

"For what, protecting our children? Don't be ridiculous. You're my hero; you always will be."

She looked over her shoulder to the master bathroom where the night before we'd turned our chariots around. The laughter, the fun, the Rocky Road ice cream, what a contrast to the violence of the afternoon. We'd been infected with the violence virus and now could only fight the symptoms, keep down the fever that came with it, a fever that tended to burn people to the ground.

Marie whispered, "What happened to that horrible man?" She'd seen me at my worst, seen what happens to me when evil men threaten my family.

I choked on the lump in my throat from her having to ask such a question in our home that was supposed to be a paradise. "He's gone."

She nodded, not needing any further explanation.

The water shut off in the bathroom. I never thought Darla Figueroa would be washing my blood off her arm in our bathroom.

"Babe, Waldo's . . . he's . . . he's gone. He saved my life."

"Ah, Bruno, I'm so sorry."

Her words finished me off, tears filled my eyes, all over a dumb-assed dog.

Darla came out drying her arms with one of our fluffy white towels, just as Marie started stapling closed the knife slash that had to be gaping like a big red smile.

Darla said, "Gaylord, you take as much time as you need. Your job will be waiting for you."

Marie stopped. "That's very kind of you. Thank you."

The IV helped stabilize my system and all I wanted to do was sleep.

Wait.

Marie had slipped me a little analgesic cocktail. That would be just like her. My words came out a bit slurred, directing them toward Darla. "This isn't over."

Darla came over, bent at the waist, and kissed my cheek. She whispered, "Baby, you were never even in the race."

Marie said, "I think it's time for you to leave our house." She didn't like the kiss.

"See you at work, Tiger," Darla called as she walked to the door with that slinky hip sway. I kept my eyes on her a moment too long, and Marie pinched my arm. I closed my eyes, slumber sweeping in to take me to another world.

I smelled coconut suntan oil as I drifted off.

CHAPTER THIRTY-FOUR

I WOKE TO my grandson Alonzo jumping on the bed beside me and Marie sleeping soundly in a big comfy chair next to the bed. The sunlight in the double French doors waned with yellows and dark oranges. I'd slept through the night and right past the next day. I grabbed Alonzo and tickled him. He screamed with laughter. The staples in my back pulled and caused a prickly pain.

Marie woke, fatigue heavy in her expression. "How do you feel?"

"Like I can eat a horse."

"What about your back?" She stood, put her hand on my forehead. "I'm most concerned about infection." She pushed me back down and pulled up my nightshirt, examining the wicked knife slice the Russian gave me. I didn't want to see it. I could only imagine the glint of the staples holding together the puffy, purple lips of the wound. Robby Wicks, my old boss, had said on more than one occasion, "Give me a bullet over a knife wound any day." When he said it, I'd always thought, why wish for either one.

"My back feels like the children went at it with a stapler while I slept." I looked around a little too anxiously.

"What?" she asked.

"I ah . . ." I leaned over, set Alonzo on the floor. "Go on, Son, let Mommy and Daddy talk." He took off running out of the room yelling, "Hey, everybody, Daddy's awake."

Marie closed the door. "Waldo didn't come back."

"Damn."

Tears welled in my eyes. Turning fifty obviously meant enhanced emotions.

"I'm sorry, and Drago called to see how things were going."

"You didn't tell him about what's going on with the nightclub and the Russians? He'll quit his honeymoon and run back here."

"Give me some credit, cowboy."

She said "*cowboy*" with a lusty voice mimicking Darla Figueroa.

I rolled my eyes. I wanted to ask if she'd told him about Waldo. That rueful job would fall to me, not her—another death notification and a difficult one.

She said, "And your new girlfriend with the fried feet called to ask about you. I don't like her, Bruno."

I threw the rest of the covers off and stood, my body creaking, bones crackling, muscles slow to respond. "Yeah, I'm getting that. What did you give me to put me out like that?"

"If I hadn't, you'd have been right back to work. You needed the rest."

She was probably right on both counts. "Thank you, babe." I came around and gave her a kiss on the forehead. "But there's too much going on to take a bed vacation."

"Wait. Look at this."

She held up the controller and pressed a button. The TV came on to the top news story, a video of the shuttered El Gato Gordo nightclub, the parking lot crammed with a host of news trucks and commentators talking rapidly into microphones.

Marie had the sound muted, but it didn't matter. Rebecca Sanchez, *News Six*, the Darling of Costa Rica, spoke rapidly, using her hand to point back to the front door of the nightclub.

I sat on the edge of the bed. "Ah shit, I guess it had to happen."

"You think Drago will see it?"

"Are you kidding? He's on his honeymoon and—" I'd caught myself yet again ready to give my lovely wife a cop's locker room description of what went on during a honeymoon, vulgar, yet funny. "—Ah, Drago never watches TV. He says it's a big waste of time, that news is all about entertainment, not information."

"You're probably right. Get back in bed. You're not going anywhere."

I pulled her in a hug, my nose in the crook of her neck, and took in a big inhalation of her scent, something I never got enough of.

Regarding rest, something else Robby Wicks used to say when we'd been on the trail of a murderer forty straight hours, "Come on, kick it in the ass, there's plenty of time to sleep after you're dead."

Even groggy I knew that was the wrong thing to say to my lovely wife who cared so deeply for me.

I whispered, "If I stay in bed to heal, this whole mess is going to bowl me over." She knew I really meant bowl over the entire family.

She nodded. "Okay then, sit. I'll give you a sponge bath."

I winked at her. "Babe, I don't think I have the strength for that."

She pushed me away, smiling, and play-slapped my face. "Sit, you big oaf." She broke away from the embrace. I instantly missed her warmth.

"Hey," I said to her as she tinkered in the master bath. "I don't want you to slip me another micky either. I'm onto that trick."

She brought a small plastic tub, the kind you soak your feet in, filled with warm soapy water. She helped me out of my clothes. "If I wanted to slip you another micky, you'd never see it coming."

"I'm not infirm. I can do this myself."

I wanted her to do the sponge bath, the guilty pleasure, an erotic activity we'd shared. I tried to focus on something else so as not to cause an unwarranted delay back to work. I needed to talk with the Ice Princess and Otis.

I stiffened, sat up straighter.

"Relax," she said.

"No, I've slept through the night and all of the day. Who's covering Otis? He's paying me to protect him." I stood. "I have an obligation."

She pushed me back down. "Not until I'm done. Good hygiene keeps infection at bay." She kissed my forehead.

I sat and waited; the anxiety doubled. "Are you studying the murder book?"

"In all my spare time? Yes, I am."

"You see anything that sparks that curious mind of yours?"

"That wicked woman is like a chameleon, one minute she's . . . she's this wonderfully nice person, the next minute, she turns into an unfeeling animal."

"You got that out of the murder book?"

"You know who I'm talking about."

"Yes, but that's not what I asked."

"Lie on your stomach so I can rebandage your staples." She climbed on, sitting across my butt like it was a saddle, so I wouldn't try and move while she gave that extra TLC nurses are famous for: tender hands around painful sites.

"Can we stay away from words like *staples* that make me cringe. You know I prefer *sutures*."

She applied antibacterial cream on the slash injury that soothed and cooled. "Did you see that there were six victims, each shot at least once."

"Yes."

"The suspect fired ten rounds."

"Right."

"Salvador was hit twice, both fatal GSWs, as was Aleck."

She was trying to lead me to her same conclusion. "That's only nine." I tried to sit up. She pushed me back down and asked, "Did they find the tenth round?"

"No."

"And?"

"They also didn't identify the mystery woman who was with Aleck."

"You think she was hit and got away."

"I'm just telling you my observations."

"This is good, really good, babe. You got anything else?" I turned to look—her eyes said she did.

"Come on, don't leave me hanging."

She dismounted me like a British Royal finishing a game of fox and hounds. "You're the detective, think about it."

I played back the short conversation we'd just had. She wouldn't have asked me to think about it had she not given me all the information to come to the same conclusion. "Everyone shot once, Salvador and Aleck shot twice. Babe, I'm an idiot, okay? I'm not tumbling to what you're trying to say."

She shrugged. "I don't know if it's correct, it's just an observation."

"Tell me."

"Salvador is a private investigator and he's shot twice."

Her conclusion hit me all at once, sparking nerve endings all up and down my back and legs. I jumped up, looking for my clothes. "You're saying Salvador was investigating something Aleck was involved in and the shooter . . . I mean those two, Salvador and Aleck, were the real targets, the others just fodder for the chaos?"

"It's just a theory."

I took her by the shoulders after I gingerly shrugged into a clean aloha shirt, kissed her on the lips. "Yes, but what a theory."

CHAPTER THIRTY-FIVE

I CALLED AN Uber for the two-mile ride to the hotel. Marie insisted—a compromise for me going to work at all. I sat in the old, but well-kept Toyota that smelled of pine trees, thinking about what Marie said regarding her theory—Salvador investigating Aleck—when the driver turned into the long drive that led to the Punta Bandera Hotel and Beach Club. Cars in line all the way out to the street, the valets running their legs off to keep up.

Felix Hurtado, the doorman, opened the door for me. I asked, "Hey, amigo, what's going on?" He was a short, squat Hispanic with acne scars and thinning black hair. He had his hand on the pulse of the hotel, knew every bit of gossip. When I first met him, I made some inquiries. He was an ex-cop from Miami with expertise in criminal intelligence. He knew how to buy and sell information and had been racked up, run off the job. Rumor had it that a criminal enterprise was looking for him.

"Mostly newshounds," Felix said, "who don't tip for shit. We're full up, not so much as a closet to let."

"I can see that. How's the family?" He didn't have any family, he lived alone, but we played the game.

"Bueno. How is yours? You really ran out of here yesterday—everything okay?"

"Everything's fine now, thanks for asking. Where's the Ice Princess?"

He smiled and quickly looked around. "I wish you wouldn't call her that while you're talking to me. I need this job."

"Oh, sorry, I didn't think." He didn't need the job. He had a chunk of money stashed away. He only used the doorman job as a cover in his new identity.

"She's been down at the Lido bar lending a hand—can you believe it? Serving drinks, working like one of us peons."

I never told him I'd been on the job, but he knew; cops had that kind of built-in instinct to spot each other.

"Who's down there working with her?"

"Chacho. Man, I've never seen him so down in the mouth. You know him, he usually has a smile for everyone, even if it's been raining two weeks straight. And you better batten down the hatches, weatherman says we're in for a long deluge."

He even had good intel on the weather.

He lifted his hand and gently moved me out of the way for another group of tourists entering the hotel. "Welcome to the Punta Bandera Hotel and Beach Club."

After they passed, he said, "Hey, you hear what happened over at El Gato? It's international news. We got newshounds from all over the world flyin' in here. Great for business." He looked over his shoulder again. "Wouldn't surprise me a bit if the Ice Princess gunned all those poor people and even planted that guy on the ninth hole just to spike the occupancy rate. Some crazy shit, huh?"

Before yesterday I might have laughed at his ridiculous postulation, but the way she'd driven like a maniac, yet still in control to get to our house, the way she burnt the hell out of her feet trying to help me and my family, those acts had humanized her. I just realized I could no longer refer to her as the Ice Princess. And worse, she was now standing on those burnt feet covering my job while I healed. Those feet had to hurt like hell.

"Thanks, Fe, keep up the good work." I shook his hand and headed for the hall to the side of the check-in desk. I'd never seen so many people in line to check in, and if Felix was right that there were no rooms, there were going to be a lot of disappointed people.

None of the five front desk clerks noticed me enter the hall. I went right to Darla Figueroa's office and used the master passkey she'd given me to handle the dead Russian with the knife sticking in his abdomen up in the hotel room. I opened her office door and slipped in. I'd been in her office before but under less than favorable circumstances. I couldn't help but feel guilt that I was somehow stabbing her in the back.

Her office was decorated in 1980s décor, all chrome and black with large paver tiles for floor covering and area rugs. Wall-to-wall carpeting didn't do well in tropical countries, too much mold. I moved to her desk first and hit the space bar on her computer. The huge screen lit up in multiple quadrants displaying row after row of windows showing every aspect of the hotel environs. No wonder she always knew exactly what was going on.

Felix was right, she was working the Lido Cabana Bar with Chacho, both frantically preparing drinks and handing out beer, never catching up. They'd need a restock soon, if not immediately. I'd been telling her she needed a bar-back position to run from the hotel to the Lido bar stocking and fixing the garnish, but she was too tight-fisted, her eye glued to the bottom line.

The password-protected computer wouldn't let me into her files. I moved over to her executive bathroom that had an essence of lilac and found a shower and a two-station sink all with upgraded fixtures, onyx granite counters, the benefits of rank and privilege. I opened her walk-in closet and took a step back, a little stunned. First item on the rack, a gray London Fog raincoat. What the hell? How many suspects were there going to be for the killings at El Gato Gordo?

I checked through all of her shoes in a wall of pigeonholes, Prada, Gucci, Jimmy Choo, and others. Food and beverage manager apparently paid better than cabana bar drink slinger. No black wingtip shoes. Wingtips were male shoes but could be filled with balled-up tissue for a woman to wear as a disguise and to throw off suspicion.

I stepped back out into the bathroom. She wasn't a tidy or meticulous person like you'd think—the onyx sink was marred with toothpaste drops from a rushed brushing. A standard hotel water glass she used to rinse sat next to the mess. I pulled the empty plastic bag insert in the wastebasket and put the glass in, only touching the rim.

I could no longer trust anyone, especially not Chief Franco Hernandez. I left Darla's office carrying the bag.

The concierge, Mary St. John, like everyone else, was too busy to pay attention to me. I interrupted and asked her if she had an overnight shipping box.

"Check the Business Center, the cabinet to the left of the silk palm tree."

"Thank you." She waved her hand and continued trying to help a family who insisted on seeing a three-toed sloth. I was about to direct them to the stool at the cabana bar where Otis sat but I hadn't seen Otis' feet for the three-toed confirmation. He definitely fit the sloth part.

In the Business Center I quickly found the cabinet to which she referred and located a box too large for the water glass, but it would do. I stuffed the box with balled-up packing paper and labeled it to the FBI main headquarters in Virginia, an address I found on my phone, and added: "Eyes Only, Dan Chulack, Deputy Director." I'd helped Dan recover his kidnapped grandchild and he owed me one. I'd never call in that favor, but this was an unusual, if not desperate, circumstance. I dropped the box off at the concierge desk. Mary moved it to the side without looking up, still trying to use diplomacy on the three-toed sloth family.

I finally felt like I'd taken a giant step in solving at least part of my problem. I needed to find something on Darla, some leverage I could use against her to back her off. She wasn't working in Costa Rica by choice. A woman of her talents could work in the best hotels in Miami, San Francisco, or Los Angeles, earning a big paycheck, profit sharing, hotel stocks. She had to have a few ghosts in her closet. A sordid affair, a labor dispute, a tarnished reputation.

I sent a quick text to Dan Chulack asking for the favor and to check the glass for fingerprints. He texted right back: NO PROBLEM. He had not even hesitated. Good friends weren't minted, they had to be earned.

Now I needed to help out Chacho. I hurried to the storeroom, loaded up the dolly with cases of beer, rum, vodka, and gin and toted it down past the crazy pool filled with kids and tourists and on down to the Lido Cabana Bar. Darla looked up from her blender grinding away at a strawberry red daiquiri and *smiled* when she saw me. I immediately felt guilty for having just prowled her office. Darla never smiled. What the hell was going on?

People stood three deep all around the bar waiting to be served.

Chacho saw me and shot me that renowned Chacho smile. "The cavalry has arrived, *gracias amigo.*"

I *was* wanted, I was needed, something every human craves.

I elbowed my way to the pass-through and made it into the bar onto the duck boards and set down the dolly. I stood on tiptoes to see over the sea of people to the beach hoping against hope to see a big dumb dog playing Frisbee.

Waldo was conspicuous by his absence. A hole opened in my chest, an emotional void. I whispered, "He was just a dumb-assed dog, get over it."

CHAPTER THIRTY-SIX

IN THE LIDO Cabana Bar, I first reloaded the beer in the ice coolers, working fast. I suddenly remembered Otis. I moved around to that side. Otis sat on his usual stool, the skin on his face sallow, sagging, with an urban street map of lines in surface blood vessels. His eyes bloodshot, eyelids droopy. Sixteen parasols lay on the bar in front of him, going for a personal best killing off grasshoppers.

"Otis, have you seen Waldo?"

His head swayed from side to side. He raised a shaky hand and pointed it at me. "You, my friend, can kiss my white blubbery ass. You're . . . You're fired."

Darla rushed over, angry at the contempt in his tone, her face flushed. She opened her mouth to say something scathing and rude. I put my hand on her shoulder and gently pressed down as I whispered in her ear. "He's drunk and one of our best customers. He lives in the hotel full-time paying daily rates." She knew all of this but needed reminding.

She shut her mouth and stared into my eyes. Hers had gold flakes surrounded by green. Her scent a whisper of hot oil and coconut that caused an electric shiver that made my staples twitch.

She nodded, reached into her pocket, and came out with lip balm; her face only six inches from mine. She didn't take her eyes off me as she applied moisturizer to her lips—very erotic.

The bar turned silent. I swallowed hard, kept my gaze on her, and whispered, "Your feet have to be killing you. I got this. Thanks for covering."

She leaned up and kissed my cheek. Some of the men around the bar groaned.

"Thanks, cowboy." She held my eyes a moment longer, put her hand on my cheek, her skin warm, soft.

She spun, said loud enough for everyone to hear, "I'm outta here, folks, thanks so much for your patience, the next one is on me."

The bar cheered and began screaming drink orders. She moved to the pass-through, stopped, and put her hand on Chacho's shoulder. "Baby, don't forget, half those tips are mine."

He looked back at her, fear in his expression. She scared the hell outta Chacho. I couldn't blame him.

I lifted the pass-through for her. She fled, her gait unimpeded by her burnt feet. She wouldn't let her pain show; no weakness allowed, not in her projected persona.

The rain came down in a deluge, pounding the beach sand flat, then just as quickly shifted to a light mist, what the locals called "pineapple juice." The bar patrons scooched in tight, shoulder to shoulder as Chacho and I continued to sling our wares. Hours passed. Night fell. The tiki torches were lit. Slowly the crowd thinned. We ran out of rum, then imported beer, Budweiser and Coors Light. We emptied the tip jar twice because it had overflowed with U.S. greenbacks. Sam Snead buried to the waist in the sand trap and the poor dead folks in the El Gato Gordo nightclub had spiked the biggest run on booze in the history of the hotel.

Sadly, murder paid dividends. Most folks ran away from death, but in a ghoulish hysteria, there were a whole lot more who ran to view someone else's bad day. Once the novelty wore off, the hotel's reputation would be irreparably damaged.

Chacho opened two Modelos and handed me one. I took it and stared at the bottle, my throat closing off with emotions. I was a silly old man.

Modelo was Waldo's beer.

I looked and didn't see Otis. He had slipped away unnoticed—fled back to his room unescorted. I didn't worry too much, two of the Russian mobsters were accounted for; the third would be walking with a bad limp.

Chacho clinked my bottle with his. "*Salud.*"

I replied in kind. I didn't usually drink, but the cold bottle in my hand made me realize my overheated body craved fluid. I slugged down half of the cool elixir. No wonder Waldo liked it.

Three couples spaced around the bar talking quietly were all that remained. We weren't allowed to drink at the bar, a bluie-worthy offense. The bar phone rang. We both ignored the summons from the Ice Princess. Bold for Chacho, who strictly obeyed all rules, even the request for him to respond to the hotel roof to service the Queen. That thought made me dislike Darla when I'd just started to come around.

I said, "How are you doing, my friend?"

Chacho's eyes brimmed with tears as he pasted on a fake smile. He turned and looked out at the beach. His voice was low as he said, "She was . . . she was my sun . . . my stars . . ." He took another drink of his Modelo. I understood. Marie was my everything as well. All I could do was put my hand on his shoulder. He gently shook as he wept. He'd been holding it in while working. Work was good for him.

He reached into his back pocket and pulled out a crumpled envelope. "Someone left this for you on the bar."

I took it. "Gaylord" was scrawled and barely legible across the front. "Did you see who left it?"

He shook his head. "No, it was just there. *Lo siento.* It was too crazy."

I checked my cellphone for messages and found one from Eddie: THERE'S NO SUCH THING AS FREE KITTENS

Eddie, in his roundabout way, was saying thank you for protecting him and the family.

"Is that your family?" Chacho must've read my expression. "You go. I got this."

I checked my watch. We worked right through his shift and he'd put in three hours overtime; it was almost eleven thirty. Time had slithered underneath us like a snake looking for a mouse. I did want to go home, but I had two and a half hours left on my shift. The cellphone in my hand rang. I answered it as I opened the pass-through.

"Wait," Chacho said. "The tips?"

"You keep them, my friend."

"You sure?"

I nodded, pressed ANSWER, and walked away. He'd need the money to bury *his sun and his stars.*

"Hey, beautiful," I said to Marie.

"Busy night? You coming home soon?"

"Busiest night I've ever worked, bar none."

"Good tips then?"

"The best. I gave them all to Chacho."

She paused. "That's for the best."

"You call just to tell me you love me."

"That, and I did some more research. I'm sending you two photos; check your phone."

At first the photos didn't make sense. One depicted Chief Franco Hernandez arriving at some big to-do in San Jose. He stood on the steps to the criminal courts building with government officials posing for the camera.

Then I got it. His blue uniform front exposed all his regalia. Off his shoulders and down by his sides hung a gray raincoat, possibly a London Fog. Ah, man.

The next photo was more obvious, a picture of a news story of how the cops in Tamarindo all carried Beretta model 92FS, 9mm, double stacked pistols.

I spoke into the phone, "Thanks. I'm starting to get run over with all the suspects in this mess."

I remembered the envelope in my pocket and took it out while I spoke. "How are the kids doing after what happened?"

"Good. Most don't even know anything happened. Eddie is a little quiet, though."

"He was the one who sent up the alert. He did a good job."

"I'll talk to him. What was he doing home from school?"

"He said he was worried about you."

I nodded as I tore open the envelope. Inside had one piece of paper with one sentence in Spanish.

Hoyo dieciocho a la medianoche.

I said to Marie. "What does this mean." I read the words the best I could.

"Why?" Her voice tense, "Bruno, what's going on?"

I closed my eyes and stopped walking. "Babe, I'm dead tired, can you just give me a break on this one, please?"

"It says, 'eighteenth hole tonight at midnight.' Now please tell me what's going on? Don't you dare go out there. You hear me? This isn't our mess. Leave it be. Please, just leave it be."

"Take it easy. You don't want me to check it out, I won't."

"You promise?"

"Really, it's come to this, I have to make a promise every time I—"

"At least promise you'll be careful." She knew I wouldn't lie to her.

"I promise. I love you. I'll be home soon." I hung up and headed out to the eighteenth hole.

CHAPTER THIRTY-SEVEN

I WALKED THROUGH the crowded lobby. Some folks were sacked out on couches and easy chairs, their luggage beside them, a few even curled up on the floor in the corners. All the other hotels must have been full. Patrons inside the hotel bar, the Beach Comber, overflowed out into the lobby, boisterous drunks, laughing, talking too loud. If I had not been so darn tired, I would've worked as bar-back for a while and stocked for the two bartenders. I didn't know if our bar stockroom would survive, but that was a problem for Darla to deal with. She needed to call the distributor in San Jose, make an emergency order and delivery or we'd lose our sales momentum.

I stepped out into the front of the hotel under the porte cochere, and of course, it started to rain; *pelo de gato*, nothing heavy. The Ticos call a light mist "hair of the cat" because it looks like fur on the windshield. Even though it was tropical-warm, I shivered. I hadn't replaced all the blood loss yet, hadn't fully recovered. If I was smart, I'd order up an Uber for the ride home to save my strength and what little energy I had left.

But there weren't many who'd say I was smart, especially when it came to skullduggery that threatened my family. I wanted to meet the mysterious person at the eighteenth hole, see what he or she had to say. This had to be related to the Russian thugs or the nightclub.

I took the road headed away from the hotel, the one parallel to the golf course, aware that Darla Figueroa was sitting in her office watching me on her CCTV. I held my hand up and gave her a backward wave.

I passed all the news vans and rental cars parked in the parking lot, not one empty slot available.

I missed having Waldo walking at my side. The rain came down hard soaking me then quit almost as if God or his wife were laughing at me.

My cellphone buzzed in my pocket. I checked it. Eddie:
PLEASE DON'T GO.

He had either been talking to Marie or he'd eavesdropped on our last conversation when she asked me to come right home and then relented and said to be careful. That kid was something else. I typed back: I'LL BE OKAY. GO BACK TO BED.

I put my phone in my pocket.

After I got out of view of the last CCTV camera, at least the last one I knew about, I cut through the shrubs onto the fairway and walked on the edge. The golf course doglegged around twice until it came close to the Pacific where the eighteenth hole had a spectacular view of the ocean. The moon came in and out of the clouds, making the shadows grow long and then disappear altogether. I cut across the doglegs instead of following the course and came out onto the driving tee for eighteen.

I stayed in the shadows and waited. I didn't see or hear anyone except for the song of night birds and the wind in the trees and shrubs, a calming ambient noise. I checked my watch instead of my cellphone that would light up my little section of the world in a globe of white; ten minutes after midnight.

The eighteenth tee had a 320-yard drive, then a loop back. Through the sparse shrubs and few trees, the smooth putting green glowed in the moonlight until clouds covered the moon and darkness fell yet again.

The cherry glow of a cigarette caught my eye. A man stood about thirty yards from the green. I headed toward the man until the cherry glow stopped and I lost sight of him. I waited.

He took another puff. This time I silently ran across the perfectly manicured grass. I made it to the shrubs and paused to catch my breath and for another break in the clouds, so the moonlight would work in my favor. The clouds cleared. The man had disappeared.

I again wished I'd carried a weapon.

"Buenos noches, senor."

I startled and jumped a few inches in the air. I hit the ground, jarring the staples in my back. A groan slipped out.

Jose Rivera, the ghost, had walked up on me.

He stank of tequila and nicotine and body odor. The moonlight came out. His eyelids drooped, and his facial features were relaxed.

"What's going on, Jose?"

"We didn't get to talk the other night, me and you." His words slurred as he waved a tequila bottle that sloshed. I had never seen Jose drink before. Salvador had been a good friend. As long as he lived, the impact of Salvador's death would be a black mark in Jose's memory that would cast a shadow over his entire world.

"Do you know what Salvador was investigating? Was he at the nightclub that night, following someone?"

He pointed with his index finger, the others wrapped around the bottle's neck. "El Gato Gordo."

"Si, El Gato Gordo. What was Salvador doing there that night? Was he following someone?"

Jose nodded, took a drag off his cigarette, and then a slug of tequila. "He was following el doctor."

"Doctor Aleck Vargas?"

"Jess . . . El doctor . . . no. No." He shook the tequila bottle. "He was following the woman, el doctor's puta."

"What? Why?"

Jose shrugged.

"Who is this woman?"

"When I find out, I will bury her to her neck like the other hombres." He sloshed the bottle, pointing out into the darkness.

I started to ask him more about the woman when what he said hooked onto one brain cell that wasn't overwhelmed with fatigue. "What . . . you said men, *plural*?"

"*Que*?"

I held up two fingers. "*Dos hombres*?"

"*Si*." He waved with the bottle and shambled through the thin shrub line over toward the eighteenth green, about thirty yards from where I'd seen him the first time.

Jose stumbled to the closest sand trap and fell down on his butt.

He patted the head of the dead man buried up to his chin in the sand.

CHAPTER THIRTY-EIGHT

I'D NEVER SEEN anything like what was happening in Tamarindo, not even in Los Angeles where I'd lived most of my life—well, maybe in Los Angeles. Tamarindo went from a quiet bucolic little town to full-throttle violent. Amoral despicable violent.

Jose had carried the dead Russian, the one from the trunk of the car, out to the eighteenth green and buried him in the closest sand trap. I lost the use of my legs and eased down, sitting in the wet sand, my body exhausted. "Jose, why did you . . . you plant this man here?" The head in the moonlight looked like something out of a Boris Karloff movie, a prop. Its pallor a blue gray, lips purple, eyes staring straight ahead occluded with a milky film.

He shrugged. "Jus' like the other."

"You buried the other one on the ninth hole?"

"No. No." He waved his finger, the same hand with the bottle, then pointed to his eye. "I see, *la otra*." He shrugged again. "So, I put this one here too."

My response slipped past my lips without full brain approval. "Dead Russian thugs aren't supposed to be buried in the Punta Bandera Hotel Spa and Beach Club sand traps."

Jose chuckled, put the bottle down. He leaned over and with a finger closed one eyelid of the dead Russian, then opened it as he said in perfect English, "When death winks at you, senor, all you can do is wink back."

Jose had seen too much death during his war experiences—dead bodies meant nothing to him. The tequila didn't help. There is no psychological force greater than revenge. He thought he was avenging his best friend's death when in all actuality the dead Russians and the nightclub massacre could be entirely unrelated. Nothing so far linked the two. But odds were, they were linked, and we just hadn't yet found the common denominator. It was too big a coincidence for it not to be.

I needed to talk with Otis, grab him by the throat, and make him talk, force him to tell me why he and I had been attacked. I'd been a fool to think it might've been me they were after or his lame excuse about tourists and random robberies.

I suddenly looked over my shoulder back toward the hotel. If the press jackals caught wind of this, that would be the end of our world as we knew it. Another dead Russian planted on the golf course would cause not only a greater international incident, it would also cross the line into a diplomatic one. Putin himself would fly out here and ride his horse on our golf course naked to the waist to prove to everyone no one messed with Mother Russia.

"Come on, help me get this guy out of here and back in the trunk of the stolen car." I fell to my knees and started digging, pulling the loose sand away from the dead Russian's chin and neck. He'd started to stink, a fecund decay like no other, overpowering the fresh scent of rain and jungle flowers.

Jose leaned back on his elbows and drank. "There are two more of these putos."

I stopped. "Two more Russians?"

"Si."

"Where?"

"I don't know, but I will find them, and then." He dragged his finger under his chin across his throat.

I half-turned, pulled up my hotel aloha shirt, and showed him the bandage. "One more went in the stream. He didn't come out. That leaves only one, not two."

He pointed at me. "You?"

"No, *mi pero*. My dog, Waldo."

"Ah, si. But there are still two."

"Have you seen my dog? Have you seen Waldo?"

He wagged his finger. "No. If he went in the stream, it comes out in the ocean. Sharks wait in the ocean at the mouth of the stream and eat what comes down. Mira."

He moved on his knees over to the man I'd uncovered down to the chest, the dead man's shirt, a shroud, plastered to him. Jose dug quickly, much faster than I had. He suddenly stood, got behind the dead man, grabbed him under the arms, and pulled. The man came free. I turned and tried to hold back my stomach contents from coming up.

Sharks had been at the man; his bottom half missing, shredded and loose. Jose gave a drunk cackle. "I found him on the beach and bury him here."

This was the thug I'd chased away from our house, the one with the injured shoulder, the one Waldo tackled and rolled with into the stream. The man chewed up by sharks.

I should've recognized him. The dead take on a different appearance after being ravaged by a land shark and then an ocean shark.

The thought of Waldo meeting the same demise, a violent death after saving my life, again caused a hole to open in my chest, a deep emotional gap.

I knew the place where the stream emptied into the ocean; the city had permanent signs posted that said, "No Swimming Sharks."

We'd made a field trip out of it, took all the kids down there to show them and explain why. With a straight face Eddie had said, "No swimming sharks? What do they do, walk, dance?"

Waldo couldn't both swim and fight off sharks. If he even made it that far before drowning. I dearly missed that damn dog.

I lifted the bottle of tequila, took a slug. The alcohol burned all the way down. A warmth started in my stomach and radiated outward. I wasn't going home, not yet. Someone killed my dog and there were two more Russians out there who needed to know I wouldn't stand for being messed with. "Jose, mi amigo, could you, ah . . . take this . . . man fishing?"

To "take someone fishing" was a term Salvador had used when he got rid of those who would harm our children.

"Si, no problem."

"Do you know where the other two are, the other two like this man?"

"Not yet. They are staying in a rented casa in Tamarindo. But I will find them."

"When you do, don't take them fishing before I talk to them."

He smiled hugely. "Si, I understand."

"How can I reach you when I need to talk?"

He shrugged.

He didn't want to be reachable.

"Thank you, my friend, for leaving me the note at the bar."

I got up, brushing off the sand. I pulled out my cell and texted Eddie that everything was fine, that I'd be a smidge later, and that I was going back to the hotel. As I walked in the moonlight, I watched the screen for his reply that wasn't forthcoming. *Pelo de gato*, a misting rain started in again. I put the phone away and hurried.

CHAPTER THIRTY-NINE

I LISTENED AT Otis' hotel room door.

He snored like Tarzan calling his faithful companion Cheetah the chimp, short, sharp barks: Ungowa . . . Ungowa . . . Ungowa.

I took out the passkey, slid it in, and eased the door open, flinching, waiting for Otis to grab up Big Bertha and hit me with fourteen 9mm rounds. He was over-beveraged and couldn't fake a snore like Tarzan. Or hold a gun steady enough to hit the target.

I peeked around the door's edge. One lamp next to the couch illuminated the room in a low-wattage yellow, an eerie 1930s kind of yellow.

The Browning Hi-Power—Big Bertha—sat on the end table. Otis lay on his stomach, one arm hanging off the couch, a long string of continuous drool, powered by the earlier slain grasshoppers, pooled on the area rug below. I eased the door closed even though a canon going off wasn't going to wake him.

First, I picked up the Browning, dropped the magazine, ejected the round in the chamber, and set it back down. Based on my experience dealing with drunks, I wouldn't be able to arouse him in any moderate way. I took the ice bucket on the counter over the mini bar and left the lid. All the ice except a few small cubes remained in cold water. I stood over Otis and slowly poured it on his face and head.

He sputtered and slapped at the water stream. Coughed. Then let out a loud yelp. "Hey, what the hell are—"

Behind me came a quick growl. Before I could react, there came a snap as sharp canines latched onto my ass cheek. "Aheee."

I spun, slapping at Waldo's jaws trying to get him to let go, and at the same time, happy to see him—over-the-moon happy to see him.

If only he weren't trying to bite off my ass.

"Waldo. It's me. Waldo, let me go. Let me go."

Otis sat up bewildered, his hair wet, matted down, his mouth open as he took in deep breaths from ice-water shock.

I shuffle-stepped over to the mini bar concession, dragging along man's best friend, took down a Snickers bar, and waved it in front of Waldo's mug. He let go and snatched the bar from my hand, preferring chocolate and nougat over African American ass.

I turned around. Waldo had a white bandage around his midsection with areas of his fur shaved down to the skin, peeking out. He too had been slashed by the Russian.

"Hey, hey," Otis yelled. "He's supposed to stay in bed for another couple of days."

Waldo grunted as he ate the Snickers, wrapper and all.

"Did you take him to the vet?"

"You're damn skippy, I did. Someone had to."

"Thank you, Otis, truly, thank you for that."

"Why? He ain't your dog. You gonna pay for it? Cost me a chunk of change, it did. He got sliced but good."

"Yes, of course I'll reimburse you for it."

My butt throbbed, and the back of my pants turned wet with blood.

"Isn't he supposed to be wearing a cone to keep him from messing with his injury?"

To keep him from lunching on my ass.

"I've gotten him two and he chewed them off both times. He's not messing with the bandage, so I said ta hell with it. How can you treat your dog like that, leave him all cut up without a doctor's care? Cruel, that's what it is."

I took a step toward Otis; the tone shifted in my voice. "It was one of your friends who did it, cut me as well. And tonight, you're going to tell me what's going on. You know, and you're not telling me."

He struggled to his feet. I shoved him back down.

Behind me, Waldo growled.

I reached, picked up the gun, inserted the mag, and charged the chamber, pulling the slide back and letting it snap home. "Tell Waldo to go in the other room or I'll shoot you in the foot."

It hurt me emotionally that Waldo took up with the likes of Otis instead of me. Stupid to be jealous over a damn dog.

"Do it, Otis, I'm not kidding." I took aim at his naked foot intending to tap the trigger, carry out my brutal intent. I was tired of not knowing what was going on.

"Okay. Okay."

He spoke some German words. Waldo looked at me then back at Otis. He slowly obeyed. I followed behind and closed the door. When I came back into the living area, Otis had stood and staggered his way to the mini bar. He'd opened a small bottle of lime-flavored rum and tilted it back.

"Get back over to the couch and sit down."

He stared at me as if trying to decide what to do. I picked up a throw pillow from the couch and held it in front of the gun to muffle the sound.

"You don't know me. If you did, you'd do exactly what I tell you or you're going to learn a hard lesson."

He straightened up, pulled his shoulders back, his expression shifting to one I had not seen before: confident, self-assured. Otis had transformed right before my eyes. "What do you want to know?"

"What's your real name?"

"Not relevant. Next question." He spoke clearly and concisely, no longer drunk.

"I decide what's relevant, not you."

"Do you want information or not? I'll hold up to any kind of torture you want to hand out. I've had the training."

I regripped the gun, which turned wet in my hand from sweat. "What are you doing here?"

"Looking for someone."

"Who?"

"A man named Genie."

"Seriously, a man named Genie, like Ali Baba and the Forty Thieves kind of Genie? All this mess is over a man named Genie?"

"That's right." He pointed to the dining area table and chairs. "I'm going to sit over there; the couch hurts my back." He didn't wait for approval, walked to the table, and sat down. "Next question."

"Who were they and why did they jump us?"

"They're brainless thugs who can't do anything without being told exactly what to do. And most times they even screw that up. Subcontractors from the Russian mafia out of Brighton Beach. They're here looking for a big payday that's owed the mob. They didn't jump *us*, they jumped me. They wanted *me*. They want the same thing I'm after. We take out the rest of 'em, Brighton Beach will just send more."

"Brighton Beach also wants this guy named Genie? That's what you're saying?"

"That's correct. That's why I hired you to keep them off me until I found Genie."

Waldo scratched at the door. Otis looked that way. "I'll get charged for that damage."

I ignored him. "What did this Genie do?"

"He cheated me and the mob out of a big score. Cheated Brighton Beach who sponsored the heist."

What he said was the first thing that made any sense in this whole mess. A rivulet of blood inside my pants ran down the back of my leg. I didn't think my ass cheek was bleeding enough to worry about.

"How much? What kind of score are we talking about?"

"Eleven million in diamonds. We ripped off a courier."

His intonation had changed slightly. "You were going to say something else—what was it?"

"You're in over your head, pal. You have no idea what you're getting into."

"Answer the question."

"I know you're a smart shitass. I did a background check on you, so you'll know the truth when you hear it. Diamonds are easier to transport—to exchange—than bulky paper money, especially when you get into the kind of numbers I'm talking about."

"Ah, shit." I eased down into a chair opposite him at the table. "You ripped off a cartel courier."

"Bingo. Like I said, you're a smart shitass."

CHAPTER FORTY

OTIS—OR AT LEAST the man called Otis—lit a narrow cigar from a pack on the table. He'd never smoked at the cabana bar. I rested the Browning Hi-Power on the table pointed at his chest. The threat didn't seem to bother him.

"Keep talking," I said.

He shrugged as if this whole scenario wasn't a big deal.

"The takedown of a cartel courier had to have cutouts or the cartel enforcers would kill their way back to the source. Like I said, the job was hired out by the Russian mob from Brighton Beach. I was hired through a cutout to orchestrate the job, that's all I know about that end. I used subcontractors for the whole thing. We never met up, we did everything through the dark web and by disposable cellphones, text messages.

"I need another drink."

"Keep talking."

He waited a moment then nodded. "This Genie guy came highly recommended, and I used him to lead the caper. I'd used him two other times before and those jobs came off without a hitch. My job: I organized the cars, the guns, the safe house, passed on all the intel including info on the courier's schedule, suggested a method, and then let Genie put together the team and have final say on the tactics. I don't know where Brighton Beach got the schedule and didn't care."

"What happened?"

He waved his hand. "What usually happens when it's not your own intel. I wasn't told—and maybe Brighton Beach didn't know—the cartel was running their own countersurveillance protection on their courier, heavy hitters who knew what they were about." He paused, his eyes wandering over to the mini bar. He was a stone-cold alcoholic—or at least he wanted me to believe he was.

"Don't stop now. Keep going."

"Do I really need to spell it out? Can't you put it together? The whole thing turned into a grade A shitshow." His brown eyes glowed with anger at his "Otis" cover being discovered—about being held at gunpoint by someone who made his grasshoppers at the cabana bar.

"Say the words. I want to hear it from you."

"It went down bad. None of the Russian contractors made it out of the parking garage. Genie did and apparently one of the counter-surveillance protection team lived long enough to tell the tale. Genie thought he'd been double-crossed and took it on the lam with all the gems. I didn't get paid. Brighton didn't get paid. The whole caper went right down the shitter along with my reputation. I'm here to correct that error on both counts."

"And Brighton Beach is now after you for screwing up the job and losing their men."

"There is that, yes."

"Who's this Genie?"

He shrugged, stood. "Shoot me if you're going to—I've gotta have another drink."

He walked without a drunken stagger to the mini bar, grabbed up a handful of little liquor bottles, and came back to the table. He twisted off the top to the green Tanqueray gin and tilted it back, draining the little fella.

I guess I'd be drinking myself into a stupor if I had Brighton Beach and the cartel both after me. He sat down at the table, dropping the bottles, which rolled and had to be chased before they fell to the floor.

I let him do it and didn't fall prey to his ploy. I kept the gun trained on his belly. The way Otis had wielded that switchblade and stuck the Russian thug in just the right place now made perfect sense.

He wasn't who he made himself out to be. He said he'd been trained in how to resist torture. He was ex-military intelligence, black ops maybe. He'd just tried to distract me with the runaway bottles, a ruse to take the gun away.

"Why are you here living at this hotel? Are you hiding or are you following a lead on Genie's whereabouts?"

He glared at me and said nothing.

"One of your Russian friends laid open my back and almost killed my dog. I'm not in a good mood."

At the mention of the knife wound, the staples in my back started to itch.

He let an ugly little smile crawl across his mug. "You mean that same dog that just took a chunk out of your fat ass, that dog?"

I took the gun off the table and pointed at his naked foot. He searched my eyes to see if I was bluffing, if I had it in me to pull the trigger.

"Okay," he said. "I backtracked my contact who recommended Genie. He said 'Tamarindo.' That's all I got out of him. Just the name of this town."

"And I suppose this contact is no longer breathing and can't give us any more information?"

He shrugged, his eyes still on mine. His mind working fast, trying to get out ahead of me.

"Why this hotel?"

"Truthfully?"

I said nothing.

"Because of you," he said.

"Me?"

"In all of Tamarindo, as far as I can tell, you're the only one with the background that could pull off a job like the takedown of the cartel courier in the parking garage and be able to walk away in one piece.

"I told you, I did some checking; that was the truth. You fit the profile perfectly and you know it. You're Genie and you're not going to convince me otherwise. All this here, this useless conversation, it's just to throw me off your scent. It's not going to work, you're the Genie."

"That's why you hired me, to get close, to see if I would slip and give myself away?"

He shrugged again. "*And* I knew those Russians would eventually catch up to me. I knew how you'd react if they did find me here. And I wasn't wrong."

"I'm not Genie. I have kids at home, thirteen of them. I'm a cabana bartender and nothing more."

He stared and again let that ugly smile out to play, this time only one side of his mouth, crooked and more of a grin. He didn't believe me.

He said, "Who else but a guy like Genie would plant a Russian operator on the ninth-hole sand trap? Pure genius. What a distraction to everything else going on."

"Not me." My words sounded hollow even to me. "What happened at El Gato Gordo?"

He shrugged again. I was getting tired of his wordplay avoiding the truth. He gave out just enough information to keep me at bay, still holding an ace up his sleeve. But a thought hit me, the shooting at the nightclub fit the cartel's type of operation; fear and tyranny. Maybe the Russians and the nightclub *were* linked after all. And it was the courier takedown that had set all this mess in motion.

The old Bruno I'd been trying so hard to suppress, the one Marie never wanted to see again, wanted to come out and play. I wanted to be a father and good husband. I didn't like the old Bruno. The blood and bone Bruno.

I leaned over and shot Otis in the foot.

The bang still echoed in my ears when his screaming started. A billow of grayish white smoke filled the room, the acrid odor a comfort, like an old friend.

Waldo rammed the bedroom door wanting out. I walked over to the kitchenette, picked up some clean dish towels, and tossed them. He sat on his butt on the floor cradling his foot, blood oozing through his fingers.

After he calmed down to a moan, I pointed the 9mm at his knee. "Keep jacking me around and you'll keep losing joints. If you don't die from blood loss, you'll be a cripple. *And*, I don't have a fat ass."

He said through gritted teeth, trying to eat the pain, "See. See, I told you, you're Genie. You shot me for nothing. We were just talking nice, and you shot me. You want me to believe that you're not, and you just shot me in the friggin' foot."

"I'm not Genie. Last chance, tell me about El Gato Gordo."

"I have no idea. I'm telling you the truth. If I knew what happened over there, I'd tell you. I don't want my ass shot off."

The hotel door clicked, then swung open. I whirled and pointed the Browning at the intruder, expecting to see one of the Russians.

Darla Figueroa rushed in.

CHAPTER FORTY-ONE

DARLA SAW THE gun in my hand, took in Otis sitting on his butt on the floor, his hands holding his naked, bloody foot. She didn't look shocked or surprised, not in the least.

She hurried back to the door, stuck her head out into the hall, and said to some unseen patrons, "It's okay, it's just a loud argument and someone slammed a door. Sorry for the disturbance . . . check with the concierge . . . she'll give all of you a free breakfast coupon in the hotel restaurant." She came back in, easing the door closed.

She hurried over to me. "Are you out of your ever-lovin' mind? Did you just shoot one of the hotel's patrons in the foot?"

She reached for the gun.

I gently put my hand on her chest and moved her back one big step. "I'm tired of playing catch-up with what's going on. I'm tired of being your patsy and now his. I'm going to find out what's going on and I'm doing it my way."

"What are you talking about? Who is this man?" She pointed at Otis, his blood filling the grout in between the tile and slowly rolling along in two different directions. After drinking grasshoppers, day after day, I half-expected his blood to be pastel green.

"I'm just here on vacation and this crazy man burst into my room and shot me in my foot."

I chuckled. "Oh, you're good. You're really good."

"Bruno?" Darla said.

Otis' face had turned pale. "Oh," he said, "she calls you by your real name. She knows all about you and you still have a job. That says a lot right there about what's going on here. You're Genie, all right, and you can't prove otherwise."

I kicked him in the butt. "This piece of shit thinks I'm some kind of diamond thief and I'm hiding out in Tamarindo. Those guys that jumped us, that guy buried to his waist on the ninth hole sand trap, they're people after him, to recover a handful of gems."

She came up close to my face. "I don't care if he was on the grassy knoll and shot JFK. Not in my hotel. You understand me?" She pointed back over her shoulder. "This place is crawling with press. Are you out of your mind, shooting him in his foot? Get him out of here; throw him out on his ear. He is no longer welcome. You getting the picture now? We need to get back to normal as quickly and quietly as humanly possible."

"I was about to shoot him in his knee. I can put a pillow over the gun if you like."

Her face flushed red, her eyes wild with anger. "Why are you going to shoot him in the knee? Are you some sort of sadist?"

"I was just asking him if he had anything to do with the killings at El Gato Gordo."

She came off her tiptoes and down out of my face. "He had something to do with that massacre?"

"No!" Otis yelped.

I said, "He has this 9mm here." I waggled it. "And a London Fog coat and wingtip shoes in his closet."

I had not thought Otis capable of being the shooter, but that was the old Otis, the drunk Otis who put on a show, day after day, down at the cabana bar where he specialized in slaying grasshoppers with pink parasols as he watched, waiting for me to slip up. After what he said about organizing a complicated heist, he could easily have had something to do with the nightclub killings.

"Excellent," Darla said. She took out her cell. "I'll ring Chief Hernandez and turn this whole mess over to him. He knows how to be discreet. We'll let his cops in through the back. The shooter at the nightclub wore a London Fog and wingtips. How do you have this information?"

I pulled her aside and whispered, "You can't call the chief. Hernandez fed me to the OIJ. He gave them your video tape, the one with me dumping the Russian across the street from the hotel property. Something *you asked me to do*. You call him, that's going to throw you into the jackpot right along with the both of us." I pointed to Otis.

She pocketed her cellphone just as Waldo barked and rammed the door again. "Is that your dog in my hotel?"

"Don't change the subject."

She said, "What do you want to do? If you think he killed those people over at the nightclub, he needs to be arrested and held accountable. That was hideous, a vicious slaughter of good people."

Otis struggled to his feet, his bloody hands dragging across his beige seersucker suit leaving a smear. "Yeah, what *are* you going to do? You know how many people have a 9mm and a London Fog raincoat? My word of honor—I didn't shoot those poor folks at the nightclub. I've never set foot in that place."

I said, "Oh, you have a lot of credibility—a thief and an armed robber."

My cell buzzed. It was Felix, the doorman. I answered it. "Yeah, Felix."

"You better get out here fast."

"Why?" He hung up just as Darla's cell rang.

She answered it and started for the room door, where she stopped, turned to us. "No more shooting in my hotel, take it off premises. If I have to come back, I'll be the one doing the shooting." She said it like she meant it and I believed her. She didn't wait for a reply; she disappeared out the door.

I said to Otis, "I'm not done here. I'll be back to finish this." I dropped the gun's magazine, cleared the chamber, and threw the gun across the room. It landed on the couch. Otis said nothing as I followed Darla who had to be headed to the same place—the front of the hotel.

I caught up with her in the long hall that would dump us out in the lobby. She talked on her cell. "And get the doctor in here, quietly. Yes, shot in the foot. You know what doctor I'm talking about, and I mean quietly. Have him see to his foot then just as quietly escort him from the hotel. Give him the boot but first make sure he's paid up." She hung up without a goodbye.

I tried to keep step with her, but my gait had a hobble in it from the ache in my ass cheek that Waldo chomped. "Who was that?"

"Who?"

"On the phone?"

"It's hotel business."

"I think I've earned a little more trust."

She stopped, stared at me. "Are you kidding me?" She began to give a list of violations and or errant behavior that had betrayed her trust, caught herself, and shut her mouth.

I waited.

She resumed her trek. "It was Chacho. He's the only one I can really trust anymore. I used to trust you." She looked over at me as I skip-hopped next to her, her long, lithe legs eating the distance to the lobby.

She wore her typical off-the-shoulder Hawaiian dress with a slit that revealed lots of leg. Not that I was looking, but she had a round purple bruise high above the knee, halfway to the hip on the outside thigh. I hadn't noticed it the day up on the roof, but then again, she had been naked and slathered with Hawaiian Tropic coconut oil that glistened in the sun. I shuddered from the memory.

She said, "Your theory about the London Fog and 9mm has lots of holes in it. I wasn't going to debate it in front of that closet turd you shot in the foot. *I* have a London Fog and a 9mm pistol."

Why would she tell me that? Had she figured out someone had been in her office?

She stopped again, looked me in the eye. "I've been looking for a hotel detective, a fixer, and thought you might fit the bill. You know how to get things done, but dumping that guy so close to the hotel and shooting a guest in the foot in our hotel proves you'd rather use a hammer than a more delicate balance of discreet diplomacy."

"*You were* about to fire me."

"As cabana bartender, sure. House detective carries with it a raise and a lot more responsibility. You're wasted as a bartender." She took off walking. "But I guess that's all you'll ever be. You don't have the common sense to fill a thimble."

"Hey, that doesn't even make sense. You were going to fire me and then give me a job with more responsibility?"

Over her shoulder she said, "Doesn't matter now, the entire topic is moo."

"You mean *moot*, don't you?"

"Another test you just failed. The boss is always right."

We came out the front door to find all the patrons who'd been sleeping in the lobby and half the ones from the bar standing under the porte cochere, all looking at some sort of spectacle, pointing and talking.

The news people with their bright camera lights lit up the night like it was midday. Rebecca Sanchez from local Channel Six shoved a microphone in my face. "Is this your van. I understand this is your van."

Last thing I needed was to have my face splashed all over the news. Rebecca Sanchez was a beauty with perfect skin and all smooth angles and eyes that could melt titanium. She'd do anything to penetrate the U.S. market and would one day, no doubt about it. The older kids at home would go crazy to meet her. She was the icon of Channel Six.

I pushed the microphone away, pushed my way through the crowd, and stopped halfway into my next step.

Marie's Volkswagen van, painted beige with different colors of '60s hippie flowers, sat in the drive-through of the hotel, the front end crumpled from a low-speed crash into the stucco support that held up the porte cochere.

Eddie stood next to it shivering in fear, a dribble of blood from his hairline running into his eye.

CHAPTER FORTY-TWO

OUT IN FRONT of the hotel I scooped Eddie up in my arms and felt him all over, looking for injuries, broken bones, or additional bleeding.

"I'm sorry, Dad, I'm so sorry."

He said it over and over. Each time the lump in my throat grew larger. Choking. Car accidents scared the hell out of me. I'd seen too many over the years, the end result agony, grief, the torn and maimed lying on the dirty asphalt. I was lucky Eddie was okay, physically.

For those who have never experienced a slobberknocker of a car crash—they are every bit as violent and unpredictable as any stabbing, gunshot, or bludgeoning. They carry the same nightmares and post-traumatic stress that can linger for years, if not permanently. Eddie had had enough trauma in his life. He didn't need anymore.

Eddie had worried about me and went against his morals and life lessons training at the Johnson residence. He'd taken Marie's Volkswagen bus. He was too short in the britches to sit on the seat and reach the pedals and had to stand to drive. When he crashed into the pillar while trying to stop, the force shoved him forward, and he hit the windshield with his face. Though not a slobberknocker, he'd still remember the accident for the rest of his life. The shock and fear as he pumped the brake, the scary feeling of no control over the unfolding danger.

And then his face mashing up against the unyielding windshield. I ached for him having to go through the ordeal, for having just minted a new violent experience to be carried in memory forever after.

I'd caused my son to worry—this was my fault—not his. He put his arms around my neck and buried his face in my shoulder. The events that brought on all the anguish to my family further proved I'd been pussyfooting around, not handling what was happening the same as I would in Los Angeles. Handling it with blood and bone.

No more.

Shooting Otis in the foot uncovered more of what was going on than all the rest of the nosing around I'd done while avoiding the real situation.

Darla stood in the driveway trying to herd all of the hotel customers and news people back inside. She stopped long enough to tell Felix the doorman to call for a tow truck and get the VW van moved, towed back to our home. Felix was nodding as he spoke on the phone.

She approached and I braced for an earful. I'd made up my mind. I gently set Eddie down, ready to sock the woman square in the face if she said one thing out of line, one thing to further enflame the guilt already heaped upon my son.

She came up close, put her hand on Eddie's shoulder as he stood close hugging me around the waist. Her green eyes with the gold flakes glowed with concern. "Is he okay? You want me to drive you to the clinic? Come on, I'll drive you to the clinic."

My breath caught. What was going on with her? "A ride home would be nice." To say it with the right tone, I had to tamp down the old Bruno.

"Of course, come on." She led the way over to her BMW still parked in the manager's slot. Eddie clung to me and wouldn't let go. I was afraid he'd regressed back to the time when we rescued him from his awful circumstances back in the States. Back then he didn't talk for a long time, not till he realized we only had the best intentions for him. I opened the BMW's passenger door, set Eddie down, pried his arms off, and knelt down next to him.

"I didn't mean to crash. I'm so sorry I took the car."

He still wouldn't look me in the eyes.

"I'm not mad. Look at me. I'm not mad, Eddie."

Darla got in on her side and now waited for us.

"You're not? How can you not be mad?"

"What have I always told you?"

He shook his head. "You tell me a lot of things. You tell me things every day."

This was a huge shift from the confident child who continually sent me text messages with jokes.

"I told you that if you had to do something wrong, something against the rules, that if you were doing it for the right reasons, it's still wrong but it can be understood and dealt with. You remember that?"

How could I say anything else without being a hypocrite? I'd just shot a man in the foot. The question was, had I done it for the right reasons?

He nodded.

"Did you do this for the right reasons?"

He nodded.

"Then I'm not mad at you for what you did. I'm a little disappointed over you not first stopping to think about the consequences. But you did do it for the right reasons, so I can't be too mad."

He wiped the tears from his eyes with his hands. I stood and used the tail of my shirt to gently daub the blood from his eye and forehead and smeared the hotel aloha shirt. The blood came from a small laceration at his hairline that was going to need a couple of sutures.

"Come on," I said. "Let's get in the car and go home. Your mom must be worried sick."

Right on cue, Marie phoned my cell. I hit ANSWER and said, "He's with me. I'm bringing him home."

Eddie got out of the BMW and stood next to me waiting to hear what his mom had to say, the verdict to his error in judgment.

"Thank goodness. Bruno, my van is missing."

"That's all taken care of. We'll be home soon."

"Thank you. Tell him I love him."

I rang off just as two Tamarindo police cars pulled into the hotel and stopped by the BMW. Someone inside had called the police for the accident, called for the little kid with blood on his face. I turned and moved Eddie, who was Caucasian, behind me, an old habit. Cops who saw a black man with a white kid getting into a new BMW tended to jump to conclusions and things could quickly get out of hand.

Three uniforms and one plainclothes agent got out and approached, their descriptions washed out from the police car's bright headlights, different gradations of gray shadows obscuring their expressions.

The plainclothes man came up and stood in front of me; the other three took up flanking positions. This wasn't good.

"Señor Gaylord Johnson, I am arresting you for murder. Please step away from the car and put your hands behind your back."

Eddie said, "Dad?"

Darla got out and came around the car. "What do you mean, you're arresting this man for murder?"

"Who are you, Senora?"

"I own this hotel and this man works for me." She'd over-inflated her position in an attempt to intimidate them. Since the manager had fled when the going got rough, she was the ex post facto leader of the ship that was the Punta Bandera Hotel Spa and Beach Club.

"I am sorry, Senora, please do not interfere or there will be consequences."

"It's okay. Eddie, this is just a big mistake."

"But he said *murder*? Dad, he said he's arresting you for *murder*."

I knelt in front of him. "I didn't murder anyone. This is all a big mistake."

"Where is Chief Hernandez?" Darla railed. "He knows what's going on. He knows all about Gaylord."

"This has nothing to do with the local police. This arrest is by order of the OIJ. Now please stand up and put your hands behind your back."

For a brief moment, the old Bruno wanted to come out and play, to take on all four of these men. They couldn't be as familiar with violence, which gave me a huge advantage. But I would be doing the wrong thing for the wrong reason, and the new Bruno won out.

I turned and put my hands behind my back.

Darla came up, her lips close to my ear, her breath hot and minty. "You want me to take Eddie home?"

"Yes, please, that would be great. Could you tell Marie something for me?"

The plain-clothed OIJ detective had stood aside and let one of the uniforms cuff me.

"Of course I will."

"Tell her, Rosebud."

That was the code to drop everything and bug out.

To head for Panama with all the kids.

CHAPTER FORTY-THREE

I SAT HANDCUFFED in a standard police interrogation room in a white resin chair. Well, not standard in some ways. No graffiti adorned the walls, the furniture wasn't new but still in near-pristine condition, the paint unmarred by loogies and spit from recalcitrant criminals. What kind of crooks did the Ticos have in Tamarindo?

The room size was about the same as in the States, eight by ten feet, small, confining, an interrogation tactic. I did two years in California prisons for killing my son-in-law, Derek Sams. The claustrophobic room did nothing to nudge my panic button.

I sat and worried about Marie. Had she and the kids safely escaped to Panama? Once the Tamarindo police pulled on that thread—finding out my true identity—Marie would be at risk as well. Then they would delve into our children, where they came from. Everything would unravel like a cheap sweater.

The fear for my family was the only reason stewing in a small room worked at all.

Poor Eddie would think his actions caused the Rosebud bugout.

Two hours later the door opened and in came a man in his fifties, dressed in a white shirt, black tie, and black slacks. He wore a goatee shot through with gray and a little too long, making him look more like he should've been wearing a painter's smock with a palette in one hand, a brush in the other.

He took a seat opposite mine and stared at me. I smiled at the tactic. He wanted me to squirm and suddenly belch out a confession. I stared back, playing his silly game until I closed my eyes and leaned back, tired of the pettiness.

"My name is Special Agent Joseph Tapia with the OIJ. I've been assigned to investigate the shooting at El Gato Gordo." English wasn't his first language; his syntax and word choice was careful and deliberate.

"Good for you, Joe. What does that have to do with me?" I didn't open my eyes and stayed in the lean and rest position. He smelled of burnt tobacco and coffee. My stomach growled, the only sound in the room.

He opened a file he'd brought with him; the papers whispered as he moved them about.

Then came the sound of paper being slid close to my side of the table. "Please look at this."

I didn't give him the satisfaction, didn't move or open my eyes.

He leaned back, his chair making a minor squeak. "Mr. Johnson, I have enough to hold you. In our country, unlike yours, I can hold you incommunicado for five days before I have to charge you or release you. Is that what you'd like?"

I didn't move.

"Maybe you will be more amenable after three days in one of our cells."

"Do I get to pick the menu? I'd like poached eggs for breakfast and some lumberjack pancakes with real maple syrup and a big lump of butter, not margarine."

I still had not opened my eyes.

His ploy did not work. He was under pressure by his superiors to get results. Three days was a lifetime when your bosses called five times a day demanding action on the one and only active shooter murder the country had ever experienced.

"Look at this photo. It is a picture of you dumping a body on the side of the road."

I opened one eye and looked. "That's not me. Why in the world would you think that's me? It's dark, you can't see if that guy is white, black, brown, or yellow. You can't see his face. If that's all you got, take me to my cell so I can get some sleep. What time's breakfast?"

His cellphone buzzed. With one eye open to a slit, I watched his expression. He read the text, got up, and fled.

Fatigue caught up to me—it'd been a busy day and my butt throbbed from the Waldo encounter. Thirty minutes passed; forty.

* * *

The door finally opened. The woman who'd tried to pass as a tourist at the cabana bar, now dressed in similar attire as her boss, white blouse, black tie, black slacks, said, "We thank you for your time, Mr. Johnson, you may go."

"That's it?"

She said nothing.

"So, I'm not your heinous killer after all?"

She stared at me.

"Can I at least get a ride home? Maybe some lumberjack pancakes and maple syrup for my trouble?"

"There is a car outside waiting for you and your humor is not appreciated. This is a very serious matter."

I stood, hesitated for only a second, not wanting to act too coy, and walked from the room. She led me to the exit to the rear of the Tamarindo police station. Outside, the night was cool, the constant *pelo de gato* rainy mist didn't disappoint. The birds sang a cheerful tune at my release. I took in a big chest full of free air. I didn't know what happened but wasn't going to—as the cliché goes—look that gift horse in the mouth and check his age from his teeth.

A Tamarindo police officer I'd seen before cruising around town opened a police car door. The silent woman held out her hand, indicating this was my ride home.

Before I made it over to the cop car, another one pulled into the back lot loaded with two people in custody in the rear seat: Chief Hernandez and another cop.

I waited a moment. The two cops in the transport car got out and opened the back doors. Hernandez slid out. He tried to rush over to me, his hands cuffed behind his back, his face bloated with rage. "Thisss is not over. You hear me? I won't let this take me down. I'm going in there and telling them everything. And I mean everything."

I said, "Excuse me, sir, do I know you?"

He looked about to explode, sputtering with bits of spit flying as he tried to get the jumbled words out. I asked one of the transport officers if I could have a word with the chief.

In California it would never happen, but this was the pleasant country of Costa Rica and the Ticos were kind and generous people.

I pulled the chief aside. He still wore his maroon satin smoking jacket with wide black lapels. I whispered in hushed urgency, "What's going on? Why are they letting me go and bringing you in?"

"You don't know?"

"Why would I know?"

"That puta, Darla, sent the OIJ video of my officer burying the dead man in the sand trap. I didn't know she had video. I did it because she dumped her hotel basura in my city. Then she retracted her statement, said that it wasn't you in the first video. And here I am. What are you, screwing her? That why she chose you over me? She made a big mistake. She's underestimated my power."

I didn't know what to say. Darla had stepped out of character— way out of character, standing up for me, getting me released. I suddenly remembered I'd told her the code word. My family, at that moment, could be on a bus to Panama. "I'm sorry for your troubles, Chief, but this time I had nothing to do with what you're talking about."

I started to walk away.

The police officer came up and took hold of the chief's arm, held him back as he tried to follow me. "Tell Darla Figueroa that she has too much power. Tell her I'm the chief of this town, not her. Tell her I'll get even." The two transport cops pulled him into the police station as he continued to yell expletives.

I couldn't argue with him—for a food and beverage manager of a large hotel, Darla did have too much power.

CHAPTER FORTY-FOUR

ONE O'CLOCK IN the morning, the cop car dropped me off in front of our home and took off before I even had the door all the way closed.

Rude.

Darla's white BMW was just driving away. Darla held her hand out the window in a backward wave goodbye. Had she been at the house the entire time I sat in jail? I didn't need her talking to Marie. Both women had claws and knew how to use them.

At least Marie hadn't bugged out to Panama with the kids.

The sodium vapor streetlights cast an orange tinge on everything, including the damaged Volkswagen bus that sat out front. Somebody—probably one of the kids—had put a makeshift splint and sling on the front bumper as if it had a broken arm, along with a couple of Band-Aids on the dents. The children all had great senses of humor largely due to Eddie, who used humor to disguise a deeper pain derived before he came to us.

I did play a lot of jokes on the kids whenever the moment struck. Humor made them smile, and smiles pushed out their past ugly worlds. The Band-Aids also carried the signature of Marie's involvement—making Eddie feel better about what he'd done. Toning down the guilt.

Marie, who must've been watching from the front window, came out to meet me on the flagstone walk that led up to the front door. She hugged me, her head in my chest as if she took great pleasure in listening to my heartbeat. I held on tight, never wanting to let go.

I said into the top of her head, "So, the Ice Princess didn't give you the 'Rosebud' code?"

Marie pulled back and looked up at me. "What? Why would she? She said she was going to take care of getting you out. I trust her, Bruno, and I don't like that name you've dropped on her. It's unjust."

I stepped back to get a better look at her. "Are you kidding me? You used to laugh at that moniker when I talked about her. I've told you how she treats the employees, that stupid 'blue slip' program, the way she fires people out of hand, rides all of us as if we don't know how to do our jobs."

"She has a tough job, running the food and beverages. Maybe she could be a little more diplomatic, a little more sensitive. She supervises a lot of people and carries a lot of responsibility that, at times, has to be smothering and lonely. She got you out of jail, didn't she? That says a lot about how she takes care of her employees."

"*She's the one that got me put in jail in the first place.*"

"Bruno, your voice just went all squeaky. I don't like it when you talk all squeaky." She smiled, put her arm around me. We started to walk toward the house, me with a sore limp. She stopped, inspected my front then moved around to the back—where she spotted my shredded ass cheek.

She said, "Ah, Bruno, you found Waldo."

She hugged me as if finding that damn dog meant something good.

"He about chewed my ass off and you're smiling."

"What did you do to make him chew your ass off?"

"Are you kidding me? Does he need a reason?"

"You love that dog and you know it."

"I don't know why. I did expect a little more sympathy, though."

She put her hand up to her mouth in mock horror. "That's right, that's where you house your brain. You could have brain damage. What's three plus four?"

"Very funny. Everyone's a comedian, while my ass hurts."

"Come on, I'll get my stapler."

"No, babe, not the stapler. Can't we use some good old-fashioned sutures. I like sutures."

"No." She said it definitively without any room for discussion.

"Guess what I found on the web today?" We'd stopped at the front door. Once we entered, the kids, if they were still up, would take center stage as they should. It was late, though—they should all be in bed.

"What?" My old bones suddenly wanted to give out, sit down in an easy chair, allow my mind to vegetate, think about all that had happened in the last twenty-four hours, rather than lying on my stomach and having my wife tinker with my ass cheek like an auto-body man fixing a dent.

She stopped and looked up at me.

"Okay," I said. "What did you find on the web today?"

"Aren't you going to guess?"

"Sweetie, please, these old bones are ready to drop right where I stand. Crumple up like—"

"Those three *New York Times* stories. I don't know why I didn't think of checking the web before, instead of asking for copies. How stupid, right?"

"You got a lot going on, babe. I didn't think of it either."

"Yes, but you're older and—"

"Only by a couple of years."

"Ten."

"As if I didn't feel old already."

"You going to guess what I found in those newspapers? What's the one thing that's consistent in all three?"

"I'm pretty sure I can guess what's in them."

"That right, Mr. Smarty Pants?"

Not Mr. Smarty Pants.

"Can I get a Yoo-hoo and a couple of Sno Ball cupcakes? My empty stomach is touching my backbone, wrapping around it, and starting to creep up into my throat." She usually thought my hyperbole humorous.

"All right, if you can guess what's in the newspapers you can have your darn old chocolate drink and stupid little pink cupcakes."

I smiled. "Really? Two packages, four cupcakes? And . . . and lumberjack pancakes tomorrow morning with real maple syrup."

Talking about them earlier had given me a hankering.

"Sure, it's not going to matter, though, you're not going to guess. Never in a million years."

I tried not to let out the Cheshire cat smile and couldn't help it. "The three articles are going to be about a shooting in a New York underground garage, in the Diamond District with at least four people shot or killed."

She play-punched me in the stomach, turned around, opened the door, and we went inside.

"Do I still get those cupcakes and Yoo-hoo?" She didn't turn back. "A bet's a bet, but your stomach is far from touching your backbone, little mister."

"Hey, you don't have to be mean."

I tried to keep the gloat out of my chuckle. "It was just a good guess."

I followed her into the quiet house, into the kitchen where she put out the glorious booty won in the bet. I ate and drank the elixir of the gods while standing next to the island. She left and came right back with her black medical go-bag. "Take down your pants."

"Sweetie, not right here in the kitchen, the kids might come—"

She slapped my chewed-up ass. "Ouch. Babe, take it easy, I'm tender down there."

She donned sterile latex gloves and gently pulled down my pants. "Ah, Bruno, he really did a job on you. I *am* going to have to use the stapler. I was only kidding before, but I think I really should."

"Come on, not the stapler. Seriously? You're just saying that, right?"

"But first, I'm going to have to clean it, scrub it real good. Why didn't you come right home after you did this?"

"I was a little busy getting arrested for murder. And for the record, *I* didn't do it."

I put my elbows on the counter and leaned over. She pushed, swung me around to the other side, the one with better overhead lighting. I kept eating the cupcakes from the carton of cupcakes and would until she realized her error letting the fox into the hen house. She scrubbed the wound a little too much with Betadine, scrubbed it until it hurt worse than when the damn dog first chomped. I put my head down on my arms and told her what had happened in Otis' room.

"You shot Otis in the foot? Are you kidding?" she said, while injecting the Novocain into the cheek of my gluteus maximus. I feared in the future it would be somewhat less than maximus.

She'd given me free rein over the pink coconut cupcakes with cream centers, the same as she would when giving a kid a sucker before an unwanted shot. She came forward where I could see her. "Now we have to wait for the Novocaine to work before I use the stapler, click, click, click.

You know . . . the way that bite looks, I think the scar might end up looking like a sideways happy face, with your crack being the smile."

"Is this you trying to be funny? 'Cause I'm not getting it here, not being bent over the counter with my chewed ass hanging out."

She kissed me on the cheek—the one close to my nose. "Quit being such a big baby. I'm letting you eat the cupcakes."

"Yeah, but they don't taste as good while you're working on my taillight assembly."

She ignored my comment. "You know that story in the *New York Times*, the diamond robbery? It means Salvador knew about it and was investigating. It means he was hired by someone to find this Genie guy."

"I know. Salvador's office was trashed. Someone else is doing the same thing we are. They're just a couple of steps ahead of us."

"And my guess is whoever killed all those poor folks did it to keep the truth from coming out."

My lovely wife Marie knew how to cut right to the chase.

CHAPTER FORTY-FIVE

I WOKE ON the couch covered with a handmade afghan, Eddie's head resting on my shoulder as he slept soundly, my bones and muscles frozen in place. After Marie completed the stapling of the "sideways happy face" I'd sat down on the couch, something I wouldn't be able to do once the Novocaine wore off. The last thing I remembered was Marie snuggling up to me with Tobias in her arms, feeling the emotional warmth more than the physical—and Marie's body could radiate some heat. In the little capsule that was our family, life was good. Eddie must've come looking for me later on.

Standing close around the couch, eleven children stared at me, obviously told not to wake the sleeping beast under the penalty of no cellphones or laptops for a week, the heaviest punishment in the Johnson household.

Eddie sat up rubbing his eyes, looking around trying to figure out how he ended up on the couch.

I stood, bones cracking, aching muscles moaning, the sideways happy face smiling. Alonzo, my grandson, yelped, "Let's play something." This was my day off and they knew it. I scooped up Eddie and held him under my arm pinned to my side like a sack of potatoes. He was ten but small for his age, a product of an inhospitable childhood back in the States. Children don't thrive while being abused.

I swung him around from side to side. "Anyone seen Eddie? I'm mad at him."

The smaller kids laughed, tickled at the new game. Eddie Crane's best friend and brother, Tommy Bascome, said, "Why are you mad at him? Is it because of the wounded hippie mobile out in the driveway?"

I spun around quick to face Tommy, swinging Eddie, who giggled. "What?" I said. "A wounded hippie mobile? What happened?"

The kids all shook their heads as they laughed and yelled, "Nothing happened."

They wouldn't rat out their brother.

"I'm gonna find that little kid Eddie and when I do . . . you know what I'm going to do?" I hunched over and widened my eyes.

"What? What are you going to do?"

"I'm going to—" I paused for effect. All of them held their breath. "I'm going to spank him."

We didn't spank in our house and the kids knew this was just part of the Bruno game.

"Noooo." They laughed and yelled. I took off running carrying Eddie under my arm, the kids in close pursuit. "Where is he? Someone tell me where he is."

Alonzo yelled, "Right there. He's right there." Alonzo fell on the floor giggling. I pretended to step on him, putting my foot on his stomach. "I can hear Alonzo, but I can't see him." Alonzo squirmed and laughed. "I'm right here. I'm right here."

I ran to the kitchen and around the island where Rosie stood making lunch before the siesta, smiling at the antics. I'd overslept, the morning gone. We made two circuits around the island with everyone chasing and ended up back in the living room. I dropped gingerly to the floor and stayed on my back to protect the recent injuries from the children as they piled on my chest. I roared like a lion and pretended to eat them.

Marie came in with Tobias in her arms, feeding him from a bottle. "Okay, all you little monsters, get washed up for lunch."

"Ah, come on, just a little bit more?"

She didn't answer, didn't have to. She worked her magic on the kids with expressions they understood, "the secret language." They took off, Eddie the last to leave. He stood over me waiting for me to say something.

I reached up and took his hand. "You okay?"

He nodded. "Are *we* okay?"

"Always. You don't ever have to ask."

Tears welled, he nodded and took off.

I struggled to get to my feet, the staples in both areas tugging and pulling. Marie said, "How's Waldo Junior?"

"Waldo Junior?"

"You know—that's what I named the new happy face. He has to have a name."

"Funny. Real funny."

She smiled, one that quickly vanished. "Ms. Darla Figueroa called. She said she needs you in to work the cabana bar."

"It's my day off."

"Apparently the OIJ brought Jaime in for questioning. I guess they can keep him for four or five days?"

"He's MS13. I would've brought him in a long time ago even though I know him and don't think he's involved. The OIJ are running a little behind the game. Scrambling, trying anything and everything."

"Bruno, when is this all going to be over?"

"Soon, I promise. When did she want me to come in?"

"Two hours ago, but I let you sleep. I don't like her using you as her personal puppet."

"What happened to liking her?"

"That was yesterday."

"Geez, I hope I never get on your bad side."

She came over, went up on tiptoes, and kissed me. "You'll know it when you do."

"Yeah, I'll probably wake up with my lips stapled shut."

She smiled. "That's a wonderful idea. Thanks, tiger. Come on, let's eat with the children, then I'll give you a ride to work."

I ate with the kids, showered, then Marie reapplied antibacterial cream and fresh bandages. She drove me to work in the wounded hippie mobile. On the way Marie told me Alisa had texted—said she was off to Rio to tell her daughter Layla, in person, that her father, Aleck, was dead. It wouldn't be long before Drago and his wife, Layla, returned, cutting their honeymoon short. Drago would be hard to keep out of the game. He'd want to defend his wife, find the man who'd killed her father.

When Marie turned into the drive to the hotel, for the first time since I started as a bartender, I dreaded going to work.

I found Darla working the cabana bar with Chacho, barely keeping up with the incessant demand. She scowled at me when I lifted the pass-through and entered.

I could always gauge how the shift would go by taking the temperature of the bar. That afternoon the conviviality rang in the air, the patrons drank with smiles, their voices loud, their laughs raucous. The tip jar would be full, and everyone would go home happy. Except, apparently, the Ice Princess.

She took off the waist apron, threw it down on the duckboards, came up and grabbed a fistful of my hotel aloha shirt, tried to yank me closer to her and couldn't. "I called you three hours ago."

I yawned. "I know, but I was *sleepy*."

"You were *sleepy*?"

The bar crowd heard the exchange and called me by apparently my new nickname, mocking her, "GeeJay was *Sleepy*?" Their laughter went up several decibels.

Always the professional, she let go, smoothed down my shirt, and said through gritted teeth, "If I don't get a re-up from the liquor distributor in San Jose, these fine people are all going to be drinking greyhounds, and then we'll see how they treat *GeeJay*." She stormed off without another word. I'd been Gaylord Johnson too long and should've changed my name. Now it had stuck.

"*Buenos tardes*," I yelled at her back. She kept walking and without turning around she raised her hand in the air, curled her fingers down shooting me that vulgar fickle finger of fate. The crowd roared and ordered more drinks . . . and more drinks.

Off on the beach, fifteen feet down on the sand, Rebecca Sanchez *News Six* had her back to the bar with the bright light from the cameraman filming a stand-up about the big story—the Russian in the sand trap—trying as best she could with her slippery words to link the Punta Bandera Beach Club and Spa to the El Gato Gordo nightclub massacre.

The hotel owners couldn't be happy about the violent association. The hotel needed to get their public relations machine fired up and change the narrative, get out in front of this mess before it churned everyone under, the employees, their families by proxy, and the hotel's bottom line.

I made sure the camera didn't pick me up. The last thing I needed was for American law enforcement to identify me.

Otis sat at his usual spot, his leg propped up on the stool next to him, his foot overly enlarged with white bandages to the size of a football. I checked myself for guilt and found none.

Eleven pink parasols lay on the bar in front of him. He chuckled. "She's really pissed at you this time. When she calls, she wants you to jump, huh, buddy boy?"

"What the hell happened? You were supposed to be eighty-sixed last night, kicked out of the hotel, branded persona non grata."

I found it odd he wasn't mad about getting shot in the foot. Maybe I should've been worried. But what did I have to worry about, a fat drunk with only one leg to stand on?

He shrugged. "Can I get another one of these." He held up his empty grasshopper. "And let me buy you one." He was one customer who would definitely not like having to shift from smooth and creamy, sickeningly sweet grasshoppers to the bitter sour of grayhounds; grapefruit juice and vodka.

I put a blender full of grasshoppers together, including the dash of peppermint extract, and poured him a new one in a fresh glass.

"Go on, try one, they're maddeningly addictive, almost like rock coke. Orgasmic to the tenth power."

"I'll drink one if you tell me how you tamed the savage beast and avoided your imposed exile." I held my hands out wide. "Banished from this wonderful place to the isle of Elba."

He grinned. "Buddy boy, it's the ol' cliché, money talks and bull-shit walks, never truer than in this broken-down Central American burg."

I figured that's what turned the head of the Ice Princess, the hotel's bottom line. I didn't like him calling our home a broken-down burg. I poured myself a grasshopper and took a sip.

Not quite orgasmic but damn close.

Chacho had his smile back but one made of cardboard in comparison to the Chacho of old; his eyes still grieved for his lost love, Gloria. I was worried about him. I'd seen people literally die from broken hearts.

San Jose's sweetheart, Rebecca Sanchez, finished her stand-up news story. The cameraman turned off the bright lights.

I relaxed. That camera made me nervous. Rebecca came over to the bar. An overly boisterous group of men on a golfing tour based at our hotel, who'd already had too much to drink, made room for her, shoving and pushing until a spot opened up. She didn't look at them and her eyes remained on mine. When it came to gossip, she knew the bartenders had their hands on the pulse of the hotel and even the town.

She intended on working her evil magic on me. She came around the bar to the only other spot open, the section that Otis' leg and wounded foot took up.

The lascivious glow in Otis' eyes as he watched her approach could've been mistaken for a hyena who'd just spotted a three-day-old zebra carcass abandoned on the African savanna. He brought his leg down, allowing her to slide her rump onto the stool.

He leaned over quick as a snake, grabbed my hotel aloha shirt, and whispered, or thought he was whispering, "In my next life I want to come back as that barstool she's sitting on." He winked as if I were in league with his vulgarity.

Otis leaned back and slapped the bar. "Barkeep, get the little lady a drink and put it on my tab." As if Otis would have any chance at all wooing her, but a man's gotta dream. Even the fat, ugly drunks in sour-smelling seersucker suits and mussed-over hair that could've been a rug.

"What are *you* drinking?" she asked me.

I held up the grasshopper glass I'd been sipping. It was more a desert than a cocktail.

She said, "I'll have one of those."

The drunken golfers mocked her, "She'll have one of those." They all yelled in unison.

I poured her one. And really shouldn't have. The simple action set in motion a series of events that would be talked about in conspiratorial whispers through all of Costa Rica for years to come.

CHAPTER FORTY-SIX

I AWOKE IN alien surroundings, a headache 9.5 on the Richter scale banging away in the inside of my skull. Sunlight streaming in through the sliding glass doors didn't help. Red shadows flashed on the inside of my eyelids in tune with the beat of my heart. How could it be daylight? I was working the cabana bar at night. If it were daylight, I was supposed to be home.

I remembered almost nothing of the last eight to ten hours, at least not right away. My eyelids were stuck closed. I forced them open and I realized I was in a hotel room. What the—?

I lifted my head and looked around. *I was on a hotel bed in a hotel room.* Hopefully, in a Punta Bandera Hotel room. It was one of the less expensive ones with the wall-sized framed mirror to make the room appear larger.

I lifted the sheet and looked underneath.

I was in a hotel room *and* naked.

Dear Lord.

My clothes lay on the floor, strewn from the door to the bed inter-mingled with a woman's clothes.

A woman's clothes?

I jumped to my feet, heart racing, legs wobbly. I struggled to remain standing, my body aching, the world spinning. I stepped on a torn open and empty condom packet, haphazardly discarded on the cool tile. I eased down to the floor, sat down to stop the room from gyrating, stop the nightmare scenario.

"No, no, no, no. What the hell's going on? What'd I do? What'd I do?"

Movement to the right.

Waldo's head appeared on the other side of the bed. He rested his chin on the bed and stared at me, his eyes glassy.

I said to him, "How could you let this happen? You're supposed to be my friend. Man's best friend. But with you, that's a load of crap, right?"

He pulled his head off the bed and lay back down on the floor while emitting a long groan. He still had his side wrapped with a bandage, now wadded up a little and dingy. I immediately felt bad about berating him—he had saved my life jumping that Russian with a knife and tumbling into the stream that was more a river.

I started over to him to stroke his coat and offer an apology when I noticed humidity drifting out the open bathroom door.

Steam rolled from the top, crawling along the ceiling, an ethereal beast. Through the doorway to the bathroom the fogged-over mirror meant the other person might still be here. "Marie?" *Oh please, please be Marie. Let it be Marie.*

I brought my hand up to rub the sleep out of my slack face and caught a scent. Oh my God, no. The scent was unmistakable, Hawaiian Tropic coconut oil. Wait. Wait, not the Ice Princess.

No, wait, she'd grabbed on to my shirt the night before, pulled me close. That was it. That had to be it. It wasn't the Ice Princess in the bathroom taking a shower, no way. *Please let it not be the Ice Princess.*

The buzz from my cellphone broke the loud silence that rang in my ears. Still naked, I crawled on all fours over to my cellphone in my pants pocket, fumbled around with shaky hands until I found it.

Seven calls from Marie and three text messages asking why I wasn't home. That was at three a.m. Why had they stopped coming in at three a.m.?

The newest text message: Let's talk. Otis.

The phone buzzed in my hand again, another message, this time a series of photos that he'd sent: me naked on the bed with a sappy grin, eyes half-open and glazed over from being drugged. More photos of a naked woman from her neck down, one breast resting on my chest, her long, lithe leg swung over mine, her hand resting on . . . on Bruno Johnson Junior.

I looked close for that circular bruise I'd seen the night before, the one on Darla's thigh, and didn't see it. But it could've been her other leg . . . right?

No, this woman in the photos had worn her swimsuit in the sun, the skin on her exposed breast and her bottom glowed white in comparison to the tan. And she was nothing short of va va voom. I enlarged the photo and spotted a small tattoo by the cleave of her bottom. Definitely not Darla.

The photos Otis had sent were smut and blackmail. I didn't want to believe Darla was in on this horrible charade to discredit me to my family, but her unmistakable scent did linger. Or it could've been my imagination, all of my senses skewed from the Mickey Finn Otis had slipped into my grasshopper.

Grasshoppers, plural. He must've done the dirty deed when he grabbed that handful of shirt and pulled me over to whisper in my ear about reincarnations as a barstool.

Flashes, images from the previous night's activities returned in full, blinding color. My God. I put a hand to my head and closed my eyes. We had one hell'va wild party. Out of control once the keeper of the peace, the bartender, joined in.

Did we really play football with an empty half-gallon jug of rum, run like crazed idiots out on the sand, tossing it, tackling each other? With a glass bottle? Talk about a recipe for disaster.

A night to remember.

The *now* kicked back in.

I was being blackmailed.

CHAPTER FORTY-SEVEN

THE REAL WORLD had steamrolled over our little town of Tamarindo. No one thought that kind of world would ever catch up and pollute our slice of paradise with the vulgar and the profane, but here it was. Do we run farther south to Panama where violence is an everyday staple or get smart in the world we'd chosen, deal with it, smooth it over?

Anger rose, flushing my face hot. I'd been wrong not to handle this whole mess when it first cropped up, handle it with blood and bone, tamp it down with fists and lead.

I stood on wobbly legs and went to check the bathroom to make sure I was alone. I stood at the threshold, peering in—at my underwear lying on the floor intermingled with a black lacy bra and a racy red thong.

Had the woman left without her clothes?

Not likely.

This was all part of the frame job. Otis wanted me to know who controlled who. He thought I was the Genie and he wanted his diamonds and his reputation back. To do it, he'd put me in a crack. And he'd succeeded in spades.

I'd give him something that he didn't want, a glass jug to that ugly face, knock out all of his teeth, along with a couple of bullet holes, one for each knee.

My phone buzzed again. I answered it without looking and said, "I'm coming for you and there's no place you can hide."

"Bruno?"

The voice startled me as I stood there naked at the threshold to the bathroom, swaying on my feet, sweat beading on my forehead and running into my eyes.

"Who's this?" I asked.

"Sounds like you need some help down there. I'll be on the next flight."

He'd spoken enough to recognize him: Dan Chulack, deputy director of the FBI and good friend.

"No. No. You don't need to come down here. I'm about to take some positive action that will resolve this entire situation."

Silence for a long moment. Then, "Bruno, don't . . . ah, don't be Bruno down there. It's your home, you don't want to mess that up. Step gently, my friend. Think it through first, please."

He was right, of course, common sense from someone not involved personally, someone without super-heated emotions. "Thank you, that's good advice."

Another long pause.

"Are you calling because of the water glass I sent you? The one I need the fingerprints checked on."

"Yes, I've been waiting for it and it hasn't arrived."

I closed my eyes and put my head against the doorframe to the bathroom. Darla must have diverted it from Mary St. John, the concierge. Of course, she did. Darla knew everything that happened in her hotel.

"That's on me. I trusted someone to send it off when I should've handled it myself."

"I understand. You sure you don't want me to take some personal time, come down there and lend a hand? I've been following the story on the news—that shooting has to be a real mess. Are you caught up in it? Is that why you sent me the glass?"

"To tell you the truth, I don't know what's going on. I'm getting close though. Are you familiar with a Diamond District rip that occurred in New York with the cartel and the Russian mob involved, nine-ten months ago?"

Another pause.

"Bruno, if you're caught up in that mess, you're going to need some help. We're tracking it. It's turned into a turf war between the Russians and the South American Cartel. Is that what happened in your nightclub? Is it spillover?"

"Seems to be. Besides the six dead in the nightclub, three Russians have been taken off the board."

"That was you?"

I didn't answer right away.

"Never mind, don't answer that. I wasn't thinking."

"There are two or three other Russians here now with more on the way if I don't resolve this thing soon."

"Do you know Chief Hernandez down there?"

"Yes, and as it turns out, he's part of the problem."

"I understand. He sent the Bureau some expanded 9mm rounds and shell casings for comparison. Hernandez has his own lab down there, I don't know why he sent them to us. I found out about it when I inquired about the water glass for fingerprints that never arrived."

"Yeah, I asked the chief to send it, but that was a shot in the dark. Now I know it's not relevant to the nightclub shooting. No way."

Anxiety started to rise. I wanted to be dressed and out of the jack-pot Otis had left me in. I wanted to get over to Otis' room and have a little talk with him, do some dirty work, punch some holes in his knees with Big Bertha, his own gun.

I moved into the room, gathering up my clothes with the phone pinned to my shoulder.

Dan said, "I don't know about that, but the bullets and casings are a direct match. No doubt about it."

The phone dropped to the floor as I wilted to my knees. Dan's voice grew small and tinny. I grabbed up the phone, staying on my knees. "Say again?"

"The two sets of bullets and casings Chief Hernandez sent in are a match. They came from the same gun."

Otis' gun had been the one used in the nightclub shooting.

His gun had killed six people.

Two of them close friends.

Otis was the killer.

How had I missed it?

CHAPTER FORTY-EIGHT

I STOOD IN the hotel room stunned at the new information relayed by Dan Chulack, deputy director of the FBI. I couldn't get my mind around it. Otis was the cold, calculated killer who shot dead six people.

Otis, a drunk, someone who sat at the bar all day, every day in the same sour-smelling seersucker suit, drinking sugary drinks. Fat, out of shape Otis. How could he have stepped up onto the bar stool, then up onto the bar that night in El Gato Gordo while carrying all that weight? How could he have a steady enough hand, one that could target six people without missing? Steely cool accuracy.

He'd said he could take any torture I could hand out. He had black ops training in his background.

Unless that was just braggadocio.

He was the one: he'd done it.

From the bathroom came a long, low moan.

"Ah, shit."

"What?" Dan asked.

"Hey, thanks for the phone call. I really have to get moving."

"I understand. You call me if you need anything at all."

"I will. Thanks again, Dan."

I hung up and peeked back into the bathroom. The ringing in my ears had masked the other low-level ambient sound from the shower spray that hit the curtain and wall. The warm water made steam that rose in the air, filling the space with a misty cloud that roiled out.

On the other side of the curtain something hit the plastic in a blurry shadow, a hand. I jumped out of the bathroom then peeked around the doorframe.

I eased into the bathroom and pulled the curtain aside. A woman, soaking wet. She barely filled the bathtub. Petite, tanned, leggy.

A naked woman.

My God, another naked woman.

She moaned again and turned to her side away from me, still unconscious from the Mickey Finn.

What was it with the women in this hotel and their clothes?

The woman's dark hair—darker with the water—plastered across her face kept me from identifying her.

On her lower back just above the cleave to a perfectly heart-shaped bottom, a tattoo of a dolphin leapt from the ocean, small, expensive, done with great detail and color and, most of all, tasteful.

I pulled up the blackmail picture Otis sent me on my phone, held it up for comparison. Yep, the same woman, thank goodness. I mean, if it had been a different one—well—I'd start looking around for Sean Connery.

The way to handle the situation wouldn't endear me to her, but I couldn't see any other way. I took the fluffy white hotel robe hanging off the back door and held it open. Then I leaned down and turned off the hot water. The cold water hit her. She held up both hands to fend off the unfair treatment, coughed, and sputtered and choked. She cried out, "Stop. Turn it off. Turn it off." She smeared the hair out of her face.

I stepped back yet again, stunned.

Holy shit. Rebecca Sanchez from *News Six*.

The Darling of Costa Rica.

Otis really put me in the jackpot this time.

She struggled to her feet, a newly born fawn on weak legs, her eyes dazed, trying to figure out what had happened, how she ended up in a strange black man's bathtub when the last thing she remembered was partying at the cabana bar.

I knew the feeling.

Her mouth dropped open when she looked down and realized she was naked. She straightened up, her eyes going steely like strong women tended to do when confronted with adversity.

She stepped from the tub. I stepped back still holding up the robe, trying not to look. I said, "Wait. Just wait a second and let me explain."

She pulled back and hit me with a palm strike to the chest. "You bastard."

"No, wait. It's not what you think."

The evil Bruno inside me took control of my eyes and wouldn't let them move back to hers, not soon enough anyway. They lingered on her wet breasts . . . her lovely wet breasts, slick with beads of water, breasts that jostled together when she gave me the palm strike to the chest.

I pulled my eyes away.

The residue from the Mickey Finn clouded logical thought, obscuring good manners. I wouldn't have peeked in normal circumstances. I know I wouldn't have.

Right?

I held up the robe and backed away from her. "Wait. Wait. I was drugged too."

She didn't hear me. Unabashed, she followed me into the bedroom, still stark naked.

In the large mirror on the wall, Waldo had risen again and rested his head on the bed, watching the domestic interplay in his front-row seat.

Rebecca swung again.

I ducked.

Her momentum skewed from the miss left her off balance. I scooped her up around the waist, tossed her on the bed, and pinned her, lying across her slippery wet body. She fought, slapping and clawing.

"Hold it. Hold it. Let me explain. Let me show you something."

"I've seen plenty enough already, mister."

She wouldn't give in and continued abusing my fifty-year-old body. I ducked my head and held on. She ran out of steam and stopped flailing, my face pressed to her chest that heaved for air, her heart racing.

I got up, recovered the robe from the floor, and covered her. My face and back and arms stung from her nails raking off top layers of skin. These new injuries would help foster a claim of rape, burying me deeper in the jackpot. Waist deep like the dead Russian in the sand trap.

She sat up breathing hard and tried to shrug into the robe. I turned my back and allowed her some privacy. The good Bruno having won out over the evil one. With my back to her I said, "I was drugged, too. We were both set up."

She must've seen the used condom package on the floor. "You bastard, you raped me." She attacked again, punching and clawing. I stood and took it, ashamed for the situation, ashamed that I'd been ignorant enough to fall for Otis and his honeytrap.

She again ran out of steam and sat down on the bed, out of breath. I found the second robe, put it on. "I didn't rape you. I was unconscious just like you, so I couldn't have . . . ah, performed even if I wanted to."

"Likely story. Of course, you'd say something like that. I'm going to have your ass in prison. You'll do twenty years."

Her words took my breath away. I couldn't allow her to report this to the police. No way could I be wanted in another country, the country we'd chosen to call our own. The country where we chose to raise our kids.

My God, what would the kids think of their surrogate father?

The old Bruno straightening my back as my now deceased boss, Robby Wicks, whispered in my ear. "Son, looks like this time you've gone shit the bed but good."

CHAPTER FORTY-NINE

I SAT DOWN next to Rebecca Sanchez, the Darling of Costa Rica, both of us in hotel robes recovering from drug-induced unconsciousness. I had to somehow work my way out of this mess. I had to.

"Don't you dare sit next to me. Get the hell away." She tried to shove me but didn't have the weight to get it done.

I showed her my phone and cued up the text message: LET'S TALK. OTIS.

"That doesn't mean a damn thing." She tried to slap the phone out of my hand. I moved it out of the way and cued up the photos.

"This came with that text message." I showed her the photos. "He's the real bastard. This wasn't me. I promise."

Confusion clouded her expression. She looked again at the photos and then up at me, searching my eyes for the truth, and found it. "Why?"

I said, "You're just a pawn caught up in a dirty game, that's all. He used you to get at me. I woke up naked on the bed and found you in the shower with the water running. I lost about eight or ten hours of time, just like you. They must've left the room as I woke up."

"Who? Why? I remember drinking at the bar last night, watching that goofy football game and that's . . . that's it." She got up, went into the bathroom, came out with a wet washcloth.

She stood in front of me and daubed at my face. "I . . . I'm sorry I did this to you." Tears ran down her cheeks. "You still haven't told me why and who."

"I'm thinking."

"About what? After what I've been through, you owe me that much."

"Yeah, maybe it's the right thing to do, blow this thing wide open."

She'd been a reporter long enough to sense a story when it rose up and nibbled at her ears. "Tell me."

"You remember last night, the guy with the bandaged foot?"

"That perv, all he did was ogle me. He's the one who did this? How? He can hardly walk on his own."

"He had help."

"Why? Tell me why."

"Can I trust you to leave me out of it? I have a wife and kids. I live and work in this community."

"Wait, what are you saying?" Her eyes came alive, anxious to hear the rest. She said, "And if I don't?"

"Promise you'll leave me out of it. I'm an anonymous source."

She pursed her lips, thinking through the options. "I don't have enough information to make that promise. Whether the information will be worth it or not."

"Oh, trust me, it'll be worth it."

"All right, you have my word."

"Shake on it." I held out my hand. She took it.

"Now give."

"You know that guy with the foot, Otis. His real name's not Otis."

She waited for the rest. Now I wasn't sure if giving her the information was the right tactic. I wished I could call and talk to Marie, she'd know what to do. She'd tell me the answer without even hesitating. "I'm working on the El Gato Gordo shooting. I guess I was getting too close."

Her eyes went wide. She jumped to her feet. "Oh, my God." She paced back and forth, her robe flapping open and closed, flashing smooth, tanned thigh. She stopped and pointed a finger. "Wait. What are you saying? You're a bartender. How can you . . ."

I couldn't tell her my background, the part about being a Los Angeles County sheriff's deputy who chased violent criminals all over Southern Cal. I couldn't risk her finding out my real name and fugitive status. I got up, went to my pants, and showed her the private investigator's ID, the one Salvador got for me when he'd tried to entice me into helping out with his business. The thing did actually have a purpose.

"You're a PI?"

"On the side, yes."

"And you figured this whole thing out when the Tamarindo cops and the OIJ haven't? That's what you want me to believe?"

I held my arms out wide. "What do you think? Why would someone do this to me, to us, if I wasn't getting too close."

The lie caught and hung on my conscience, a coin about to drop in a sewer grate. Dad had drilled into me that an omission was the same as a lie. I hadn't told her all of it. About the gun, the ballistics comparison match. About how Otis thought I was Genie, a gem thief wanted for the murder of four men in an underground parking garage in New York.

She sat down on the bed beside me and placed her hand on my thigh, trying to work me. I liked her a lot less for it.

She said, "Tell me the rest."

She wanted the story—the biggest one to hit Costa Rica in decades. She'd be able to name her price the next time her contract came around. She might even be able to parlay the story into a seat at the big table in the U.S. networks.

"I don't know for sure; I won't speculate. What I *can* do is promise you that I'll give you an exclusive as soon as I know."

"No chance. I'm in this now." She pointed to the phone in my hand. "Those pictures can ruin me."

"Not if you get out in front of it."

"What are you sa— Wait. Wait, you're saying I should tell the world that . . ." She stood and paced again. "That I should come out ahead of these pictures and say . . . and say what? Wait, that I was investigating the shooting, *and like you* got too close and the bad guys are trying to blackmail me?"

She grabbed the phone from my hand. "Here, type in your code. I want to see them again, the photos."

I did as she asked.

"She moved the phone from side to side looking at herself naked lying across a black man in a hotel room bed, trying to imagine the story. "These aren't bad pics of me, not really . . ."

"Come on, you know you look sexy as hell."

"This could be big, I mean huge . . . Wait. But what if we can't get this guy Otis to talk, to admit that he's trying to blackmail me . . . and you, of course? Then these pictures turn back into exactly what they look like—a drunken tryst."

"What other option do you have?"

Her words "drunken tryst" hit like a gut punch. I still had to explain this mess to my poor dear wife Marie. My misstep would hurt her terribly. The anger rose and flushed my face hot. Otis did this, he created all this pain and grief. I needed more than anything else to have a talk with him, whisper in his ear what was about to happen before I shot him in the knee.

"I'll get Otis to talk. You have a tape recorder?"

She jumped up, ran to her discarded purse. "Of course I do." She came back with a small digital recorder and handed it to me. "But you have your phone, that works as a recorder."

"If—no—when he talks, he'll want control over my phone." Not really, just more fodder to make her believe the scenario.

She sat back down next to me, this time her naked thigh touching mine, her skin hot to the touch. Made me wonder how many times she'd used the same ploy on the more gullible.

"How do I know you can get him to talk?"

"You know why his foot is all bound up?"

She shook her head.

"Because *I* shot him in the foot."

Her expression shifted from enchantress to fearful innocent. She slowly eased away from me, the color draining from her face. She'd caught a glimpse of the old Bruno. The blood and bone Bruno.

CHAPTER FIFTY

I STUCK MY head out the hotel room door and checked both ways down the hall, making sure no one would see me exit. Rebecca Sanchez agreed to wait ten minutes before leaving. We'd both dressed on opposite sides of the room with our backs turned, pulling clothes on under our robes.

From the big mirror I caught Waldo on her side watching her every move. Maybe my old boss Robby Wicks *had been* reincarnated as a dog named Waldo. It wasn't the first time that thought had occurred to me.

Pure sci-fi, mentally unstable ideas.

I eased the door closed and headed for the elevator, headed to the ground floor, to Otis' room, a large helping of blood and bone tartar on the menu. Waldo came along and sat next to my leg. I pushed the button to call the elevator car and waited as the memory from the last twenty-four hours sped past, including the conversation with Dan Chulack, what he'd said about not being "Bruno," a direct contradiction to what needed to be done. And then what the deceased Robby Wicks had whispered in my ear: "Son, looks like this time you've gone shit the bed but good."

I put my head against the wall and closed my eyes. Of course, it was the wrong tactic going to Otis' room. For one thing it's what he'd want, what he'd expect. In the days of old, that wouldn't have mattered. I would've bulled my way through, ambush or not, laid down the law, made him pay what he owed for his actions against me and my family.

But we'd just had a baby—a lovely baby boy named Tobias. I also had twelve other kids who depended on me . . . and Marie. I had to think about her first. I had to talk to her, show her the blackmail photos before someone else, like Otis, used them against me to hurt her worse. I needed to take the fangs from the blackmail photos by showing Marie. I didn't want to hurt her, but there was no way around it.

The elevator arrived. I got in, the blood-red revenge in my eyes having dissipated. I took the car to the lobby and headed out, headed for home. I stopped at the concierge desk where Mary St. John covered the shift. "Hey."

"Hey, yourself." She had the most marvelous hazel eyes that complemented her smile, the perfect job that fit her personality, easygoing with a kind voice.

She had a crazy boyfriend named Hector, who talked about himself in the third person as "Jimmy." She deserved better.

"Did you by chance mail off that package I left on your desk?" I could still use that leverage on Darla, something to bring her around at least a little to my side. She'd be a formidable ally.

"What package?" Her eyes shifted to regret. She started opening drawers. She froze when she opened the second one down, left side.

There sat the box with the water glass that had Darla Figueroa's prints. "Oh, Bruno, I'm so sorry. I'll go do it right now. Hey, this is addressed to the FBI in Virginia."

I quickly looked around to see if anyone heard. She caught my consternation and put her hand to her mouth. I almost reached for the package, said that I'd take care of it, but higher priorities prevailed. I had to get home to Marie. "Would you mind, please?" I asked.

She held my eyes a moment longer. "Sure, not a problem. I'll run it over there right now." She locked her desk and then answered the phone.

She was one of the smartest people I knew, but at times, her mind spun a million miles an hour and things could slip through the cracks.

Over by the front door, the doorman, Felix Hurtado, held the door for Chacho, who came through lugging a dolly loaded with boxes of top-shelf liquor headed for the Lido Cabana bar. I should lend a hand but didn't have time.

I said, "Why are you taking that through the lobby instead of through the loading dock?"

He shook his head and nodded back the way he came, the move clear in its explanation. There could be only one reason: the Ice Princess. According to her, "Nothing went through the lobby except patrons," a bluie-worthy violation. But today it did make sense, all that alcohol going directly to the depleted cabana bar rather than into the storage room first and then out to the Lido Cabana, where the booze could be immediately deployed.

I let Felix hold the door for me. Outside at the edge to the porte cochere sat a huge delivery truck with a hydraulic lift loaded with cardboard cases, beer and liquor, enough booze to party for days.

My headache pounded worse just at the thought. Our supply had been seriously eroded by the violence in our little town. The night-club massacre and the dead Russian planted in the sand trap, all the imbibers trying their best to smother the world's unfortunate reality.

Darla Figueroa stood by holding a clipboard and pencil, marking off every bottle and can that entered her fine establishment.

She never let one detail get past her. I guess if I owned a hotel I'd want someone like her looking out for my interests.

She looked up from the clipboard and glared at me. "That damn dog."

I pretended ignorance. "What dog?" Waldo sat right next to my leg, his haunch on my foot. In his good moods he always wanted to be touching me.

Her eyes suddenly shifted away from me. She said, "Mary, where do you think you're going? You're only halfway through your shift."

Mary had tried to slip out the front door to her little red Honda without being seen. She hesitated, not knowing what to say. "I . . . ah forgot to mail this. It's ah, a personal thing but it's time sensitive." Her eyes slid over to me. She'd just lied to the Ice Princess, a rare violation, like pilfering, that carried instant termination.

Darla held out her hand. "Here, leave it with me. I'm going that way as soon as I finish this."

No one moved, all three of us checking each other out like we'd just stepped into an Alfred Hitchcock thriller and didn't know which way to jump for cover. Cue the suspense-filled music.

How would Ms. St. John explain the package addressed to the FBI with the hotel as a return address? It wouldn't go well.

I wouldn't let her take the rap. I'd fall on the sword first and cop out to the package. But in all likelihood, it wouldn't matter in the Ice Princess' world. Mary would get canned as well, a coconspirator in the lie.

"That's okay." Mary wielded the box like it was no big deal. "It's my mom's birthday present, and I really need to get it in the mail."

Darla gave her a crooked smile that had danger written all over it. "What, you don't trust me with a little geegaw you're sending your mom? Really?"

Mary had told me once that people who said "Really?" as a question really got on her nerves.

"What about your shift at your desk? Who'll cover it?"

Mary was not a good liar. If I saw the lie plain on her face, so did the Ice Princess.

Mary lowered her already-too-soft voice and said, "I . . . ah, ran out of . . . items I need at the *drugstore*." She squinched her eyes and nose when she said it trying to give her reply a top secret meaning only known between women.

Not much of a code to break. Mary was just too innocent to pull it off.

"Fine, just hurry. You can make up the time by staying later."

Mary nodded, hurried away. "Yes. Yes. I will. Thank you."

Darla turned her glare back to me. "Well, cowboy, you almost found your skinny hips in the unemployment line for fraternizing with the guests, drinking and getting blitzed while at work. And if—"

I cut her off. "If it hadn't been the biggest sales night in the history of the hotel."

It was only a guess. She'd obviously replayed the video of the night's activities and witnessed all the drunken debauchery.

I really needed to see that recording, see what happened at the night's end, see how I'd made it back to the room with Rebecca Sanchez. I could only guess that Otis had the two Russians on his side now working with him to get the diamonds back, to recover his nefarious reputation by tossing me into the jackpot.

Darla sauntered up to me, moved her mouth close to my ear, and whispered, "You surprise me, cowboy."

"Me? Really?" I tried to pull away, but she held onto my arm.

"Yeah, I thought you were a happily married man."

Visions plagued me, her tanned and slathered body with Hawaiian Tropic oil, long and lithe; her cool and unabashed demeanor on the hotel roof flashed back and caused me to swallow hard.

Sweat broke out on my brow. I had no other cards to throw and played dumb. "What are you talking about?"

She leaned in even farther, took my earlobe in between her teeth, and gently bit, her warm moist breath sending a shiver up and down my back. I pulled away.

"Come on, cowboy, don't be that way."

"I have to get home."

I tried to walk away.

She followed, her high heels clicking on the cobblestones behind me. In a hushed whisper she said, "What was she like?"

A vulgar, locker room question. "But more important," she said, "what does Rebecca have that I don't?"

I took off running for home. I needed to see Marie, beg her forgiveness.

Behind me, the Ice Princess let go with a haughty laugh.

CHAPTER FIFTY-ONE

THE ENTIRE TWO miles walking home I continued to replay the words needed to explain what had happened. My severe error in judgment, drinking while on duty. No words worked, every one of them came out harsh and hurtful. Ignorant even. I had only intended to sip that damn grasshopper and ended up drinking two, one of which Otis had spiked with the Mickey Finn.

Marie would believe me. Sure, she would. The pain on her face would hurt the same as a spear through the chest.

She didn't deserve it.

I had to slow several times for Waldo to catch up. He didn't feel well. I needed to get him to the vet. Probably an infection from the knife wound, the slash along his side. He also needed his bandages changed. The night before he seemed okay, playing vodka-bottle football with all of us, romping in the sand.

I slowed and came to a complete stop as I approached our estate. Parked out front sat a white Mercedes coupe, Alisa and Aleck's car. Well, just Alisa's car now. Last I heard she was headed down to Rio to tell her daughter about her father's brutal death while he sat in the El Gato Gordo nightclub entertaining a strange woman.

"Well, boy, time to face the music," I said to Waldo. He looked up with sad eyes, watery eyes. I patted his head.

He nipped at my hand.

I yanked it from harm's way just in time. His jaws clacked on empty air. "You're not that sick. Come on, we'll get Marie to change your bandage and give you some antibiotics."

I opened the front door wishing I had a hat to throw in ahead to test the water.

Marie appeared around the corner to the great room holding Tobias, gently rocking him in her arms. I took him from her, smiling to hide the severe trepidation about being out all night without calling . . . as well as the other small thing, the naked woman in the hotel room . . . the Darling of Costa Rica, Rebecca Sanchez.

Marie gave Tobias over, went up on tiptoes, and kissed my cheek, left her hand there a moment longer.

"What have you been into? You get scratched on the bougainvillea again? I told you before, you should pay someone to trim those, someone who knows what they're doing."

Heavy guilt darkened my day. I didn't deserve her.

"Oh, and I don't know how to trim simple flowering plants?"

I tried to make it sound light, like our usual banter, and missed the mark.

"What?" she asked. "What's going on?"

She'd caught my emotional shift.

"I'm sorry for staying out all night."

She shrugged. "The Ice Princess called and explained about the big party and that it was going all night. You must be exhausted. Come in and say hi to Alisa."

She said the last part loudly so Alisa in the great room could hear. Marie whispered, "She has something to tell us but wanted to wait for you. She wants both of us to hear, said she couldn't bear to say it a second time."

I whispered, "Seriously?"

Marie whispered back, "I know. It's been killing me too."

She took hold of my arm and tugged me along. "Come on."

Emotions rose up inside me. I wanted to tell Marie about what happened in the hotel room, but the evil Bruno on my shoulder whispered that I might get away with it if I just kept mum.

I could never do that.

Could I?

No.

I had to tell her and soon before the secret turned septic and poisoned my blood.

I thanked the Lord for Tobias, warm and cuddly in my arms, the cutest baby ever. He tamped down those heated emotions and made life tolerable at least until I could get Marie alone to tell her.

Alisa sat in the great room, the big couch enveloping her, dwarfing her petite figure. She sat, her hands clasped in her lap, dark half-moons under her eyes. She'd aged ten years since the last time I'd seen her—since Aleck had died in the nightclub killings.

I recognized her terrible dilemma. She too carried a beast on her back, a dark secret that had to be told or she'd be consumed by it.

Alisa's appearance and demeanor forced down my issue even further. I wanted to help her anyway I could.

I sat in the loveseat across the coffee table from her. Marie sat close to me, her leg touching mine. Her body heat a warm comfort.

No one spoke. Finally, I said, "What's going on, Alisa?"

Fat tears chose that moment to roll down her cheeks. Marie got up, grabbed a tissue box, and sat next to her. Put her arm around her, pulled her in tight.

I was jealous, a stupid reaction under the circumstances. I wanted Marie's arms wrapped around me, consoling me over what happened the night before. As if I, too, were a victim of some vicious circumstance instead of ignorantly falling prey to a fat, smelly man in a seersucker suit.

The only sounds in the room came from Alisa sobbing and Tobias happily gurgling; as a child he had nothing to worry about but food in his stomach and messy diapers.

Lucky little guy.

We waited some more.

Alisa broke the consoling embrace and moved inches away from Marie.

"I'm so sorry we fell out as friends over that silly relationship with Drago and Layla. We prejudged Drago—I mean me . . . and Aleck. We know that now. After we saw how he treated Layla and Daphne we felt like absolute fools."

She still used "We."

Marie knew enough not to interrupt once she started talking and gently patted Alisa's hand.

"Part of it—" Alisa said, and stopped. "Part of it was that Aleck and I were not doing well. In fact, we were talking about divorce."

For the briefest flash, I plugged Alisa in as the shooter for the El Gato Gordo slaughter. Spouses always popped up as number one suspects.

I quickly dismissed the stupid idea, her ability to step up on that stool, her small hands holding that big gun, the ability to tactically handle the moving targets—no chance.

"Oh my God, Alisa," Marie said. "I'm so sorry. We didn't know."

Now Marie gripped Alisa's hands in both of hers.

Alisa stared into Marie's eyes. "You and Bruno didn't know?"

Marie sat back a little. "What? Of course not. Why would we know?"

"I just thought that Aleck might've confided in you. That you . . . that you were better friends with him than . . . me."

"No, that's not the case at all. You and I are best friends. We would've talked to you if Aleck had said anything to us. We are so sorry for what's happened."

Alisa sobbed. More tears ran down her cheeks. She nodded, agreeing with Marie.

Marie stood. "Let me get you some iced tea."

Alisa reached out, put her hand on Marie's, stopping her. "Wait, please. That's not what I came here to tell you."

Marie sat back down, shot me a quick look, and wagged her eyebrows. Alisa stared at Marie as if trying to decide to spill what really bothered her.

"It's okay," Marie said. "We're here for you."

I sat there more a ghost, a fly on the wall watching the scene play out.

Alisa said, "I did something terrible and the guilt is eating me alive."

Her and me both.

"Nothing is that bad," Marie said. "It's always better to get it out; it'll unburden you. We're your good friends. You can tell us anything."

I hoped Marie felt the same way after I unburdened my blunder.

Alisa reached into her clutch purse and took out her cellphone. She gripped it until her fingers turned white.

We waited for her to tell us.

"I . . ." she said and stopped. We waited some more.

"I . . . ah, hired Salvador Rivera to follow Aleck."

She broke down and wept, letting out a little moan that was more a wail.

I sat back on the couch, stunned. Salvador was at El Gato Gordo the same night as Aleck. Salvador was there to peep Aleck to see who Aleck was meeting?

Had to be.

CHAPTER FIFTY-TWO

I SET TOBIAS down on the couch and left my hand on him so he couldn't roll off. He was too young to roll, but I needed the added peace of mind. "What's on your phone?" I said to Alisa.

Marie shot me the evil eye, meaning I wasn't supposed to push Alisa in her delicate state.

I said, "She held out her phone—there's something on it she wants to show us. Isn't that right, Alisa?"

Had Otis texted the photos of me and Rebecca Sanchez intertwined, naked on a king-sized bed? Was that what she was hesitant in showing us? That would explain her trepidation. But it was a non sequitur with what she'd just revealed about Salvador following Aleck.

Paranoia clouded common sense.

"Bruno?" Marie said, her tone going up several octaves right alongside my blood pressure, my heart at a full gallop.

Alisa looked from me to Marie. Alisa rode the fence whether to tell us the rest. She needed a little nudge.

Instead, we waited some more.

Alisa finally tapped in her code and opened the photo app. She stared down at the device in her hand, still afraid to release her demon to the world.

Alisa handed Marie the phone.

Marie looked up at me, now unsure if she even wanted to know. I picked up Tobias, handed him off to Marie, and took the phone from her hand.

I stood by them both and hit the little arrow on the frozen video frame that started playing.

I immediately recognized the location, inside El Gato Gordo—night with low mood lighting and flickering candles on the tables. I brought it closer to my eyes. This was the night the active shooter rained down death on the unsuspecting. I recognized the people from what they wore, how afterward the way they looked inert, fear carved in their granite-like expressions.

Based on Salvador's video, he sat at the bar surreptitiously filming while the bartender talked with him.

The bartender came into the frame.

Jaime Lopez.

What the hell was Jaime doing working at El Gato Gordo?

Then I remembered something he'd said a long time back. He had a large family in Mexico he supported. He was a hard worker. He must have been working every open slot he could find. No wonder the OIJ picked him up and were holding him for investigation.

Salvador's voice was difficult for me to hear. He had been a good friend, gone now forever.

They spoke about the local soccer game, argued about which country's team was better, as the phone video panned the room and stopped over in the corner.

I used two fingers to enlarge the scene.

My God. I looked up at Alisa. Tears ran down her cheeks, her chin quivered. She nodded.

"What is it?" Marie reached up and pulled the phone down where she could see it.

Aleck sat at a round, two-person table with a white tablecloth and red roses in a vase. No other table had red roses. Aleck still wore the suit he'd worn to the wedding on the beach hours before, Layla and Drago's wedding. Aleck's elbows on the table, he held the hands of a beautiful woman. He pulled her over close and kissed her lips, a deep adoring kiss. An unmistakable kiss wrapped in love, that same emotion returned in kind.

The woman:

Rebecca Sanchez.

The Darling of *News Six*.

No wonder Rebecca wanted into the El Gato Gordo story—what better way to control it? Everybody involved in the shooting seemed to be churning round and round in a mysterious vortex, all suspects dancing, waiting for the music to stop to grab a chair.

Marie gently bounced Tobias in her arms. "That's Rebecca Sanchez. Oh my God, that's actually Rebecca Sanchez."

The bottom dropped out of my world. If she reacted like that to the video, how would she react to what I had to tell her?

And my story involved nakedness and a hotel room with the same woman.

Aleck was stepping out with Rebecca Sanchez. Salvador Rivera caught it on video from the bar while he talked with Jaime as a cover. Then how had Salvador ended up over by the table with Gloria, both dead on the floor?

Gloria was a waitress who had access to the entire place. Coincidence and circumstance hand in hand also danced together that night.

The phone video changed the dynamic of how I'd pictured the shooting going down. Jaime Lopez, MS13 member, could easily come from the back dressed in the London Fog, the black wingtips, hat and scarf around his face and blasted those six people. He worked at the Lido bar and had access to Otis' room, or could have if he really wanted.

But he needed a motive, a reason why. I couldn't ask him—the OIJ had him sequestered. The OIJ would never get a confession out of a hard-core gang member. Jaime would know the game better than his captors. Someone had paid him to do the dirty deed. But who?

The video left no doubt of Aleck's intentions with Rebecca.

Rebecca had conveniently left out the part about being in El Gato Gordo the night of the shooting, the part about how she'd witnessed the entire event and slithered out in all the chaos. She too was playing a dangerous game.

Marie sat down next to Alisa, still gently bouncing Tobias, and put her other arm around her. She whispered to Alisa, "It's over now. It's all over. I know it hurts right now, but time will heal the pain. Just take it one day at a time. Okay?"

Alisa nodded and wept. "Thank you, you are good friends. It does feel better already, telling someone about what I did, not trusting Aleck and having him followed. I just couldn't go tell Layla about what happened until I told someone. The secret was poisoning me. I was sick about it. Thank you."

"What you did? What are you talking about?" Marie said. "You did nothing wrong. Aleck did this."

"And that slut Rebecca Sanchez," Alisa said, a wild fire returning to her eyes in a sudden burst.

"Yes, her too."

Oh, dear Lord. My turn was next to barf out a confession that involved Rebecca Sanchez.

I backed up to the love seat, my legs hit, and I sat-fell. I busied myself watching the video three more times, memorizing the people, where they sat, the table and chair configuration.

When I came out of my trance, I sent the video to my phone.

The time stamp placed the video occurring moments before the shooting. Salvador must've texted the video to Alisa seconds before he was shot and killed. That may have been the distraction that kept him from seeing the threat unfold.

He didn't know he was about to be shot.

I envisioned how it went down. The suspect climbed up on the bar on the left side of Salvador, while Salvador recorded the tryst off to the right, his fingers manipulating the phone, sending the video to Alisa.

I could easily imagine how, at the first shot, the loud retort, Salvador backed up from his place at the bar and bumped into Gloria Perez, Chacho's girlfriend, the waitress, holding a round serving tray filled with cocktails. Salvador's first instinct was to protect her against the threat. He was that kind of man. He moved to cover her with his body. The movement caught the shooter's eye and Salvador took two bullets to the back.

But the real question, the most important one: Who was the first person shot?

And who paid Jaime to do the deed?

The answer was as obvious as the nose on my face. Alisa was rueful over hiring Salvador Rivera to follow her husband.

No, the second half to the ugly secret she had not yet revealed was that she'd hired Jaime Lopez, an MS13 member, familiar with meting out violence.

Alisa couldn't have known Jaime would shoot five other people to cover his tracks. The guilt, ugly and black, had to be smothering her.

Death worked that way, a malignancy that ate a person like a fast-acting cancer.

CHAPTER FIFTY-THREE

Marie calmed Alisa and sent her on her way twenty minutes later. I sat with Tobias asleep in my arms. I should've stopped Alisa, kept her talking, weaseled out of her the whole truth about hiring Jaime Lopez. That's Interrogation 101; once a murder suspect starts talking, you don't stop them.

But that could wait. I was more concerned about my wife. I could call Chief Hernandez later and tell him they had the right guy in custody and that he needed to bring in Alisa.

Marie disappeared into the other room and returned with her medical bag. She knelt next to Waldo. "Poor guy." She gently stroked his fur, checked his eyes and his mouth, his heartbeat.

"I know. He's not himself. I'm glad you're taking a look at him."

She clipped off his old bandage while she talked. "What's going on, Bruno?"

"What do you mean?"

The woman could read me.

"You have that look about you, like a kid who stole a candy bar from the store and the guilt is killing him."

I'd chased murderers for years, lived through many violent confrontations, knew how the criminal world worked, and she could bring me down with a candy bar analogy.

"How's Waldo?"

She looked up from applying antibacterial cream on the wound, the sutures.

He got sutures. I got staples.

"He's fine—he's hungover, Bruno. Dogs aren't supposed to drink alcohol. Tell me about your candy bar, little man."

The last part, her calling me "little man," pulled me from the sudden revelry regarding the previous night, Waldo running around in the sand with the golfers playing vodka-bottle football, only stopping long enough to slurp down another Modelo beer.

Otis' comment about the sound generated by his slurp: "That sound reminds me of sloppy sex."

I swallowed hard, my voice coming out in a choked whisper. "It's much worse than a candy bar."

"I figured as much; it always is with you."

I wanted to say, "That's not fair," try to defend myself, and couldn't. Not with her. She deserved so much better.

She was right, though.

I don't remember her ever being wrong about anything. She was my life, the very breath in my lungs.

I waited while she finished bandaging poor Waldo who lay there panting, his big pink tongue flopped out on the cool tile. Marie came over and took Tobias from my arms and disappeared with him into the kitchen; Rosie's room was right off the kitchen.

Marie came back empty-handed and sat next to me, wrapped her arms around me, her head on my chest, her words muffled. "You're a good man, Bruno Johnson. I never have to worry about you. You don't have to be afraid of telling me anything."

Words I'd read or heard in movies, parents talking to their obstinate children. I wasn't a kid, and yet I continued to fall into mischief like that damn Dennis the Menace. No, maybe more like John

McClane in *Die Hard*. Heavy-duty mischief. Yeah, a black Bruce Willis.

Marie patted my chest. "Come on, quit stalling. Tell me."

I nodded even though she couldn't see it. "Otis slipped me a Mickey Finn last night. That's why I'm late getting home. I was out cold."

She pulled away from me, concern in her expression. "You don't drink. Why were you drinking?"

I shrugged. The answer escaped me because there wasn't one.

She put her hand to my head, then my cheek, she checked my eyes. Just like she had with Waldo. "So, Darla Figueroa, the Ice Princess, called and lied for you, is that it?"

I nodded again.

"Bruno, use your words."

"Otis did it to blackmail me."

The meaning struck her hard, her expression going slack, her eyes no longer seeing me as her mind ran through the ramifications to my statement. She leaned back and looked at me, waiting for the rest of it. She knew there had to be more.

"Tell me."

I choked when I tried to talk. "It's not good."

She said nothing.

I pulled out my phone. She didn't grab it from me, a bad sign. She gently took it from my hands and typed in my security code.

I didn't have any secrets from her.

I watched her eyes as she looked at the photo, me naked with Rebecca Sanchez. All the air left Marie's body the same as a giant character at the end of the Thanksgiving Day Parade in New York. She deflated, not physically, but emotionally. Her pain and guilt smothered me, took the breath from my lungs. I struggled to breathe.

Tears filled her eyes. She stood, an automaton, turned, and walked away. Tears burned my eyes and heated my cheeks, my face and neck. "Babe, wait. Let's talk about this, please?"

She didn't turn around and kept moving down the hall. "Not now, Bruno. Not now, for God's sakes."

She disappeared down the dim hall. The door to our bedroom eased closed.

I wished her reaction had been different—screaming and shoving, asking why, slamming the door.

This way was far worse.

Anger rose up and replaced fear and regret and sorrow. I headed for the front door, blood-red rage in my eyes. I'd fix Otis for this. I'd finish this whole mess once and for all.

I passed Waldo on the floor. "You coming, asshole?"

He groaned and struggled to his feet. His ailing shifted my emotions yet again. I held the front door open, waiting for him. I reached down to pet him. "I didn't mean to call you an asshole. I'm sor—"

He snapped at my hand, his jaws clacking shut as I yanked my hand clear.

I closed the door after him. "You know what? I'm going to start calling you Robby Wicks. That's my old boss' name—he was a grade A asshole. What do you think about that, huh?"

"Grr."

CHAPTER FIFTY-FOUR

I ENTERED THE Punta Bandera Hotel and Beach Club through the front door, Felix holding it for me. He said, "Smile, we're at full occupancy, everyone's making money, the tips are killer. The Ice Princess is happy. Enjoy it while you can."

I grunted. "Sorry, I'm just hungover."

"Yeah, I heard about the party on the beach last night, some wing-ding, huh? You shoulda seen some of those golfers when they checked out this morning. They didn't need a taxi to the airport, they needed an ambulance. That party's going down in the annals of this hotel's history. Next time call me, huh? I thought we were pals."

"You see Otis?"

"Couple of times. He had three thugs with him. Couple of 'em are real mouth breathers if you know what I mean?"

I nodded and kept going, headed for Darla's office.

"Hey, Gaylord?"

I turned around.

"Ah, just so you know, the Ice Princess said that it was my ass if I let that dog in one more time."

"What dog?"

He looked confused for a moment, smiled, pointed at me, snapped his fingers. "Gottcha."

My phone buzzed. I checked the text message from Marie:

SORRY FOR ACTING SO CHILDISH, PLEASE COME HOME SO WE CAN TALK THIS THROUGH. I LOVE YOU.

I typed back:

I LOVE YOU TOO AND I'M TRULY SORRY OVER WHAT HAPPENED. I'M AT THE HOTEL. I'M GOING TO FIND OTIS AND WHISPER IN HIS EAR.

Blood and bone speak for breaking a few of his bones in penalty and retribution.

*   *   *

I entered Darla's office without knocking. She sat behind her desk, the chair tilted back, her long smooth legs crossed, her feet in Jimmy Choo heels up on the desk. She smoked a fat Cohiba Cuban cigar, the smoke more blue than gray. She took the stogie from her painted red lips.

"I saw you coming. That's it—Hurtado, he's through. I warned him about letting that asshole dog in here."

"My dog's not an asshole. And you're not going to fire Felix. He's a good friend."

"Oh, so now I can't fire someone if they're a friend of yours?"

She brought her feet down from the desk, losing her evil grin, shifting to pure anger. "That right, fat man, well you're fired too. What do you think about that?"

I moved around to her side of the desk. She held her ground. I shouldered her away from the computer keyboard and fired up the historic video data from the night before.

"Hey, what the hell do you think you're doing?"

I ignored her and found the videos from the beach party, but there were several hours of them to go through.

Darla's hand moved quick as a snake, opened the desk drawer, her fingers wrapping around the stock to a 9mm pistol. I grabbed her around the throat with one hand, rolled her in her chair until she hit the wall. I squeezed, my nose touching hers, no fear in her eyes as I cut off her oxygen.

She stuck the gun in my side, shoved it hard into a rib. Not unlike the way Sonya, Bosco's mother, had six months earlier, when she'd pulled the trigger and shot me point blank. Only she'd used a small caliber, a .25 auto. This was a 9mm—it would more than do the job, blow my heart right out my chest.

"Waldo!"

I didn't have to see the chomp when he bit her. The crunch sounded loud in the quiet room. Her eyes shimmied as she ate the pain, still without displaying any fear.

She choked and gasped from my hand clamping down on her throat, a natural instinct or she'd have suppressed that as well.

I whispered. "You get it now? I'm done with your 'tote and carry' bullshit. We just entered the real world, the Bruno Johnson world where blood and bone rules the day. Now, you can be a part of the problem or part of the solution, your choice. What's it going to be?"

Her face turning blue, she finally relented and nodded as she tapped my hand on her throat. I let go and stood back. She coughed and choked, both hands holding her throat, one bleeding badly from the Waldo bite.

I tore off a long strip of my aloha shirt. Used it to wrap her hand. Then I tore off another long strip and made a sling to go around her neck to keep her hand elevated. Blood seeped through the material in fat splotches. She'd had perfect delicate hands, long, lithe fingers, now mangled. She hadn't deserved that from me.

The entire time she stared, searching for my eyes as I worked on her. When I finally looked at her, she smiled. "I've never been so attracted to you. Can I have my gun back, please. I'm going to shoot you in the dick." She said it, anger rising in her tone.

"Oh my God, woman, give it a rest."

I picked up the gun where Waldo had let it drop and threw it hard across the room. It banged off the wall, leaving a dent, and slid to the floor.

We stared at each other.

"I know what you're here looking for."

"You do?"

"Of course, I do. This is my hotel. Nothing happens that I don't know about."

She elbowed me out of the way, rolling her desk chair closer to the computer keyboard. She slid a yellow Post-it pad over and checked the numbers she'd written down earlier—time sequences. The woman was meticulous to a fault. She then used the mouse to cue up a scene sequence listed on the pad. She found it and froze the screen.

The scene from the out-of-control party the night before. It showed when I turned my back on Otis one too many times. She caught the video frame perfectly with his hand over my grasshopper glass dropping in a round white pill.

The insidious little culprit.

My jaw ground teeth. It was one thing to have circumstantial evidence and another to have physical evidence, catching the low-down conniving bastard in the act. I wanted to pinch his head off.

I said, "How'd he get me and Rebecca to the room?"

She stared at me again, her eyes green with gold flakes, almost feline. She said, "I didn't know what had happened until I came in today and viewed the tapes. That's the truth. I would've intervened had I seen it in real time."

She didn't bemoan or cry about her damaged hand. She was a woman carved from a block of steel.

"I believe you. Now show me. Please."

Her good hand moved the mouse and cued up another sequence selected through the on-screen clock. Two men, who looked Russian, similar to their partner, the one who'd been buried waist deep in the sand trap, laughed and joked with me and Rebecca, our arms over their shoulders for support while they escorted us away. My arm around Rebecca's waist.

We stumbled and almost fell when Rebecca leaned up and kissed me on the mouth, her tongue like a little prairie dog popping out of its hole. I didn't push her away and accepted her prairie dog and even looked like I enjoyed it. I remembered nothing, the scene surreal as if from another world, someone else's life.

What a fool I'd been.

I said, "Erase this."

She dragged the icon, dropped the file into the screen trash can. "What's the big deal?"

I pulled out my phone and showed her the photo, the naked Rebecca draped over the naked me, her hand on Johnson Junior. She took a closer look, shook her good hand. "Sweet baby bald-headed Jesus, that woman has it going on. Look at that heart-shaped butt, that perfect tan."

"Really, that's what you take from this?"

"What?" she asked without taking her eyes from the phone.

"Never mind."

I was an ignorant fool. I couldn't help being a little jealous that Darla had commented on *Rebecca's* flawless attribute.

CHAPTER FIFTY-FIVE

I PUT MY cellphone back in my pocket and headed for the door, moving fast. Time to find Otis and deliver a little payback for the Mickey Finn and the photos intended to hurt my family. Maybe a lot of payback.

"Where do you think you're going, cowboy?" the Ice Princess called after me.

"See a man about a horse."

"Gaylord, no more heavy shit in this hotel, you hear me?"

"Yeah, yeah, yeah. Come on, Waldo."

He caught up and stayed at my side. Behind us, her Jimmy Choos clacked on the tile as she followed. The noise stopped at her door. She didn't continue to follow. With her surveillance cameras, she'd have a front-row seat back at her desk—and she'd have plausible deniability.

I'd find Otis sitting on his stool at the Lido Cabana bar with Chacho feeding him grasshoppers. There'd be three cameras to handle that area so she could watch and at the same time deny being a witness.

*   *   *

Rebecca Sanchez was standing in the center of the lobby, the check-in desk as a backdrop, microphone in hand, doing a stand-up news item. When she saw me, she ran her bladed hand across her throat telling the cameraman to cut the shot. "Give me a minute, Joe." She tossed the mic to him and hurried over to me.

"Gaylord, we need to talk." She eyed my torn and shredded hotel aloha shirt, my tee shirt underneath spotted with blood from Darla's chomped hand. I looked a mess.

I tried to go by her. "No time now, maybe later."

I had an urgent appointment with a fat man in a sour seersucker suit.

She grabbed onto my arm and dug in. I didn't slow.

"Please, I need to talk to you." Her voice a harsh whisper. "I was still drugged this morning when I agreed to . . . to getting out in front of our little . . . problem. I could never do that, it'd ruin me. Please, hear me out."

Ruin her? She'd stepped out with a good friend, Aleck, and hurt a lot of people in the process, some of them even killed. When she'd said, "Please," a little sob squeaked past her ruby lips underneath those big brown eyes. I was a sucker for a woman in distress. And after all, we had experienced the same trauma—waking naked—her in the tub, me on the bed, both parties to a despicable blackmail scheme.

I stopped, said, "Two minutes."

She tugged me over to the corner of the lobby away from everyone else. Ten or twelve couples stood in two lines at the front desk: a line to check in; another to check out. Three desk clerks helped them as fast as they could, service the number one edict from the Ice Princess.

Mary St. John sat at the concierge desk. Felix Hurtado opened and closed the front door for folks coming and going. Waldo jumped up onto a lobby couch and stretched out, still nursing a Modelo beer hangover. He burped.

I looked up at the camera in the lobby, shot Darla a faux smile, pointed to my dog, and gave her the thumbs-up.

Darla's voice came over the PA, "Gaylord, come to my office. Now!"

She wouldn't want to be seen with her arm in a sling—bad for her image.

Rebecca shook my elbow. "This isn't funny, Gaylord. This is serious business."

I turned my attention to her, her big brown eyes fierce now.

"That right?" I said. "I'll tell you about serious. Someone paid Jaime Lopez, an MS13 gangster, to kill all those folks in El Gato Gordo, all because of your little tryst with Aleck. Those people went there for a drink and a quiet dinner, to relax and have a good time, and they got killed for it."

Her mouth dropped open. She took a step back. "What are you talking about? That's not true. That wasn't . . . not because of me. No. No. No."

She came out of the trance for a second, looked at Joe the cameraman, and yelled, "I said cut, Joe, damn you. If you got any of this, delete it, now."

I called up the video I'd sent from Alisa's phone to mine, the one with Rebecca and Aleck kissing in the nightclub, and showed her.

Her big brown eyes welled with tears. "It's not true. That horrible thing didn't happen because of our love for each other. No, it couldn't have. Our love was pure and beautiful." She put a fist over her heart.

I wasn't a trusting soul, not when it came to power alliances, the way they corrupted all they touched. Aleck was set to be the next governor. With her position in the media, they would complement each other in their rise to power and fame.

Her words made me ill and at the same time I understood how love was a lot like fate—a lonely hunter.

If there even was such a thing as pure love.

I again showed her the video in the phone. "There are only three true motives for murder: greed, love, and revenge. Here, take another look at you two in a public place, in front of God and everyone making goo-goo eyes at each other. Kissing like a couple of high schoolers out by the smoking tree. I think this video qualifies on two counts, love and revenge, and maybe even greed once the entire incident came to light."

It wasn't until that moment I realized if Alisa hired Jaime to do the deed she would be going away for a long time. And worse, she had something to trade: she knew my background, my fugitive status. She could trade me for less time in prison.

And worse yet, she knew all about the kids.

When had life gotten so difficult?

"Gaylord?"

I turned. Otis hobbled in the side door from the pool area, the bandages on his foot dirty and brown, blotched with dried blood that had bled through. He'd come in from the cabana bar, his eyes bloodshot and grasshopper-glassy. He grinned. Proud that he'd backed me into a corner with the salacious photos of me and Rebeca in a compromising position. He wanted his diamonds from Genie and his reputation restored and didn't care who he hurt to get it done. Along with him came three thugs who looked Russian, real meat eaters just like Felix had said.

Waldo sat up, climbed off the couch, went over, and let the pancake and sausage man pat his head.

The turncoat.

The guests in line sensed an atmospheric shift and turned their eyes on us. A couple even raised their cellphones, started recording.

In the other direction, down the hall off the lobby, Jimmy Choos clacked on the tile floor and reached a crescendo. The Ice Princess popped out from the hallway yelling, "Take it outside. Take it out front. Not in my hotel. You hear me!?"

Now the folks in line at the front desk moved back, bunching up by the desk, not knowing where to go, confused lambs among the wolves, the scent of violence thick in the air.

Otis said something in what sounded like Russian. From the looks on his friends' faces he'd just told them I was the one who'd killed their other two friends, the one with the knife Otis stuck in and the one Waldo knocked down into the stream, the shark bait.

All three Russians fanned out, their eyes locked on me. I had nothing in my hands and those guys knew their business. They busted heads for a living, dropped brutalized innocents in fifty-five-gallon drums into the river.

Felix Hurtado, the doorman, the ex-cop, not afraid to mix it up, came inside. His posture said he'd be involved.

Otis pulled out the Browning Hi-Power, the gun used in the killings at El Gato, and pointed it at Felix. "This little problem is between friends. Stay out of it or involve yourself at your own peril."

The staples in my ass and back started to itch—they were about to get torn out.

Otis turned the gun on me. "You going to tell me where the diamonds are, Genie, or do we do a little dance?"

By the thugs' expressions, telling them where the diamonds were wouldn't make one damn bit of difference. They wanted their pound of retribution.

CHAPTER FIFTY-SIX

DARLA STOOD A few feet from the front desk. She raised her arms high in the air, her injured hand wrapped in a bloody rag. "All right, hold it. Just hold it one second."

Everyone froze, even the Russians, and looked at the beautiful woman with her arms raised in the air.

She brought them down and directed with her hands, the bunched-up customers at the desk. "You folks move back out of the way. That's it, move over there. Everyone checking in and checking out, these folks here all get a free stay on the hotel, meals included."

One bold, cheap bastard said, "Golf? How about free golf?"

"Fine," she said, "but then I get to borrow these." She pulled out two clubs from his bag, a nine iron and a three wood. She tossed the three wood to Felix Hurtado and kicked off her Jimmy Choos. "If you four"—indicating Otis and his Russian dogs—"won't take it outside, you're going to regret coming into my hotel."

Otis said, "Dumb broad brought a golf club to a gunfight." He waved the Browning Hi-Power, pointing it at her. "Just so you know, it's not beneath me to shoot a woman. Even a beautiful woman."

Otis was right. He was holding all the trump cards.

Darla spread her bare feet on the cool tile and pulled the club back over her shoulder, ready to swing. She looked out of place in her Hawaiian-style dress. She said, "Rebecca, fire up your news camera and aim it at the fat stinking bastard with the gun and don't take it off him. See if he wants to shoot someone while on live television. Spend the rest of his life in a Costa Rican prison."

I let out the breath I'd been holding. That camera idea would defuse the whole mess. They'd all back down and—

The closest Russian, built like a small bull, lowered his head and bum-rushed me. I barely had time to get my feet squared and braced when he hit, driving me backward. We both flipped over the couch and landed on the floor.

The gun exploded. Otis had fired. In my peripheral vision, I caught a glimpse of Darla going down, grabbing her abdomen, flopping on the floor, pain ruining her face.

The Russian had me around the chest squeezing the life out of me.

Otis screeched. With it came an undertone from Waldo growling and mauling.

I tried to get enough breath to yell and could only muster a harsh whisper that came out all but inaudible, lost in the clatter of mayhem—people screaming, grunts, moans, steel thudding against bone and muscle. "Waldo! Waldo!"

He was my only hope to get the guy locked onto me in a death grip. The guy must've been a wrestler in a prior life, Olympic class.

Bright lights and stars sparked in my vision. I was going out. I struck uselessly at the bullet head locked against my chest just below my chin.

Looking from the floor level with blurred vision, a mirage appeared running through the front door.

Marie.

She scooped up the nine iron Darla had dropped. She looked around, saw my dire situation, let out an Apache war cry, and attacked.

She struck my Russian again and again on the back, the thuds the same as a ball bat on a watermelon. Nothing. No reaction.

I tried to say, "Head. Hit him in the head," but had no breath left. She was a physician's assistant and sometimes her Hippocratic oath got in her way meting out the appropriate amount of blood and bone.

With the last strength left in my hand, I pointed to his head. She nodded. Her tongue came out to the side of her mouth and stayed there, her eyes fierce as she pulled the nine iron over her head and brought it down hard. She clubbed the guy like a catfish flopping on the boat deck.

Still nothing.

She hit him again. The second thunk resonated through his skull and into my chest.

The man turned slack.

I shoved him off.

Air rushed into my lungs.

I tried to get to my knees to help and couldn't. Two Russians had Felix, one holding his arms, the other pummeling him with brutal fists. Waldo had Otis by his good leg as Otis tried, without success, to drag himself and the hundred and thirty pounds of teeth and fur out the poolside door.

Darla was down on the floor clutching her abdomen, her hands slick with oozing blood, her eyes pleading for relief and filled with regret. She was a hotelier and not a street thug, not someone practiced in blood and bone.

Marie tended to me. I waved her off, pointed and whispered, my voice a harsh rasp, "Those two, they're the ones who posed me and Rebecca."

Her concerned expression turned violent.

She picked up her nine iron and let go with another Apache war cry. She attacked. She clubbed the man who pummeled poor Felix's face right across the head. He went down, lights out. The other Russian holding Felix pushed him and fled out the front door.

Fifteen, twenty seconds max, and it was over. All caught on the *News Six* camera with Rebecca Sanchez, the Darling of Costa Rica, commentating the blow-by-blow description.

I kept my back to the camera, but it really didn't matter, too many patrons had their cellphones out, downloading what just happened to the net. The Punta Bandera Beach Club and Spa would again be infamous in international news items.

I struggled to my feet, made it over to Marie, and hugged her. She glommed on. I was the last life preserver on a sinking ship. "I'm sorry, Bruno. I'm so sorry. I shouldn't have acted that way. It wasn't your fault. I know it wasn't your fault, that you had nothing to do with it. You were just a store dummy in the display window."

"I'm sorry you had to go through it. But man, oh man, am I glad you showed up." We sounded like a couple caught up in some cheesy B movie with third-rate dialogue.

"Wait, a store *dummy*?"

I slapped my leg. "Come here, Waldo. Waldo, come."

He stopped worrying Otis' leg, looked up, his jaws red with blood. Once released, Otis fell into the pool exit door and out onto the landing. He crawled on hands and knees, trying to get away.

"Babe," I said, "you have to help Darla, she's been shot."

She nodded and hurried over to her.

CHAPTER FIFTY-SEVEN

THREE DAYS LATER my chest still hurt when I took a breath. That Russian cracked a couple of ribs. Marie treated me like an old man and dropped me off at the hospital entrance while she went to park the dented hippie mobile. She didn't want me walking too far.

Outside Darla's hospital room, I found Chief Hernandez demoted to a slick-sleeve patrolman guarding her door, a demeaning job for someone with such stature. Otis and one of the Russians still hadn't been found and the OIJ couldn't afford anything else to happen to Darla Figueroa, a woman who had, in her short time managing the food and beverages at the Punta Bandera Beach Club and Spa, become a Tamarindo power broker to be reckoned with.

The chief stood when he saw me coming, put down his newspaper, and took off his cheater glasses. His face remained expressionless.

I held out my hand to shake. He didn't move to take it but stared at me with hard, black eyes. Angry.

I said, "Why are you mad at me? I'm innocent. I didn't do a thing to cause any of this. You pulled me out of the ocean when all this started and asked for my help. Remember?"

He shrugged. "I guess you are correct. I'm lucky I am not in prison eating frijoles and tortillas."

"What kind of case do they have on my chef Jaime Lopez?"

He shrugged again. "They do not keep me in the loop. They've had Alisa Vargas in their interrogation room for three days now. She won't admit to having her husband killed."

"What a sad mess this whole thing turned out to be."

I started to go past him into Darla's hospital room when he put his hand on my chest.

"I thought you would extricate me from this, that you would figure out it was Jaime and Alisa long before OIJ. I was wrong—you are nothing but a cabana boy bartender."

I held his eyes for a long moment then looked down at his hand on my chest. He removed it.

I didn't have the need to defend myself . . . or maybe I did. "I wasn't given all the information."

He wagged his finger. "No, you cannot say that. I did just as you asked. You had everything you asked for. You held back from me. And don't try to deny it. What happened to those bullets I sent to the FBI like you asked. I called, and they would not tell me. They said they were still processing them. I say *caca de toro*."

I did feel sorry for him, ending out his career as a slick-sleeve patrolman. I reached behind my back and brought out the Browning Hi-Power from my waistband and handed it to him. I'd scooped it up from where Otis dropped it in the lobby when Waldo mauled his leg and before the police arrived.

"This is the murder weapon. You call the FBI and ask for Deputy Director Dan Chulack—he's waiting for your call. He'll have the ballistic information you need. It belonged to Otis Brasher, a guest at the hotel. Jaime had access to Otis' room, and his London Fog raincoat, and black wingtip shoes. Jaime has a record for violence and the lack of conscience that's needed to shoot innocent people."

He took the gun with shaking hands, tears welling in his eyes. His job defined him. To lose it made him less than a man, a nonentity.

"*Gracias. Gracias, mi amigo.*"

"I just wish I could do more."

I again tried to go past him. He said to my back, "You asked me who was shot first."

I turned and said, "Aleck was shot first." An assumption I'd made based on the revelation of Aleck and Rebecca's tryst.

He didn't take his eyes off the Browning, marveling at the piece of evidence that could reinstate him as chief. "No, Señor, the waitress was shot first."

"The OIJ is mistaken."

Or, at the very least, Jaime had panicked when Salvador, sitting at the bar, videoing the tryst, reacted. All very logical.

He shrugged as he took out his phone and dialed the OIJ to negotiate his terms to return as chief.

While he waited for them to pick up on the other end, I said, "You might have to get tough, threaten to go to the media."

"I may not be the best investigator, but I know politics." He turned his back to me and started talking into his phone.

"Is that you out there, Bruno?" Darla said from her hospital bed, her voice lacking her old command and control. Her confidence. The bullet to her abdomen had broken her emotionally. I knew the feeling. When Sonya shot me in the chest point blank with the .25 auto, in a microsecond I recognized life's simple thread that all humans clung to, how our tenuous existence could slip through your fingers with a snap—a smooth pull on a trigger. A life-changing event made a person savor every day afterward, every minute.

I entered the room that belonged to my old boss, Darla.

She lay in the bed, the back elevated, propping her up, her skin sallow, no longer tan and vibrant. She'd have died had it not been for Marie's quick action.

Tubes and wires connected Darla to the machines that monitored her vital signs. Her left hand was bandaged where Waldo had bitten her to get the gun. Today was the first that she'd been allowed visitors and then only for five minutes.

No family had come to see her.

She raised her good hand. I hurried over, took it, and found it cold to the touch. Now she truly was the Ice Princess.

That was rude and unfair. She'd turned out to be kind and caring and, most important, a true friend. When I needed help the most, she'd stepped in swinging a golf club, going up against a gun.

I tried to smile at the disheveled woman and said, "I passed your wrestling coach on the way in. He said he's really going to put you through your paces today."

My feeble attempt at humor fell miles short of the mark. I wished Eddie stood beside me whispering his near-perfect observational humor to help cheer her up.

A crooked smile, one heavily dosed with painkillers, crept across her face, revealing a mere whimper of the woman she used to be. She squeezed my hand. "You're a real asshole, you know that?"

"I've been called worse." I sat on the edge of her bed, still holding her hand. The memory, the image of her naked, her tan skin shimmering with Hawaiian Tropic sun oil, made a large lump rise in my throat and my eyes fill with tears. I'd caused this mess.

She squeezed my hand. "What's the matter, cowboy, someone pee in your Wheaties?"

"I came to tell you I'm sorry. You're here in this bed because of me. This is all my fault."

"You're an arrogant fool. You think the whole world rotates around you. I knew what I was doing. I knew the choice I made when I picked up that dumb-assed golf club. Climb down off your high horse. We have business to discuss."

I sniffled and smiled. There was the old Darla Figueroa I knew. I nodded.

"Since you're foolish enough to be sorry for something I did on my own accord, you can take over my job as food and beverage manager while I take this little unscheduled vacation."

"No problem. Don't worry about a thing. I got it."

"Wait—don't get all rosy and cheerful yet, cowboy. You're going to do my job in addition to yours."

"I understand."

"Quit interrupting me. You're also going to do it for the same wage."

I smiled.

She said, "What's so funny?"

"As food and beverage manager, I'm tasked with the books, the ordering, paying the bills, the petty cash? Sure, I'll do it for the same wage."

She chuckled and coughed. "You're an asshole, Bruno Johnson."

"Don't tell my wife. I have her snowed."

Her eyes filled with tears and she squeezed my hand. We stared at each other without saying anything. She finally broke the moment. "I got a cute little bullet hole that's parallel to my navel and a not-so-cute curved scar underneath. It looks like two eyes and a smile. So I guess I made out okay."

I wanted to tell her about my smiley face on my ass, with my butt crack as the smile, tell her we were now twins, but it wasn't appropriate, wrong time, wrong place. Probably never would be.

I needed to change the subject. "When is Herb Templeton, the hotel manager, coming back?"

She shook her head. "He's not. The owner fired him. You have to pick up his slack as well. You up for it, cowboy?"

"For the same pay?"

"What do you think?" She smiled.

CHAPTER FIFTY-EIGHT

I CAME OUT of the hospital to bright sunlight that immediately clouded over, shadowing the day, the dark clouds moving in fast to crowd out the sun. Rain spattered down as I looked for the dented hippie mobile with Marie.

A white Mercedes coupe pulled up and stopped. I recognized the car. It belonged to Alisa Vargas. Two days prior, shortly after the melee at the hotel, Alisa was arrested for six counts of murder including her husband, Aleck. The OIJ must've gotten into Salvador's phone. The video of Aleck kissing Rebecca Sanchez played all over the news. The whole sordid affair hit the national media market and several true crime shows had made an appearance at the hotel shooting B-roll in anticipation of signing media deals with the primary players: Alisa, Jaime, Chief Hernandez, and "the black cabana bartender named Gaylord."

That last one was never going to happen.

I leaned down in the rain and looked in the passenger window to the Mercedes coupe. Jose Rivera, behind the wheel, reached over and opened the passenger door. "Amigo, let us go for a ride."

I wasn't sure I wanted to get in the car with him. I'd just started breathing easier now that everything had wrapped up. All I had to do was lie low for a while. Change my name from Gaylord and deny,

deny, deny. Jose was a rough customer who tended toward violence. I hesitated, getting soaked from the rain, and finally got in and closed the door.

The interior smelled of Alisa's expensive perfume, Chanel No. 5. Jose Rivera took off, driving too rapidly in the rain, wipers working hard but not hard enough.

"Where are we going?"

He drove, didn't speak or look over at me.

I trusted him. Well, for the most part anyway.

We wound in and around the homes in the area, the rain pounding down a flood, getting worse against the windshield. I was still having difficulty getting used to the constant rain, having lived my entire life in Southern California—basically, a desert. I did enjoy all the greenery and sweet-smelling flowers with their bright colors. The greenery and flowers needed lots of water.

Jose pulled down a long private driveway with tall shrubs on both sides, the narrow asphalt strip only wide enough for one car to pass. The long driveway opened to an expansive grass yard and a mansion with Southern architecture that I had no idea existed in Tamarindo and in no way fit with the other style of houses.

He parked right in front. I expected a man dressed as a butler to appear and to open our doors. Jose got out and walked up the front steps to the big double doors. I followed, holding my arm across my ribs, the steps giving me pain.

Inside, the house reeked of dust and mildew, all the furniture covered in white sheets, turning dusty and dingy yellow. It'd been a long time since the owners had been here.

Jose took a hard right from the entryway, manipulated a solid wall panel that opened the wall to a disguised entry. We descended some stairs down into the inky-black basement. I stopped at the bottom, fighting vertigo from not having a point of bearing.

A weak yellow light came on from an overhead naked bulb with a hanging dirty string. The light swung, creating shadows that grew and receded with each pass.

Two men sat in expensive dining room chairs, antiques from another century. They wore black hoods. I recognized one from his sour body odor and light blue seersucker suit coat.

Otis.

The other had to be the Russian who'd escaped the day of the fight in the hotel lobby. I'd forgotten that I'd told Jose I wanted to talk to the Russians.

They were both bound, hands behind their backs, their feet tied to the chair. A rope hung over the support beam, tied around their necks to thwart any attempt at escape. Jose knew his business. They had to sit upright, backs straight, or risk choking.

He pulled off both hoods at the same time. The men had gags— dirty rags tied around their mouths. The Russian's eyes bulged as he groaned, an unintelligible plea to be released from the madman, Jose. Both their faces brutalized, swelled with purples and reds, their eyes mere slits. Otis sat there the same as if on a stool at the cabana bar sipping his grasshoppers, proud and confident.

"Please take off the gag on that one."

Jose pulled down the dirty rag around Otis' swollen and bloody mouth.

He exercised his bloated lips. The swinging light lit his face then shaded it, aging him twenty years, making him more monstrous.

"Thank you, Gaylord. You've finally come. I thought you might let us die down here. An appropriate penalty for what I've done. For what happened in the hotel lobby. You'd be within your rights."

He was good. He knew how to soften an interrogator, work the interrogator around to his own agenda.

He said, "You have all the diamonds. You've neutralized the threat. What are you going to do with us? Though, I can imagine. You want your pound of flesh. Or wait, maybe you don't know how to stop the flow of Russian thugs coming your way to make your life miserable. I do hope they at least do half as much to you as this ignorant thug has done to us."

"Shut up, you're giving me a headache."

I looked around and found a wooden stool to sit on. I couldn't stand too long without my ribs throbbing. "Do you agree that I'm holding all the cards right now—at least Jose is?"

He nodded.

"So, I have no reason to lie. I do not have, and never have had, your diamonds. I was never a part of any kind of heist."

"And I suppose you're not Genie either?"

"Correct. This is just a bad set of circumstances, the nightclub massacre and you thinking I'm some sort of heist expert. I've never robbed a bank or armored car or anything like that."

"You've obviously mistaken me for an idiot. Underestimated me yet again. I told you I did a complete background on you before coming down here. I talked to your cohorts, one in particular, someone who acted like an intermediary not unlike what I do. Put the jobs together. He told me you've ripped off trains filled with computer chips."

The name slipped past my lips before I could stop it. "Jumbo."

"Yes, exactly."

"That was theft, not robbery—there's a big difference."

"Hmm, that right?"

"Your initial intelligence is wrong. You said your guy gave you the name Tamarindo and you took it from there, made a huge leap to get to me. Since I fit the bill, you're like a dog with a bone you won't give up."

"Would you, if you were me?"

He had a point.

I said, "If I can't convince you, I guess we've gone past the talking part of this little soiree."

He shrugged.

I said, "You came at me when I have done nothing to you. You tried to blackmail me to my family. My family is sacred. You can do whatever you want with me, that's the game I joined many years ago." I pulled up my sleeve and showed the tattoo on my shoulder, "BMF." "But you crossed the line. You tried to hurt my family."

"Yes, I see that now. I didn't think it through and I'm sorry."

I held out my hand to Jose Rivera. He reached to his back waistband, took out a .357 Magnum, and handed it to me.

"So, you're just going to shoot me like a dog?" He said it without a quaver in his voice, a proud man who lived by the sword, knew the rules, and willingly accepted his fate.

I got up, moved over to him, my eyes not leaving his. I stuck the gun under his chin. "You understand what you did wrong?"

He nodded. "Family is sacred. I know that now."

"You come at me again. You come at me, not my family." I pulled the gun from under his chin and shot him in the leg just above the knee. The explosion horrendous in the empty basement. Otis passed out from the pain.

I moved over to the Russian, pulled down his gag, stuck the hot barrel under his chin. "You speak English?"

"A little." His eyes wide, sweat running down from his hair into his face.

"You tell your friends I had nothing to do with the diamond heist. I'm a family man just making my way in life. You understand?"

He nodded.

"You tell them my name. My real name is Bruno Johnson. Tell them about this tattoo. Have your people call their people in LA, ask about me. If Brighton Beach comes down here again looking for me, I'll come up to Brighton Beach and they won't like it. You tell them."

"Yes, I will."

I handed the gun back to Jose.

The Russian said, "You're not going to shoot me?"

"Did you blackmail my family?"

"No."

"You're a liar—you helped." I held out my hand again. Jose handed me the gun. I shot the Russian in the leg in the same place as Otis. The man yelled and screamed. Jose put the gag back in his mouth. I handed the gun back to Jose. "My friend, if it's not too much to ask, could you dump these two in front of the police station before they lose too much blood?"

"No, they killed Salvador."

"No, they didn't. It was Jaime from the hotel. You know Jaime. He's in police custody and you can't get to him."

"You sure?"

I didn't answer him right away. A thought hit me square between the eyes. Salvador could easily have been Genie. He had the skill set and could have pulled off a job like the one in the underground garage in the Diamond District of New York. Why had I not thought of it before? I knew him as a friend, a kind person. The more I plugged in what I knew about Salvador, the more it made perfect sense and linked everything together nice and neat.

"What did you say?" I asked Jose. "Ah . . . yes, I'm sure Jaime did it. Just dump this trash in front of the police station. It's over."

I turned and left, taking the stairs up slowly one at a time, glad life could finally get back to normal.

CHAPTER FIFTY-NINE

MARIE DAUBED ANTIBACTERIAL cream on my back and buttocks in preparation to rebandage both. "Another couple of days we can leave the bandages off and let fresh air help to heal." I was on my stomach naked on the bed. I watched her eyes in the mirror, my love for her flushing my skin with warmth.

On the opposite wall, also in the reflection, I saw the police report pages and photos, the El Gato Gordo nightclub shooting unable to leave us alone. Not us really, just Marie.

"Would you please take down those photos on the wall? I'm starting to have nightmares and PTSD." I didn't have those things. I had other ghosts, vile and brutal, to deal with in the dream world.

Whenever the thought struck her she'd again tell me no way could Alisa contract Jaime to kill all those people. Something nagged at her like an itch she couldn't reach. I wasn't with her on this one. For me everything fit nice and neat into an ugly jigsaw puzzle of mayhem created by jealousy.

"I don't believe it. I don't, Bruno." She slapped my bottom. "The police won't let me talk with her. I need to talk with Alisa, look in her eyes, and have her tell me herself."

Marie had her own polygraph built into her six senses.

"I'd really like it if the kids can again have full reign of the house." With the gruesome photos up on the wall, they'd been restricted, not allowed to enter.

She slapped my naked butt again. "There. Get dressed."

I rolled over and gave her my best Burt Reynolds nude pose from *Cosmopolitan* magazine. "You know, the bedroom door is locked."

She smiled, stepped away from the bed, repacking her black medical bag. "You want to mess up the bandage job I just finished?"

I reached out for her hand. "You said they could use a little fresh air to heal."

"I said in a couple more days, tiger. Power down on the throttle."

"You're telling me you don't want some of this?" I held out my hands.

She chuckled. "How could a woman resist such romantic overtures?"

She came to me. I pulled her into a hug. We kissed. We both started breathing hard as the human hydraulic system powered on without direct orders from the brain housing group, the autopilot taking us in.

I froze, stopping just before the point of no return, before nothing could stop us short of a bucket filled with ice water.

Marie pulled back. "What? Did I hurt you?"

"No, sweetie. No."

I struggled to my feet and stood by the bed naked. Something had flashed behind my eyes, an idea. More a sense really. Something I'd missed. A thought just at the tip of my brain that I couldn't grasp.

I'd learned long ago to listen to that spidey instinct—it had saved my ass more than once.

"What, baby?" Marie said as she stood, putting her bra back on and buttoning up her blouse. "What is it?"

I stared at the collage she had made on our boudoir wall, one composed of violence and bloody mayhem. How many couples let that kind of ugliness into the bedroom? Was that what caught me, the incongruity, making love while violent remnants looked on?

No.

I stood there naked and stared at that wall. My mind had caught onto something and wouldn't let me move on until I reconciled the mystery.

Marie stood beside me holding my hand while my eyes scanned the wall again and again. Each time a little slower with each pass, examining each item a little longer.

My eyes fell on the photo with Salvador standing next to his boat holding a decent-sized fish—not big by anyone's standard—but his smile told the story. It didn't matter what other people thought, his medium-sized fish no different than if he'd caught a thousand-pound marlin.

I started to smile at his smile and froze. I backed up until my legs hit the bed's edge, and I sat down hard. "Ah, shit."

"What?" She looked at my eyes and tried to follow them to what I saw. "What, Bruno?"

"Ah, shit."

I slugged the bed again and again. Then I hurried to find my clothes.

CHAPTER SIXTY

I PULLED UP in the Volkswagen van, the hippie mobile painted beige with sixties-style pastel flowers, hand-painted, covering all sides except the top, and parked at the Tamarindo harbor. Not the kind of vehicle driven by slick-talking PIs. I worked at a cabana bar serving drinks to fat drunks who accused me of misdeeds I didn't own, though I'd done my share of others.

I got out and walked down the pier along the berths, past all the expensive sailboats and motorboats and yachts, the night misting, trying hard to rain, creating yellow halos around the parking lot lights. The air thick with jungle humidity.

Thick with treachery.

A storm far off on the dark horizon lit the night with lightning, the thunder barely a rumble.

I had not told Marie where I was going. She didn't need anything else to worry about. Or maybe I hadn't told her because my chase was a foolish idea—too ludicrous and embarrassing to share with her.

I looked for Jose Rivera but couldn't find him.

So I went alone.

I didn't want to be right. Why push it? Why not let the sleeping dogs lie?

I'd had enough. I wanted it all to be over, but sometimes a person couldn't help getting crushed by the weight of truth. Something I couldn't walk away from, not and still live with myself. Not and still look my kids in the eye.

I adjusted the .357 revolver in my back waistband, then reached in my pocket and turned on the small digital recorder I'd gotten from Rebecca the morning we woke together naked in a hotel room.

I didn't know which berth, but I'd recognize the boat from the photo with Salvador holding up his fish. The boat named *Glory*.

Salvador, my good friend. He'd never told me he had a boat. What was he doing with a boat that size? Dad always said boats were just holes in the water where you throw your money.

Salvador lived a modest life, quiet, under the radar, until the job other people paid him to do turned ugly, the noise tamped down, the problem crushed and swept under the carpet. He was paid well for his discretion. But well enough to buy a boat big enough to motor across an ocean?

He'd died on the nightclub floor. I'd seen him there, no breath, his blood coagulating in a puddle around him. No way for a man to end. For that matter, no way for anyone to end.

I spotted the boat I wanted, a light on outside and inside with someone moving around loading stacked supplies from the dock, unafraid of being seen. Preparing for a long trip at sea.

I stopped.

Chacho startled, looked up, caught himself, regained control of his emotions. But not before I spotted something behind his eyes scamper away to hide.

Truth.

He shot me that huge Chacho smile and waved his arm. "Come aboard, mi amigo. Have a beer." He grabbed a bottle from the case he set down on the boat deck. He twisted off the top and handed it to me. My stomach rolled at the thought, the memory of drinking one too many grasshoppers the night of the beach party still too vivid.

I stepped on the boat, not familiar at all with how they worked, never having been aboard one, took the bottle, and tilted it back. The warm beer tasted sour and bubbled up once it hit my stomach. I moved around the back of the boat, keeping him in front of me. "Chacho, where are you going, my friend?"

"Fishing." He laughed and mimicked holding a pole fighting a huge fish. He shifted to excitement. "You want to come, my friend? I have beer and food enough for three. Come with us."

"Us?"

"Who's with you?"

"Ah, a good friend of yours, I think. Go see. Down in the main cabin. Go on. I'm going to load the rest of this stuff." He climbed back up on the dock and arranged some dry goods, consolidating some boxes.

I stepped down in the saloon and froze.

On the floor lay Rebecca Sanchez, naked. Her blood gently rolled back and forth as the boat moved with the incoming tide. Her eyes stared straight, fixed on me.

I pulled my .357 and spun to take on Chacho and never made it.

The light behind my eyes winked out.

CHAPTER SIXTY-ONE

CHACHO STOPPED WHAT he was doing when I came to. He was wrapping Rebecca's feet together with gray duct tape. "Ah, I thought maybe I hit you too hard. You been out for an hour, amigo. You probably have a concussion. Need a CAT scan." He chuckled. "Yeah, you need medical attention." He stopped and drank from a beer bottle. His image blurred, doubled, and came back to normal. He was right about the CAT scan.

I tried to struggle up, but he'd taped my feet and hands. He went back to his work, tying a thick yellow rope with an anchor attached to Rebecca's feet. "This bitch found me just like you did."

His words, his demeanor, was nothing like the Chacho I knew. I thought I was a good judge of character, but I'd missed the mark on this one by several miles, maybe even by a continent.

My shirt at the shoulder soaked up some of Rebecca's blood that leaked from the gash in her throat. I'd had enough blood and bone to last me two lifetimes. Her face only inches from mine, her eyes occluded, the waxy film of death that invaded all parts of the body yellowing the skin. What a horrible loss.

"You going to say anything?" he asked.

I watched his eyes, still trying to rectify the different men, the two faces of Chacho.

"How did you find me? I thought I was home free. I thought that street punk Jaime would take the fall. I set it up that way. Too bad about Alisa, though." He shrugged. "What do you call that?" He chugged down the rest of the beer and flung the bottle out the opening to the sea that rose and fell, the large boat a small bottle on a rising sea. "Yes, that's right, an act with unintended consequences. Right, amigo? Isn't that the way it goes?"

He spoke differently, with a larger vocabulary, more articulate when he wanted to be.

The boat rose and fell and rocked, the motor a constant hum. We were headed out to sea.

My God, we were headed out to sea.

I shook off that fear. "Why is Rebecca naked?" My voice hoarse.

He shrugged again. "Why waste a good slice of woman like her? You know what I mean? When in Rome." He turned his forearms out for me to see. Long raking claw marks scarred his arms, the blood drying. "*Dios mio*, did she put up a fight. But in the end, I got what I wanted, and she . . . Well, she didn't." He sat on the seat for the half-dinette, breathing heavily, and opened another beer.

"Who's driving the boat?" I didn't know how boats worked, if someone had to be driving or if it had autopilot.

He kicked my legs. "You don't get to ask the questions. How did you find me? I have to know."

I stared at him then said, "There was a photo in Salvador's office, a photo of this boat, him standing beside it."

"So? I saw that photo when I trashed his office."

"The name on the boat."

He kicked me harder, this time in the ankle. Pain shot up my leg.

"Quit being a puto and tell me. What about the name of the boat?"

"*Glory*. It's short for 'Gloria.' Salvador named his boat after his lady, his love."

He stood, threw his beer bottle against the wall. Green glass shattered everywhere, mixed with white foam. He pounded his chest, a beast from the animal kingdom. "She was my woman. Salvador, my best friend, stole her from me! Two people I loved. Went behind my back. He bought this boat. They were going to run off to South America, leave me here. Go without telling me. Made me out for a chump, left me here with my dick in my hand."

He stopped and looked down at me, his face bloated red with rage. "That's it? You found me here because of that photo?"

"That and the fact you shot Gloria first that night at El Gato Gordo."

He fell back to sitting on the settee. An evil little half-grin crept out. He pointed to Rebecca. "That's how that bitch found me out. Said she's an investigative reporter. You believe that shit? A reporter and a dumb-assed bartender figured me out—and the cops?"

He held his arms wide. "Where are the cops? You believe that? Tripped up by a chickenshit bitch and a dumb-assed bartender. That evil bitch Fate was not my friend, not this time. I knew I shouldn't shoot Gloria first, but she betrayed me. Damn. My only mistake. A small one but still a mistake."

The beer worked on him, causing him to ramble. Or it could've been just a ploy. He'd proven to have that level of intellect and cunning.

"You're ex-military, aren't you? Intelligence, counterinsurgency? Central America?"

He nodded. "What do you think? Who else knows what you know? Who did you tell? You tell that cute little wife of yours about this boat and the name? You don't worry. I'll find out what she knows."

The boat rose higher than the other times and fell hard, the structure creaking. I bounced and splashed in the blood. The boat started to roll on its side.

"Don't go anywhere. I'll be right back."

Shooting Gloria wasn't his only mistake. All the beer he drank clouded his common sense, gave him a false sense of security, the kind of bravado that gets men killed.

His other mistake—he'd taped my hands in front instead of in back. I searched around with my hands until I found a big enough piece of green glass from the broken beer bottle. The bottle bottom had broken away, its round edge jagged.

He might have made a mistake taping to the front, but he'd taped my hands too tight. I couldn't get the sharp glass down to my wrists to the tape. It'd take me hours. I didn't have hours. He'd be back in minutes, if not sooner.

Cold fingers touched mine. I startled. A shiver ran up and down my back. Rebecca gently took the glass from my hands. Her hands were taped like mine, but she could work the glass against my tape where I couldn't.

"I thought you were—"

"Sssh."

She'd lost so much blood—how could she still be alive, let alone be conscious with enough strength to help. She'd been playing possum, biding her time.

My hands popped free. I took the glass from her and cut the tape from my feet. I struggled upright. The heaving boat made it easier to lie down than stand.

My shoulder banged off one cabinet as I looked around for a weapon. I coughed hard. Searing pain in my ribs. Blood came up into my hand. A broken rib must have punctured a lung. He must've kicked me, or it happened when he tossed me down into the saloon. I'd need medical aide sooner than later. Rebecca a lot sooner.

"I'll be right back to help you."

Rebecca raised her taped weak hands, waved me to go, get on with it.

Rain poured down on the deck. Lightning lit up the night in jagged flashes that cut through the black beyond. I held one arm under my ribs and tried not to cough, though the rain and engine drowned out all other noise. I stepped out on the fantail and looked up to the flying bridge. Chacho, his back to me, fought with the wheel using the throttle to power up and over the swells, the ocean angry and littered with whitecaps. Thousands, millions of them.

I couldn't fight him, not in my condition, especially not on a heaving deck in a storm. I had no idea what he'd done with my gun, but he'd left the digital recorder in my pocket. Probably figured the anchor tied to my feet would take it to the bottom along with me.

I again looked around for a weapon and spotted a long pole with a wicked curved spike on the end, a fish gaff.

I unhooked it, moved with it through the opening to the saloon, and balanced with one hand on the door's edge, watching and timing the rise and fall of the boat on the swells. My vision blurred again and returned.

Chacho could look back at any moment. I was losing strength fast. I'd only have one try at it.

I dropped the pole on his shoulder. Before he could react, I grabbed the pole with both hands and yanked backward. The hook caught him in the throat, skewering him all the way through his neck.

Chacho fell to the deck and flopped like a freshly caught fish, flinging blood everywhere, lit up by lightning. The rain diluting the red to pink.

I stepped on the pole, holding it in place as his hands tried to pull it free. He choked and gagged. I walked on the pole down to him and double-knee dropped on his chest. I found my .357, stood on wobbly legs, and shot him three times.

I tossed the gun overboard and then tossed him overboard.

I went back to help Rebecca and could only hope it wasn't too late.

CHAPTER SIXTY-TWO

I DIDN'T REMEMBER how I got the boat back to Tamarindo. I knew heading west was out to sea and heading east was toward land. I got the boat turned, the wind now in our favor, and smoothed out the ride. Then I made it down to the saloon and bandaged Rebecca's neck. Chacho had slit her throat when he was done with her. A true miracle that she survived. I picked her up, laid her on the bunk, and covered her with a warm blanket. My coughing started in earnest and I spat more blood. I got up on the flying bridge, shivering, staring into darkness. Right after that—that's when I lost track of time and woke in the hospital.

* * *

The police interviewed me twice. Fortunately for me, I had the digital recording to back up my side of what happened. The police said that Rebecca died within minutes, probably seconds, of having her throat cut and no way could she have cut me loose from my bonds.

I'd developed a fever from my infected injuries, and they wrote off that part of my statement as fever delirium and concussion.

* * *

Marie brought the kids in a few at a time. She let them stay a bit longer as I continued to heal. She would not let me have my cellphone. "Not until your body says it's okay."

"How can my body say it's okay? My body can't talk. That doesn't even make sense. Gimme my phone, please?"

She pointed a finger at me and gave me the slanted brow—the look all the kids feared the most.

She brought Waldo on the fourth day, so I could see him out the window. He didn't seem that excited when I tried to yell and wave. Didn't even look up. He walked over to the shade and laid down.

On the fifth day, Marie sat on my bed, holding my hand after having checked my chart. I rolled to my side and pulled up my hospital gown and showed her my naked rear end, the stapled dog bite and the butt crack smile. I changed my voice, made it higher, squeaky like you might think a butt crack would sound. "Please give Bruno back his cellphone."

"See, that's my body saying it's okay."

Marie laughed so hard she turned red and tears rolled down her cheeks. It was good to see her laugh. She relented and gave me my cell. I scanned through the text messages, most of them from the kids telling me to get well soon, most of those from Eddie with some of his best observational humor.

Then I came to the one sent by Dan Chulack:

RE: THE FINGERPRINTS ON THE WATER GLASS:

THE FINGERPRINTS COME BACK TO JEAN ELIZABETH REGAN FROM BOSTON MASS. HISTORY OF ARMED ROBBERY, EXTORTION AND MAINLY BUNCO SCHEMES. A MEMBER OF AN ACTIVE CRIME FAMILY. CALL ME IF YOU NEED MORE DETAILS.

My turn to laugh. I laughed and laughed. Marie said, "What? What's so damn funny?" She'd read the text message and didn't get it.

I started coughing with intermittent laughing. She patted my back. "Take it easy, you'll cough up a lung."

"Is that a real medical diagnosis?"

She shoved the cellphone my way. "Tell me."

"It's the name."

"Bruno?"

"Her name is Jean E."

Marie's hand flew to her mouth. "Oh my God."

AUTHOR'S NOTE

Working the street, I ran into many villains whose unmatched evil elevated them above our justice system—animals too sinister and violent to be left among the lambs. I could do nothing about their presence, hindered by rules and laws and moral obligations.

Not so in my books. I can finally get satisfaction through my pal Bruno who goes around the law to champion the rights of children and rid the world of the villains who continue to haunt my dreams.

In each novel, I draw from my life's experiences and blend them into the plot. In *The Diabolical* I used a harrowing event from my past that helped me create one of the last scenes in this book.

In 1980, I was a newly minted street cop at Ontario Police Department when my friend Randy asked if I wanted to go on a scuba diving trip to Catalina. I was a novice diver and was happy to be invited. There would be four of us on the trip: Bob, Rick, Randy, and me. We would be using Bob's uncle's huge sailboat. Once I said yes, they informed me that my price of admission was my stepfather's truck, which was needed to tow the boat. There was a six-wheeled trailer under the largest boat allowed to be hauled. The truck had bald tires, and I told them I refused to drive it at all—especially not to tow a boat. Bob said he'd drive the truck. I rode with Randy in his grandmother's red station wagon.

With the sun low on the horizon, we dropped the boat in the water at San Pedro and motored out to open water. A few minutes out of the harbor, I asked, "Aren't we gonna put the sail up?" Bob replied, "I don't know how to sail."

At that moment I should've said, "Turn this thing around and take me back."

We continued on.

I loved the wind, the rolling sea, and promise of adventure. The *promise of adventure* in this case translated to *young, dumb, and lucky to be alive.*

It took us two hours to cross the channel behind a 35-horse outboard motor. We stopped in Goat Harbor on the lee side. First thing, we donned our scuba gear and set the anchor lines fore and aft, burying them in stacked rocks.

The sun was setting quickly, shutting down the light. We divided up the fishing: I would use a Hawaiian sling and go after sea bass; Bob would go after abalone; Randy, lobster—I forgot Rick's assignment. We split up—that young and dumb thing again. I chased sea bass and brought back three beauties. When I surfaced, I found that everyone had scored. But Randy had stuck his hand in a hole looking for a bug—lobster—and got hit by an eel.

We'd towed an inflatable Zodiac rubber boat. We took it to shore, cooked our ocean's bounty, drank wine and beer, and had a great time.

Many hours later I woke inside the sailboat being banged hard against the bulkhead. I stumbled over, pulled the overhead back, and climbed out into a raging storm. The ocean roiled and roared.

Our two anchors had pulled loose. Big rollers with white caps slammed into the boat, each time almost capsizing us. The others stuck their heads out with the look of pure fear. Bob yelled over the wind, "We gotta start the motor and turn us into the swells." He didn't know how to sail but it made a lot of sense. He came out, started the motor, and turned us. He yelled for us to pull up the bow anchor—we were dragging it. Rick and Randy were busy pulling up the stern anchor. Everyone stopped and looked at me. The front of the boat kept rising on the swell and crashing on the other side. The front of the boat—dangerous bucking bronco. I crawled forward, hyperaware that if I went over the side, the three stoodges in the back of the boat wouldn't know how to come about to rescue me.

I didn't have a life vest on.

With a great deal of difficulty, I got the anchor up.

We'd left all of our gear back on the beach. Bob wanted to go west, thinking that we had drifted out into the channel. I wanted to go east because if we missed the island, we'd hit the mainland somewhere between Seattle and Baja Mexico, a much bigger target.

I was outvoted, Randy and Rick siding with Bob.

In 1980, all we had was a compass.

We motored for an hour until the visibility improved. We looked back and saw Catalina. We had missed the island completely and were headed for Japan.

BOOK CLUB DISCUSSION QUESTIONS

1. Do you think it was intrinsically wrong for Bruno and Marie to have illegally rescued children from toxic homes in the U.S.—places where, had the children stayed, they'd have faced a low probability of survival?

2. Do you think that Bruno and Marie have the right skills to raise thirteen children? Do you see other alternatives?

3. Do you accept the premise that Bruno Johnson, who has prided himself on a violent career of "blood and bone," now intends to settle in a safe spot, abandon violence, and raise his complicated family?

4. How do you think Bruno is doing in this transition from a violent world chasing criminals to a hotel employee in Costa Rica? How about Marie?

5. As the story progressed, did you think that Marie had anything to worry about with Bruno when it comes to Darla Figueroa?

6. What did you think of Otis and his relationship with Waldo, the dog? And Bruno's relationship with Waldo? Have you known a dog like this?

7. With the new criminal element in Costa Rica, do you think that Bruno should stay or move his family to Panama where there is no extradition treaty?

8. Before the violent scene on the boat, had you been suspicious of the villain that attacked Bruno?

9. Did you suspect the revelation at the end or did it come as a complete surprise?

10. If you have not read prior Bruno Johnson thrillers set in Los Angeles, did you feel that you were missing key information to allow you full immersion in the story?

NOTE FROM THE PUBLISHER

We hope you enjoyed reading *THE DIABOLICAL,* the eleventh novel in the Bruno Johnson Crime Series.

While the other ten novels stand on their own and can be read in any order, the publication sequence is as follows:

The Disposables (Book 1)

Bruno Johnson, ex-cop, ex-con, turns vigilante—nothing will stop him and Marie as they rescue battered children from abusive homes.

"I really loved *The Disposables.* It's raw, powerful, and eloquent. It's a gritty street poem recited by a voice unalterably committed to redemption and doing the right thing in a wrong world." —Michael Connelly, *New York Times* best-selling author

The Replacements (Book 2)

Bruno and Marie, hiding out in Costa Rica with their rescued kids, are pulled back to L.A. to hunt a heinous child predator.

"While laying low in Costa Rica, former LAPD detective Bruno Johnson must return to California—and risk everything to stop a ruthless kidnapper. The action won't slow down"   *—Booklist*

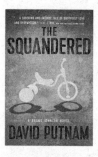

The Squandered (Book 3)

Again, Bruno and Marie leave the kids in Costa Rica with Bruno's dad to intervene in the L.A. County prison system—and face a murderous psychopath.

"Putnam puts his years of law enforcement experience to good use in *The Squandered*, a shocking and intense tale of brotherly love and redemption realized in the midst of moral decay. It's a raw and gritty story I couldn't put down."   —C. J. Box,

New York Times best-selling author

The Vanquished (Book 4)

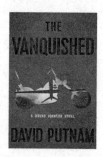

A woman from Bruno's past lures him and Marie back to L.A.—the result is an unspeakable tragedy that will haunt Bruno for the rest of his life.

"Bad Boy Bruno Johnson comes out of hiding to battle a vicious biker gang that threatens his family. Bring an oxygen tank with you when you read *The Vanquished* because you'll be holding your breath the whole time."   —Matt Coyle,

Anthony, Lefty, and Shamus Award–winning author

The Innocents (Book 5)

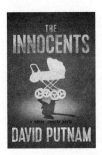

The first of the young Bruno prequels—Bruno is a new cop when he's handed a baby girl, becoming a single dad. Meanwhile, he's working a police corruption case—infiltrating a sheriff's narcotics team involved in murder-for-hire. Family and professional life for Bruno collide violently.

"*The Innocents* is a terrific read, reminiscent of the best of Joseph Wambaugh. David Putnam provides an insider's knowledge of the Los Angeles Sheriff's Department. His characters and settings are rich and authentic, and his dialogue is spot on accurate."   —Robert Dugoni, *New York Times* best-selling author

The Reckless (Book 6)

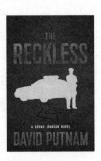

The second of the young Bruno prequels—Bruno tackles the roles of the single dad of a two-year-old daughter and an L.A. County Deputy Sheriff in the Violent Crimes Unit. He is assigned a law enforcement public relations nightmare— apprehend a gang of teenager bank robbers without killing them or getting killed.

"Reading a novel by David Putnam is almost as good as riding shotgun in a patrol car. He writes what he knows and what he knows is that justice on the mean streets isn't always black and white."   —Robin Burcell, *New York Times* best-selling author

The Heartless (Book 7)

The third of the young Bruno prequels—Bruno has stepped down from his beloved position in the Violent Crimes Unit to be able to spend more time with his teen daughter, Olivia. Now a bailiff in the courts, he gets a frantic call to extricate Olivia from a gunpoint situation in a L.A. gang-infested neighborhood—thrusting him back into violent crime mode.

"David Putnam's *The Heartless* is terrific—a smart, well-written, relentless account of a battle against evil, fought by a protagonist who has a real man's flaws, but also shows us the kind of heroism that's real."

—Thomas Perry, *New York Times* best-selling author

The Ruthless (Book 8)

The fourth and last of the young Bruno prequels—Bruno is plunged back into the Violent Crimes Unit when his friends, a judge and his wife, are murdered. Bruno's daughter is now the mother of twins; and the father of the babies is a drug-addicted criminal—abusive and brutal. This is the set up for Bruno's time in prison as he takes justice into his own hands.

"Dark, disturbing, and all too believable, this is the tale of one man's quest for atonement in a world where innocence is a liability."

—T. Jefferson Parker,
New York Times best-selling author

The Sinister (Book 9)

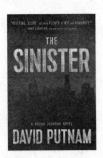

Bruno Johnson and his wife, Marie, hide in plain sight from the law in an upscale L.A. hotel as Bruno heals from a run-in with a brutal outlaw motorcycle gang—and the loss of his son—a son he didn't know he had until it was too late. Bruno is shaken to the core, but still a formidable force when it comes to saving a child.

"Riveting, scary, but with plenty of wit and humanity, author David Putnam brings ex-cop Bruno Johnson's world alive in a way that only another ex-cop could. In Putnam's capable hands, the characters jump off the page—even the dog."   —Janet Evanovich,
New York Times best-selling author

The Scorned (Book 10)

Ex-cop, ex-con, and now fugitive, Bruno Johnson pays back a serious debt as he hunts for a kidnapped child concealed deep inside a Los Angeles criminal organization—then he must escape capture and fight his way out and back home to his family in Costa Rica.

"Breathless action and a deeply humane hero."
                                        —*Publishers Weekly*

We hope that you will read the entire Bruno Johnson Crime Series and will look forward to more to come.

If you liked *THE DIABOLICAL*, we would be very appreciative if you would consider leaving a review. As you probably already know, book reviews are important to authors and they are very grateful when a reader makes the special effort to write a review, however brief.

For more information, please visit the author's website:
www.DavidPutnamBooks.com

Happy reading,
Oceanview Publishing
Your Home for Mystery, Thriller, and Suspense